<u>Stig Dalager</u>

Born in Copenhagen 1952, Stig Dalager is the author of fifty different works including novels, drama, poetry, essays and documentary films. Several of his novels and plays have been published and/or staged internationally, appearing in twenty-one different countries.

His best known novels include the acclaimed *Journey in Blue* (about Hans Christian Andersen, nominated for the UK Impac Prize 2008) and *Two Days in July* (about the Stauffenberg plot to kill Hitler during WWII).

As a playwright, he had an international breakthrough with *I Count The Hours,* staged in New York, followed by *The Dream,* also staged in New York and *An American Electra,* first presented in Madrid (May 2009) and due to be staged in New York.

Dalager was for several years co-editor of the Danish-Jewish magazine *New Outlook.* His documentary *Darkness and Reconciliation* (2003) offers a personal account of the Israeli-Palestine conflict through portraits of people on both sides of the conflict.

Stig Dalager has lived in Leipzig, Vienna and New York and now lives with his two daughters in Copenhagen.

D1347213

Other titles in this series include:

Black Mail by Thomas Feibel
ISBN 978-09551566-2-5
£7.99

Coming Back by David Hill
ISBN 978-09542330-2-0
£7.99

Junk Food Hero by Pat Swindells
ISBN 978-19065820-2-9
£7.99

Letters From Alain by Enrique Perez Diaz
ISBN 978-09551566-4-9
£6.99

My Brother Johnny by Francesco D'Adamo
ISBN 978-09551566-3-2
£6.99

Sobibor by Jean Molla
ISBN 978-09546912-4-0
£6.99

Thistown by Malcolm McKay
ISBN 978-09546912-5-7
£7.99

Tina's Web by Alki Zei
ISBN 978-09551566-1-8
£7.99

www.aurorametro.com

David's Story

by

Stig Dalager

Translated by Frances Østerfelt
and Cheryl Robson

AURORA METRO PRESS

First printed in 2010 by Aurora Metro Publications Ltd
www.aurorametro.com   info@aurorametro.com

We are grateful for financial assistance from The Kobler Trust.

Production: Rebecca Gillieron

With thanks to: Caroline Hennig, Richard Turk, Neil Gregory,
Lesley Mackay, Sumedha Mane, Jackie Glasgow, Stacey Crawshaw,
Pagan Mace, Reena Makwana.

Trade distribution

UK: Central Books 020 8986 4854 orders@centralbooks.com

USA: TCG/Consortium N.Y. 212 609 5900 tcg@tcg.org

Canada: Canada Playwrights Press Toronto 416 703 0013
orders@playwrightscanada.com

Printed by JF Print, Sparkford, Somerset UK

ISBN 978-1-906582-04-3

The sky is slate grey, the morning chill, as he makes his way through the village in his thin jacket and worn boots. The path is muddy from the constant rain they've had for the last two days. No one notices him as he moves among the silent houses, apart from the crows that dart up from a puddle and flap away noisily over the rooftops. He stops to watch them as they glide in the wind and disappear like two black spots over the fields.

He always watches the birds, especially the crows, which nobody likes, not even his father. "They're only trouble," his father says. In the summer, their feathers gleam as if oiled. Sometimes he imagines himself flying like a bird.

From a distance, he can see a large piece of paper nailed to a barn door. He knows what it is, he's seen one before − a public notice. At the top, there's something printed in German and then the same thing printed below in Polish, only smaller. The words aren't hard to follow as he can read them in both languages.

The boy rushes to the door, tilting his head to get a

good look at it. The last time he read one of these, his father had asked him, "Do you understand it?" He nodded.

"So what does it say?" Proudly, he replied: "It says that it's forbidden for Jews to go on the train."

"Do you know what that means?"

He nodded again. But it was as if his father wasn't completely sure he understood – he had that look. His father bent down to him and took his hand. His father's large, wrinkled hand completely covered his own small hand and he usually did this whenever there was something he particularly wanted to impress upon him. He wanted his son to remain calm and to trust him. He shouldn't be afraid. He should listen carefully and do as he was told. But lately, he'd noticed that whenever his father took his hand that he was trembling slightly. Maybe he was frightened, too.

His father told him: "You mustn't take the train, no Jews may go on the train, if you do, you'll be punished."

"Not even to Kielce?" he said. "Do I have to walk to Kielce?"

"We can probably find someone to give you a lift," said his father. "But you don't take the train, understand?"

Yes, of course he understood. He just didn't know why, all of a sudden, Jews mustn't go on trains. And when he asked his father, he was told: "That's how it is. We'll talk about it later!"

They'd always talk about it 'later', when his father needed to think about something or when he thought he wasn't old enough to understand.

But of course he knew what was wrong. It was the police. It was the Germans. Because of the Germans he had to wear an armband with a star, because of the Germans he couldn't go to school any more, he had to stay at home alone and read his books. Sometimes Jakob came by and they worked out some problems from the book. He was good at maths, it wasn't that hard, and if they couldn't figure it out, they could ask his father. But lately his father had taken to coming home at the strangest times. Then he'd sit for a long while, reading or writing, before suddenly going out again. He didn't know what he did. He wasn't a teacher any more. There wasn't any school.

His mother wasn't home, she cleaned house for some of the other families in the community, among them the Schliefersteins who had the grocery store by the square. She left early in the morning and came home late. He had to make his own dinner if his father wasn't home. And even if he was home, it was often the boy who put the food on the table. Sometimes when he called his father, he didn't come to the table. He'd go into the sitting room and stand beside him and say, "Dinner's ready." But his father just waved him away. "I don't have time," he'd say. Or "I'll be there soon." Sometimes he left the house without saying a word. Other times he just sat and stared out the window. He felt like he didn't know him any more. One day Jakob said: "I think your father's doing something dangerous!"

"What do you mean?" he asked.

"My father says he's a communist."

"No, you're crazy," he said, "he's definitely not a communist, there aren't any communists here!"

"My father doesn't lie," said Jakob. "He's seen him in Kielce with some other communists!"

"That's not true," he said confused, "how does he know they're communists?"

"You can tell!"

They started to quarrel, but just then his father came in and they fell silent. His father nodded 'hello' and went into the kitchen. He was wearing his black overcoat, the one he always wore for special occasions. Jakob smirked, quickly pulled on his jacket and dashed out.

The boy stormed in to the kitchen, tugged on his father's sleeve and demanded: "Why won't you tell me what you're doing?"

His father turned and hushed him.

"Jakob's father says you're a communist, but you're not, are you?"

His father took his hand and led him further into the kitchen. He sat down on a chair, still holding his hand, "Listen, it's best that you don't know what I'm doing."

"Yes ... but why?" he said disappointed.

"There's a war on, David, you know ..."

"Of course," he said.

"We have to be very careful. You have to watch

everything you say, and the less you know the better." But he wasn't satisfied.

"You've always said that I should know everything, that I should learn languages and keep my eyes open!"

"Yes," said his father, "but this is something else. You still have to keep your eyes open, but there are things that you should avoid, and there are things that, for your own sake, you shouldn't know anything about. It could be a matter of life or death. Understand?"

He nodded, but didn't really understand. What he could see was that his father was restless, that his mind was caught up in a crisis that he couldn't put into words. This crisis had taken him over so completely that the father he'd once known had almost disappeared. It was as if a shadow had embraced him.

That cold, grey morning, he reads the rain soaked announcement on the barn door: "It's forbidden for Jews to travel in cars." He reads it over again before turning and looking around at the deserted square. He's alone. He's freezing. He starts running, he runs and runs – he has to get home.

*

A few days later he wakes up with a start, and can hear sounds from the sitting room. It's a bright day, so he throws the heavy quilt aside and hops out of bed realizing he must have slept in. From his window, he can see the two great ash trees at the far end of the small garden. The branches are interwoven, black and bare; one branch has a strange round hole. Last spring a robin built a nest in the hole, and every morning when he woke up he could hear the cries of the young birds. Even though he knew the bird couldn't hear him, he often tiptoed over to the window and stood there, entranced by its song. He wondered how such a small bird could sing so high and clear.

He stands a moment and looks over the fields past the trees. In the distance Tomachevski is driving his horses, the cart moving slowly over the ruts in the road. Once, he'd been allowed to ride on the brown horse while Tomachevski watched him go around in the yard. Growing dizzier on every turn, he'd have fallen off if Tomachevski hadn't grabbed hold of him, laughing: "You'll never be a farmer!"

The clock in the hall strikes nine. He pulls on his clothes and walks into the sitting room. His mother's at the table eating. She turns towards him and smiles. Her dark eyes follow him around; she doesn't look as tired as usual. Suddenly, he notices that there's meat, cheese and pickle on the table.

"I don't have to work today," says his mother, "Mr Schlieferstein gave me some extra money so I'm taking a holiday."

As he eats, she sits quietly and watches him. She turns the cup round in her hands as she often does when she's thinking about something pleasant. Then she gets up, in a sweater that's too big for her, with her curly black lashes and dark eyebrows etched against her pale, open face. How many times he'd looked into those bright eyes at bedtime, when she'd come into his room, sit on the edge of his bed and say evening prayers with him.

Occasionally, she'd purse her lips, as if biting her tongue, only to open her mouth again in a wide smile. When a thought occurred to her (unlike his father) she had to share it: "Spring's on its way," she'd say, "Can you feel it?"

She leans across the table and ruffles his hair.

"You're all right being left alone here, aren't you?"

"Mmm ..." he says, lying a little.

"Next month we'll go with your father to the woods like we used to."

"We can't, Mama."

"No," she says, "but we'll do it anyway."

"But, what if *they* come ..." he protests but he can't say *the soldiers*, he doesn't want to imagine soldiers in their forest.

"Don't think about that," she says, "I've talked to your father. And he says it's a good idea. He says that they shouldn't be allowed to ruin everything for us."

He knows that they want to make it all right for him, that they pretend they're not frightened for his sake. He moves around the table and hugs his mother.

Half an hour later, he's beyond the village striding along the winding road to Kielce in his tightly laced boots. As he passes one small farm after another, fields and trees and hills seem to melt together. He hasn't seen a soul on the road so far and wonders where all the people have gone. In spite of the bitter wind, he's built up a sweat. When his legs begin to ache, he takes a break by the side of the road, and sits there, scratching the ground with a stick, until the roar of engines somewhere in the distance, forces him to jump up and hide behind a tree. A moment later, a convoy of motorcycles, trucks and armoured cars rumbles past him, leaving snatches of words and laughter hanging in the air. He stays safe behind the tree until they pass and then steps out onto the road.

At a bend further down the road, the last truck unexpectedly pulls in beside a clump of pines and stops.

Quickly, he hides behind a tree, closing his eyes and pressing his cheek up against the trunk. His heart's racing, his hands are sweaty, but nothing happens. In the descending mist he can only hear remote, incoherent sounds from the distant truck.

Finally, he sticks his head out and looks up the road: a man with boots and a grey cap has gotten out and opened the back of the truck while three others with steel helmets jump down and drag something out from the darkness. He can't see what it is – it looks like bundles of clothes or sacks of potatoes. The man with the grey cap points to a spot in the brush and the three soldiers throw the bundles away. One of them lights a cigarette, they stand a while and talk, but he can't make out what they're saying. The man with the grey cap brushes something from his shoulder then casts a quick glance up and down the road.

David presses himself right up against the tree and digs his nails into the bark. With his eyes shut tightly he waits until he hears the truck start up and drive away.

Silence surrounds him, like a strange dream. Suddenly, he's startled by the sound of something rustling in the undergrowth. When he turns around he notices a squirrel watching him, calmly, before it darts off among the trees.

Not knowing what he's doing or why, he walks up the road towards the pines. Immediately, he can see the bundles lying where they were thrown amongst the bushes. Two canvas bags tied at the top with thick cord. They have a strange shape. He bends down and tries to lift one of them, but can't, it's too heavy. He happens to notice his boots, one of them is covered in a strange liquid, he bends down again and feels it with a finger – it's red, looks like something he's seen before. It looks like blood. It's only now that he notices that the bottom of one of the sacks is covered in blood. Frightened, he jumps back, looks around anxiously, but there's still no one around. He grabs a handful of grass and desperately tries to clean his boots, but no matter how much he rubs, there's still a trace of blood.

What should he do? He looks back and forth from the

sacks to his boots. But as his panic mounts, he remembers what his father told him ... that sometimes ... sometimes, farmers dispose of sick or dying animals, and he thinks: 'It's not people, it's pigs.' And then: 'The Germans must have stolen some pigs and discovered they were sick, so they threw them away. Yes, that's all it is. Now he'll just look in one of the sacks and then go on to Kielce and tell his uncle all about it.'

Somewhat relieved, he unties the cord on one of the sacks, opens it and looks in. He hasn't seen it, he won't see it, and yet he stands there staring at it, his hands frozen to the edge of the sack. Three long fingers stick up from inside the dark sack, a glazed eye and an open mouth twisted to the side in a deathly pale face, its cheek pressed against a shoulder, blue veins protruding from the thick neck, the body slumped in a heap ...

With a start, as if he'd been stung, he drops the sack; it falls back into the brush with a faint dry sound. He stares at the two sacks for a moment, then walks out onto the road and continues to Kielce as fast as his legs can carry him. He sees nothing, just walks. A little way down the road he stops suddenly, grips his stomach, runs over to a field and vomits.

Once again he takes some grass, wipes his mouth and sets out onto the road on his way to Kielce.

Gradually, as he's walking along, thoughts return to him, and the image of the body floats before his eyes. Something in him is about to burst, a wave of feelings rush through him, he's been hit by something greater than himself. He struggles to believe that it wasn't really a corpse. He won't believe it, and under no circumstances will he tell anyone about it, not his uncle, not his father, not his mother. He won't frighten them, no, why should he? They're frightened enough as it is. And anyway, his uncle would only say that it's something he's made up. "He has a lively imagination," he'd say. And then he'd say: "May God protect you, David, lest that imagination of yours gets you into trouble one day."

In the great dark house in Kielce, his cousin Anna opens the door, but she isn't smiling like she usually does, she just nods, quickly lets him in and immediately locks the door again.

"Why are you locking the door?" he asks, but instead of answering she says: "We're all in the dining room. Come in and have some *borscht*."

She puts her hand on his shoulder and leads him through the house to the dining room, where everyone – his uncle, his aunt and his cousins – is seated around the table eating. They turn silently towards him as he comes in, his uncle gestures to him to sit down on the high-backed chair next to him. The menorah is lit and the curtains are closed, he doesn't understand why, but he says nothing.

His cousin serves him some *borscht* from a tureen; he starts eating immediately, but he can't help thinking of the man in the sack and puts the spoon down again. A haze descends, he feels dizzy, but clings on to the chair tightly. It soon passes.

"You must eat something," says his uncle, looking anxiously at him, "why aren't you eating?"

He doesn't know what to say, so he just says: "I have a stomach ache, I can't eat anything."

"How old are you?" asks his uncle.

"Eleven," says his aunt before he can answer.

"You must eat something," says his uncle not looking at him any more, "we all have to eat, we'll need all the strength we can get."

"He doesn't know what you're talking about!" says Isak, his cousin who's eighteen years old and soon moving to Warsaw to go to university.

"That's no way to talk to your father," says his aunt, glancing at Isak, who throws up his arms.

"I think we ought to tell David what's happened, and if you don't − I will."

They all look silently at his uncle, nobody is eating. Anna gives him a small, sad smile and shakes her head slightly then stares down at her half-empty bowl.

His uncle takes a white napkin and slowly dries his grey-bearded mouth. He places the napkin on the table and continues to stroke his beard. His uncle's hands are long and graceful, the hands of a physician. Once, when he had a high fever and thought he would die, his father brought him to his uncle's house, where he laid in bed for weeks while his uncle gave him medicine and cold compresses. While he stayed there and slowly recovered, his uncle used to come to his room and watch over him, even though he was always busy. His uncle had many patients, wealthy folk in furs, as well as patients who had almost nothing, who could only give him bread or even nothing at all.

One evening his uncle told him all about the Garden of Eden, while sitting on a chair in front of the window in his dark suit. His voice wasn't stern as it sometimes could be. Every now and then he'd be afraid of his uncle because he expected so much, but that evening his voice was soft and low, perhaps he was dreaming, perhaps he was really talking to himself. He told David about the lion and the lamb that grazed together, about the grass that was so green that it hurt one's eyes to look at it, about eucalyptus trees whose leaves glistened in the sun, and about music, strange music that could be heard everywhere like a murmuring on the breeze, and the rush of the clear springs more refreshing than anything else you could imagine. "But why did Man leave the garden?" his uncle asked rhetorically and breathed deeply. "Is it because Man is evil?" he asked in the darkness before answering again: "No, Man isn't evil, he's impatient. He's too impatient to bear happiness."

Now in the dining room, his uncle said: "You must tell your father what's happened: they're starting to throw Jews out of their homes, they call it 'Resettlement'. It's happening right here, some people have already been put in the gymnasium, others have been moved, mostly to small flats, where people are packed together. It could be our turn next. We don't know what to believe. Rumours are rife. Some think they'll set aside a special area, others say that we'll have to leave town, but no one knows. They could knock on our door tomorrow … you see?"

David nods, his cousin Anna looks at him again, she seems even sadder than before. He, too, is sad.

It's as if they're all waiting for something, a sign, a movement, or maybe a visitor to suddenly walk into the room and say that it's all a bad dream and that it's time to wake up. But nobody comes. The oak cabinets, the paintings, the doors all remain still.

His uncle gets up and goes into the next room. A moment later he returns with a book. He sits down and opens it, quickly finds what he's looking for. He reads:

"And give us, Oh Lord our God,
That we might sleep in peace,
And awake again to life,
Oh, Almighty God,
Raise Your tent of peace over us
And lead us with Your wise counsel,
And help us in Your name
And free us from our enemies, plague, war,
hunger and sorrow,
And turn us from the Devil
Who is before us and he who is behind us."

*

That night he can't sleep, suddenly he can't breathe, he gets out of bed but soon crawls back again and covers himself with the blanket. He lies there staring out through the dark window to the courtyard. Distant sounds from the town reach him, sounds like horses' hooves and dogs barking, but he hardly notices them as his mind slowly turns to strange dreams – he's walking through the town but can't find his parents' house, he asks at the square, but no one has time to talk to him, everyone's busy with their own affairs, even Jakob. Finally, he finds the house, far out on the horizon, on a mountain. It's burning. It's burning against the bright blue sky. He shouts, but no one hears him.

He gets out of bed again and goes to the door and listens, maybe someone's still awake, maybe his uncle hasn't gone to bed yet. The cold from the wooden floor goes right through him; he leans on the doorknob, opens the door and tiptoes into the dining room, stops next to the dining table and listens again. He can't hear anything, no one's breathing. The silence roars in his ears.

He rushes out to the hallway and finds the white door to his uncle's bedroom, he puts his ear to the door and now he can hear them – one breathing quickly and one breathing slowly. They're there. They're sleeping. His uncle and aunt. Relieved, he goes back to the small room and closes the door behind him. But there's something under the bed, something white, a white face. He doesn't dare go back to bed, he has to check. He kneels down and nervously feels around in the dark under the bed.

But there's nothing there. He lies down again, pulls up the blanket and slowly falls asleep with his arms folded across his chest.

David is quieter than usual, he's stopped asking so many questions. He prefers to sit by the window and read his books, but sometimes it's too hard to concentrate, so he just sits and looks. Now and then he goes out for a run across the fields with Jakob under the wide spring sky. Jakob's always the fastest, but he's the one who can go the longest; he can run and run.

They have their own spot behind the dilapidated shack on Tomachevski's field, where they've shot at bottles with all sorts of stones, where they've whittled things out of wood with Jakob's knife, where they once built a Noah's ark out of some planks of wood so rotten they were no good for anything else. When they were finished and ready to go on board and choose the animals, they started arguing. Jakob wanted both of his grey cats and David wanted his black cat, but as there could only be two of each kind, they decided to break the rule for the cats. But when they got to family and friends, it all started over again – they couldn't agree on leaving any of them out, so the voyage on Noah's ark never actually happened. They renamed the ship and sailed off.

Now the rotten planks lie in a jumble on the ground, and while Jakob still whittles, David sits and draws. He draws his friend, the dilapidated house, the trees and the clouds on some lined paper that he's borrowed from his father. He's good at drawing – faces, houses, mountains, and he can draw things from his imagination, things he's never seen, but which come to life as he draws them. He's only ever seen pictures of the sea, but he can fill pages with foaming white waves. And these seascapes are littered with rocky coasts where ships with high masts lie at anchor.

"Why are you so quiet?" asks his father one day while he's sitting doing sums in his book.

At first David pretends not to hear him, so his father takes him by the shoulders and gives him that look, but he shakes free and goes back to his arithmetic.

"Has somebody done something to you? What's the matter?" asks his father, sitting down in front of him. David stares at the numbers in the book until they swim in a haze before him.

"What're you afraid of?" asks his father, "you know you can tell me everything."

He looks at his father, but says nothing. He mumbles a few words and searches desperately for others. Suddenly, he looks up and says: "It's a secret."

"You're not old enough to have secrets from your father!" he says, getting angry, and he can see from his father's face that he really wants to know.

"You keep secrets from me," says David stubbornly.

His father shrugs his shoulders and takes out a cigarette. While he's lighting it, it's as if he's far, far away.

"That's something else," says his father, "When I keep secrets from you, it's to protect you. You know that. Why should you keep secrets from me?"

"Because ... because there's something I don't want to think about, so I'd rather not talk about it."

"Not even to me?"

He shakes his head, stubbornly. His father gives him a long look then suddenly gets up, goes to the hall and puts on his coat. When he comes back into the room he looks tired. He stands by the desk and rummages through some papers which he then rolls up with a rubber band, sticking them in his pocket and turning to the boy with a smile. His father doesn't often smile. A moment later he's serious again.

"If anyone hurts you or if anyone ever tries to, you must tell me at once," he says and buttons up his coat.

His face is pale, maybe he doesn't sleep well at night. Sometimes David wakes in the dark and hears footsteps in the sitting room. He's sure that it's his father who's just come home.

"D'you understand what I'm saying?" his father says, walking towards the door.

"Yes," he replies, nodding his head.

His father lays his hand on his head and goes out. David sits there for a long time, listening to the sound of his departing footsteps.

*

A rumbling sound wakes him, like something shaking the ground, but it's a long way off. He can't understand it. He can't make it out and before he's fully awake the sound returns, closer. Frightened, he jumps out of bed and runs to the window. His small body stiffens: on the field, some metres from the fence and the ash trees, a tank rolls past, its dark silhouette pointing towards the leaden sky, a troop of German soldiers with raised guns quickly following. As far as he can see into the distance, the field is scattered with tanks, personnel vehicles, men on horses and soldiers running. At short intervals there are explosions then blue smoke rises from the ground and floats over the field. From far off, he can hear a cracking, ta-ta-ta-ta. For a moment he's rooted to the floor, he thinks: 'It's war, it's war!' Then he shouts, "Mama! ... Papa!" and rushes towards the door at the same time as his father opens it and comes in. His father is calm and holds him tight.

"It's manoeuvres, David, only manoeuvres, they're not doing anything!"

"They're shooting, they're shooting!" he cries, clutching his father frantically, tearing the button off his shirt cuff.

"They're using blanks, David, it's not dangerous. Stay here, it'll be all right."

But he doesn't believe him and keeps gripping his father's arm. Carefully, his father frees himself and leads him over to the window. Silently, they stand together and look out at the swarm of military men in the fields.

"See," he says after some time, "no one's fallen, no one's been hit."

"Yes, but why are they doing it?" he asks nervously. "They're not allowed to drive over our fields like that."

"They don't have to ask for permission," says his father.

"Why doesn't anyone stop them?"

"We can't, they're much stronger than us. They're the ones who decide. And if someone tries to stop them, they'll kill them. They've already killed a lot of people."

He closes his eyes. Now he understands. They must have killed the people in the sacks, and they'll take people's houses and send them away and probably kill them, too. They do it because they're the strongest and because they hate Jews and Poles. But he doesn't know why.

"Is that war?" he asks, looking up at his father. But his father just nods and keeps on looking out at the dark fields.

One day in June while he's washing his hands at the kitchen sink and the sun's shining through the dusty kitchen window, there's a loud knock, like someone beating the door with a stone. He runs into the front room and looks out of the window to the street. A man in a blue uniform with a gun is standing back and looking at the house. David cocks his head to one side and notices another man just in front of the door. Another heavy knock and a voice shouting, "Open up, open up at once!"

He goes into the small porch, unlatches the bolt and opens the door. A stout policeman with a brown shoulder strap and pistol in his right hand, which is pointing towards the ground, stares at him for a moment before realising that it's just a boy standing in front of him. He smiles in a patronising manner and with a swift gesture calls the other man to the door, "House search! Is your father home?" he asks.

David shakes his head, and before he knows what's happening, the fat man gives him a shove and they both push past him into the room. He closes the door and thinks, 'Don't say anything, don't say anything.' He doesn't even know what it is he mustn't say and although it's the first time, the thoughts come to him as if he'd thought them a thousand times before.

In the sitting room, one of them has already begun pulling drawers out of the corner cabinet, and with a trained gesture he runs his hands through the cutlery and over the cups. Then he's opening boxes and throwing them onto the floor. Next, the policeman opens the cupboard and his eyes fall on his father's prayer shawl, which he roughly crumples up and throws into the far corner of the room. The other man shoves the books off the table by the window, pulls a notebook out of his breast pocket and sits down on a chair. David is standing in the middle of the room. The fat policeman beckons him over to the chair, grabs him by his shoulders and with a peculiar smile that makes his cheeks puff out, he asks, "What's your name?"

"David Rubinow," he answers, shrugging his shoulders, trying to free himself, but the hands clench even tighter.

"I think he's afraid of me!" says the fat one, chuckling, looking in the direction of the other officer who's on his way to the kitchen. Irritated, he turns back and says, "Let him go and let's get this over with!"

He goes out to the kitchen and opens the blue cupboard. Surprisingly, he lets David go while he writes something in his notebook. Then, he glances at the boy again. "You needn't be afraid of me," he says. "Just tell me what you know, OK … We're looking for some rifles and guns that are hidden in the neighbourhood. Do you know anything about them?"

David shakes his head and stares into the face that's no longer smiling.

"Listen! A Jew boy like you wouldn't lie to the local police, would you?"

David silently shakes his head, frozen.

"Can't you talk?"

"Yes," he says, looking into the large round eyes in front of him.

"So out with it!" says the fat man, irritated, bending closer to him.

"I don't know anything about rifles or guns, I don't!"

The fat man scratches his thinning hair, opens his mouth with its bad teeth, and turns away slightly, looking out of the window. At that moment, a truck filled with soldiers drives by, maybe the fat man's thinking about what he'll do with him. Suddenly, he turns and gets up. For an instant, David thinks he'll hit him and has already shut his eyes, but once again he's taken by the shoulders and shoved down on the chair.

"Sit there and think about it!" yells the man and then he goes to find the other man in the kitchen.

They look everywhere – in drawers and cupboards, behind doors and in the clothes chest in the bedroom. They open the hatch to the attic, the fat man goes into his room – he can hear him moving his bed, throwing something at the door. For a moment, he considers running away and edges towards the porch, but maybe there are more of them outside and maybe they'll catch him and take him somewhere far away and dangerous, where they can't find him, his father and mother, why don't they come home, but maybe it's good that they aren't here, maybe they'd take his father with them, yes, he's sure they would. They'd take his father. So he has to stay calm.

He sits on his chair until they've searched the whole house, they're in the kitchen for some time and as the door is half-open, he can see them drinking the milk and eating bread. When they come back to the room, the fat man has two of his mother's pots of jam under his arm. The thin man walks past him without saying a word, but the fat man stops, shakes his head and says, "Let this be a warning. Tell your father we'll be back!"

David doesn't want to look at him, turns away, pretending that he's looking at something out on the street.

"Look at me, boy!" says a voice behind him. Slowly, he turns and looks down at the man's boots.

"Did you hear what I said?" demands the fat man, moving towards him.

But David doesn't hear, he doesn't hear anything and just keeps staring at the boots. With an angry gesture, the fat man puts down one of the pots of jam, sticks his fingers into the other and takes a handful of jam and smears it over David's face. He then wipes his fingers on David's hair. David doesn't move.

With a small satisfied grunt, the man turns towards the door and leaves. David hears the door slam. Everything is quiet once again. He sits very still for a while, then gets up, goes into the kitchen and finds a cloth to clean himself. Carefully, he wipes his skin clean, rinses the rag under the tap and dries himself off. He washes his hair under the tap and dries that, too. He goes back to his chair by the window, gets a book and begins to read. Tears come, but he wipes them away and carries on reading his book although he can no longer make any sense of it.

For half an hour he stares at the dancing letters, leafing back and forth in the book, trying to find a passage he can read, but he understands none of it. A sudden fatigue overwhelms him, he fights it, but finally leans over and falls asleep with the book under his head. He dreams that he's swimming in a wide, blue lake, he keeps on swimming and the water enfolds his limbs and face like silk. He's thinking: 'This is where I'll stay forever' and then he wakes up all of a sudden, confused, and looks around. Is this where he lives?

He looks at the mess that the police have made of the house, gets up slowly and starts putting things away.

That evening while they're having dinner he tells them what's happened; but when he sees how upset they become he says nothing about the jam.

"Did they threaten you?" asks his father, clenching his fist.

He shakes his head and forces a smile. And then he has to go through it all over again, because his father wants to hear every detail. But when he gets to the jam pots, he stalls.

"The one who took the pots of jam," says his father. "Did he say anything?"

"Yes," says David, "he said he'd be back soon."

"And you're sure he didn't do anything to you?"

He nods.

"Leave him alone," says his mother, getting up from the table and putting her hands around his shoulders.

Once in a while his mother would stand behind him and put her hands on his shoulders. He doesn't really know why, but it's as if she wants to do something nice, even though she's probably frightened, too, she grips his shoulders and can barely let them go. When she holds him tightly, his father goes quiet and he knows he shouldn't say any more.

That evening, his father gets up from the table, takes out some paper and sits down at the table by the window and begins to write. David helps his mother clear off the dining table and wash up in the kitchen with its lingering smell of onions. They don't turn on the light, but stand there in the shadows looking out of the window.

It's twilight and the silhouettes of the ash trees in the garden look like great, blue ghosts waving about. Far out over the fields burns a crimson sun and clouds float across the heavens like purple banners. His mother dries her hands on her apron and hangs it on the wall, and he can smell something strong − maybe it's the perfume his father gave her because it was summer and to remind her of something beautiful. When she reaches for his hand and leads him into the sitting room, he's almost forgotten the two policemen and the sticky mess in his hair.

Later, when David's lying on his bed, his mother comes in and sits on the edge. They look out at the trees which are barely visible now, only shadows, like things half-hidden, events that have not yet taken place, rustling in the leaves, whispering in the cool breeze. David has laid there and listened at night, his ears like shells in which the ocean roars, echoing his own breath, half-dreaming in the darkness. They quickly pray together, but as his mother gets up to go, he holds her back. "Tell me about David and Goliath," and he looks excitedly at her.

She smiles faintly. She's told him the story of King David a hundred times, and he's read the story himself, but it's their favourite bedtime ritual. Sometimes she's too tired, so he recounts the meeting at Engedi or describes the Oracle from Endo himself. Or she might tell him about the shepherd who was sent to Saul's palace to play his harp to soothe the king's pain, or about the battle with Goliath dressed in heavy armour, or about Jerusalem and the Ark of the Covenant, which his father loves to describe in great detail. He might ask his mother, "Why did David only have five stones for his slingshot?" Or, "Why did Saul say, 'You show me kindness, while I am wicked towards you.'" Sometimes he couldn't grasp the full meaning of the words then his mother would bring his father in to answer his questions. At other times she'd suddenly say, "That's enough, time for sleep!"

It's months since they last talked about King David, and this evening he's quiet as his mother tells the tale of David's battle with Goliath.

"No questions tonight?" she asks, looking puzzled.

He wonders, "If God is always with David, is God with us, too?"

His mother seems taken aback — she looks away, maybe she's looking at the trees outside the window but he can't see her eyes.

"Yes," she says, looking right at him, "He's with you too." He wants to ask more, but can't find the words. His mother gets up to go; he blurts out, "I got a letter from Jan …"

A strange look comes over his mother's face.

"A letter?" she asks. "Why doesn't he just come and visit?"

"Since the school closed, he hasn't visited me once."

"Didn't he move … to Krakow? That's why," she says smiling, relieved. "Oh, I'm silly. What did he say?"

"He wrote … he wrote to tell me that even if I go to Krakow one day, we couldn't play together, we couldn't even talk to each other."

"Of course you can talk to each other, why couldn't you?"

"Because I belong to a doomed race," he says and turns his face away.

His mother sits down on the bed again and takes his hand. He can hear her quick breathing.

"Don't you believe that," she says. "No matter what Jan says, don't believe it."

He looks at her again and wants to believe her. She's smiling her familiar smile. But there's more, much more, that she's not saying.

"Jan says his mother's married a German and that Germans know how to get rid of Jews. Jews are the misfortune of the German and the Polish people."

"Now that's enough," says his mother looking angry. "You don't believe that, do you?"

He keeps hold of her hand and stares at a spot on the wall that looks like the head of a troll.

"No ... but why ...?" he says.

"You mustn't think about it," says his mother. "You're too tired; sleep now and we'll talk about it in the morning."

Oh, he wants to sleep, more than anything else, because when he's asleep the world's different, and now he's upset his mother. He doesn't want to upset her so he nods. She lets go his hand, turns off the light, waves and goes into the sitting room.

A little later he hears them talking. They whisper but he can hear most of it. His mother says, "It's no good leaving him to sit here alone all day. He's frightened, can't you tell?"

"What do you want me to do?" says his father.

"You have to stop your activities, it's too dangerous."

"I can't."

"And we need money," says his mother. "You could get work at Schliefersteins – I've talked to them ..."

"I can't just give up, the group needs me ... is that what you want? For me to sit back and let them destroy our country?"

"It's not our country any more," says his mother.

"It's our country as long as we live here," says his father.

"How much longer do you think they'll let us? In Kielce, they've thrown your brother and his family out of their house – and hundreds of others. You don't even know where he is at this moment, do you? The other day they threw a rock through Schliefersteins' window – people from the town. No one wants us here any more."

"It's not our neighbours, it's not the Poles, it's the Germans we're fighting against!" says his father, agitated. "You don't know who threw the rock, do you? And much worse is happening than rocks being thrown. In Bodzentyn, the Germans shot a Jew on the street. It's that sort of thing we –"

"Shh …" says his mother, "he can hear us, I forgot to close the door."

He hears her footsteps across the floor. She opens the door quietly letting in a crack of light but he closes his eyes and lays still. She stands there a moment and looks at him then he hears her breathe in deeply.

"He's asleep," she whispers and closes the door with a click.

They never had their picnic in the woods. Days and months pass, shadows lengthen and the north wind races across the open fields. Twice they've been registered in the congregation and twice the Jews of the village have elected a council of elders. Some people disappear suddenly. From one day to the next, houses become vacant, rumours go round, that they've fled to Warsaw or Kiev — even to Palestine, but what good does it do? Everywhere there's war and most people only have a Jewish passport. So most of them stay where they are. They carry on hoping, closing their eyes.

Every day people are going past the house, strangers in shabby clothing with pale faces. They beg for food, and although there's little enough, David fetches a few crusts of bread from the kitchen and hands them out on the street.

He feels trapped. He's not allowed to go out. But he doesn't cry, he won't cry. Instead, he spends the day sitting at the table by the window, reading or thinking. He starts keeping a diary. One day he writes, "When I think about the war going on in the world and how many people are dying every day from guns, bombs, diseases and other enemies of mankind, I feel like giving up on everything."

His father is working for the Schliefersteins now. He was arrested on his way to Kielce. They took him to the station in Bielino where they beat him up and made fun of him, but they let him go. They didn't get anything — they had nothing on him. But he can't ride his bicycle, he can't go anywhere, he should be a 'good Jew'. It was a warning.

That's why his father's working for the Schliefersteins, as they can't give people food on credit any more. That's why David's at home all alone.

Nearly every day patrols are driving through the village and the din of their trucks and motorcycles bounces off the walls. Soldiers dressed in leather coats with driving goggles scuttle around like dangerous beetles.

Once in a while, a patrol stops at the square, no one knows why. People try to get home before they're singled out for abuse. Not too fast, not too slow, in case the worst should happen. But people don't always get away in time.

One day in October, a patrol stopped in front of the Schliefersteins' shop and a police sergeant and a constable went into the shop while two others stood out on the street. Inside the shop, the sergeant ordered all the employees and customers to go outside, including David's father. Among the customers was Antek Blum, Head of the Council of Elders, and Samuel Franter, Secretary of the Community, both of whom were there to shop and talk with Mr Schlieferstein. The police asked the women to move to one side and the men to form a line. They weren't sure if this was to be their last hour on earth, but the Germans laughed and the atmosphere was fairly relaxed, so they stayed calm.

With a flick of his hand, the sergeant ordered Antek Blum to step out of the line and put on his hat, which he'd taken off as soon as he'd seen the Germans. Blum put on his hat, but neglected to bow his head.

"You're putting on your hat in the presence of a German?" laughed the sergeant, moving towards him, pointing a finger.

"You yourself asked me to do it," said Blum calmly and removed his hat again.

"Don't you know that a Jew never looks a German straight in the eye?" said the sergeant, still in a friendly tone.

"No, I didn't," said Blum, bowing his head, as the

laughter from the policemen washed over him.

"Let's try it again," said the sergeant, who didn't look a day over twenty. "Now I'll turn around and you put your hat back on. When I turn around again, you'll have taken your hat off – and God help you if you look me in the eye."

The sergeant quickly turned his back on Blum, the old man put his hat on just as quickly, and when the sergeant turned back round again, not only Blum but all the men in the line gazed steadily at the ground.

This went on for some time, with the police trying out a few of their own 'ideas'. Finally, one of them took a large pair of scissors from a bag on one of the motorcycles, and then the sergeant and one of the police took turns cutting off the men's beards. They even cut off Schlieferstein's bangs.

The men let their beards be cut off without saying a word. When they got to David's father, who didn't have a beard, and Rimorski, who wasn't Jewish, but being a peasant, had no identification, they ran out of ideas. Finally, the German police drove off on their motorbikes just as abruptly as they'd come.

* * *

It's early one morning in February, 1942. Frost glazes the windows, snow blows across the fields, and during the night, snow drifts of all sizes have appeared on the deserted street between the houses. Snow whirls through the air and the roofs are decked with snow. All around is the blinding white glow of the snow against the grey horizon, cutting off the village completely. The trees outside the window are like an icy wall and the water in the taps is frozen solid right down into the cold earth.

His parents are still asleep. He's freezing as he wanders about the house, even though he's put on two pairs of socks inside his shoes. He's got a fire going in the fireplace, but the wood is slow to burn. Wrapped in a blanket, he sits at the window. He notices a man further down the road, struggling against the snow and wind. It's the warden.

He flings off the blanket and quickly pulling on his coat and boots, rushes out into the street. The wind slaps his face, almost knocking him over, but he manages to trudge down the road through the heavy snow, until suddenly the wind is at his back, pushing him forward – he falls, gets up again, brushes the snow away and carries on. The warden, who's seen him coming, stops and waits for him.

"What're you doing out here, David? You'd better get back home again!" he shouts even though he's close by. He wants to cross the road, but David's ahead of him, grabbing his arm. Together they shelter behind the door of a barn. "Well, what do you want?" asks the warden impatiently, stuffing a bundle of public notices into the large pocket of his coat. His weathered face is moist from the snow and he sighs gruffly as he surveys the buried town. He was born here in this village and knows everyone, he's used to posting up announcements of good tidings, but now it's just bad news. He'd rather ignore the boy than tell him a lie, but what good would it do? It's the eleventh hour and soon no one will be able to do anything.

"Any news?" asks David, tugging his sleeve.

The warden nods without answering. But David wants to know.

"What's in the notice, Mr Schumin?"

The warden looks away, before he replies in a low, gruff voice, "All Jews in all villages are to be moved!"

A white mist descends. He's frozen to the spot for a moment, he doesn't really understand, and yet he does, but maybe he's heard it wrong, yes, he must have heard it wrong. Again he tugs at the warden's sleeve, but the warden pulls himself free, wraps his coat tighter round his body and walks off towards the road now buried by the snow.

"Why are you going, Mr Schumin?" asks David still standing there.

The warden doesn't answer. He's already far out on the road when David shouts to him, "All villages, Mr Schumin?"

But the warden doesn't turn; he puts his head down into the storm and disappears in the falling snow.

David rounds the corner and runs like mad against the wind, down the road, home, home, but when he reaches the house and grabs the doorknob he can't go in. As the wind whirls around him and his bare fingers are about to turn to ice, he stops and thinks. Maybe Mr Schumin made a mistake? After all he drinks vodka, much too much vodka, only a few days ago he saw him go back and forth across the road like a headless chicken, and he heard his father say: "That Schumin won't last long; he's too old to run around with public notices." No, Mr Schumin can't remember, he's …

David pushes the door open and goes into the sitting room. It's quiet in the house; his mother and father are still asleep. He takes off his coat and scarf, removes his boots and tiptoes to the bedroom door, carefully opening it a fraction to look at his parents in the grey morning light. He notices his mother's small, white face, his father's large head with its messy hair. He doesn't really know how to tell them or what he should do. Even so, he opens the door and walks over to the front of the bed. He knocks softly on the wood, but neither of them wakes up. He knocks a bit harder and this time his mother turns over uneasily and suddenly opens her eyes. Startled, she sits up a little.

"Oh, it's you," she says relaxing visibly and smiling as she reaches her arms out for him.

"Why are you up so early?"

"Because, because …," he says, "I couldn't sleep."

Now his father is awake too, lying there, looking at him, but he still can't tell them.

"Nothing's happened, has it, David?" his father asks, looking anxious.

"Yeah …" he says, "I met Mr. Schumin out on the

road, no, well, I ran after him and −"

"And what, David?"

"He's putting up new notices everywhere and we all have to get out of here. Mr Schumin says that all Jews from all villages will be moved."

"That can't be right, David?" says his mother, hiding her face in the quilt. He nods.

"So it's our turn now," says his father, closing his eyes.

"Yes," he says but they're not listening any more.

He goes into the sitting room, not knowing what to do with himself, so he sits down by the table and waits. It's never been so quiet in the house, apart from the incessant howling of the wind.

But he needn't wait long. His mother and father get dressed quickly and come into the room. His mother motions him to come closer, and together the three of them stand there, silently holding on to each other.

"People will panic now. We must be strong, we must pack our things," says his father, before falling silent. David nods, looking up at their faces and suddenly feels closer to them than he's ever felt before.

"Where will we go? And for how long?" he asks his mother in a whisper. But none of them can answer, none of them knows anything.

They separate. His father goes out to the kitchen. He stands there, shaking his head, agitated, searching for something in his pockets.

*

The next day, at four in the morning, just when the wind has dropped and the night is at its coldest, just when he'd managed to fall asleep, that's when it happens. Despite all their preparations, they're not ready, despite all their plans, they're defenceless.

He's woken by his father standing fully dressed beside his bed and calling him. Then he can hear noises from the road, the sound of engines, loud voices shouting in German, dogs growling, and for an instant he imagines the house is full of soldiers; his arms and legs stiffen, he can't move but when his father passes him his clothes and goes into the other room, he can tell that they haven't arrived yet, that it's only his mother and father. He pulls on his clothes and goes into the sitting room, where his parents are pacing up and down. All their baggage and bedding is lying on the floor. They're talking together in low tones, he doesn't understand what they're saying, he's not yet fully awake. He doesn't want to be.

"Sit down there," his father says, suddenly pointing to a chair, "and don't say anything, no matter what happens!"

He sits down and a light from outside shines in through the windows, lighting up the room, reflecting in their pale faces – and then it's gone again.

"Where'd that light come from?" he asks, looking at his father, but he just shakes his head and carries on tying the cord tight around the bundle of bedclothes.

His mother is busy in the dark kitchen, she brings him a cup of soup and some bread, and then he realises — they've been up the entire night, sitting and waiting.

He takes the cup and bread and begins to eat, when all of a sudden the light returns, their faces are again white as ghosts, and someone's shouting loudly just outside their window. His mother stiffens and stares into the light, then there's a crash at the front door, the walls shake, all three look toward the little porch and suddenly there's a man in a black leather coat holding a pistol, addressing them. David's father gets up and walks hesitantly towards the man, who shouts "Halt!" stopping him in the middle of the room. Two soldiers with helmets and heavy coats barge into the room armed with rifles. David clutches his cup and bread, staring into faces that are like stone. Maybe we're going to die? The cup slips from his hand and clatters to the floor. One of the soldiers instantly turns and points his rifle at him.

"Easy, Schwartz," says the SS man, "they're completely harmless."

Schwartz grins, but doesn't move the rifle.

The SS man holsters his gun and stomps about the room, searching the bedroom and David's room too, like a bloodhound. David watches him, his quick movements, his sharp nose, his smooth neck. He's no longer interested in them, doesn't talk to them.

Outside the dogs are barking louder than before, they hear a shot in the distance, then some shouting close by, while the constant hum of the engines goes on out on the road. David tries to look out of the window, but is blinded by the light. His mother beckons him to come closer and holds him tight, he can feel her hands shaking.

The SS man with the leather coat stands for a moment assessing their luggage.

"What have you got hidden?" he asks coldly, nodding at his father. And before his father can even reply, he continues: "Gold, bonds, jewellery, money, put everything there on the table, *schnell, schnell,* hurry!"

And while his father and mother empty their pockets and rummage through their baggage for money and jewellery which they place on the table, the SS man takes out a notepad and a pen from his bag and hands it mechanically to one of the soldiers to list the items. Just as mechanically the soldier hands the list back to the officer, who passes it with an impatient gesture to David's father.

When his father looks up from the baggage on the floor, he is unexpectedly hit across the neck with the book, losing his balance, and crashing to the floor. Seeing this, his mother cries out but immediately she covers her mouth to stifle the sound. Getting up again, his father is somewhat confused.

"Stupid Jew, I said *schnell!*" said the SS man, shoving the notepad at him again.

A small gesture from the SS man and his father silently takes it and signs the list. The SS man surveys the room one more time when something catches his eye. He goes over to the glass cabinet, opens the door and takes out a porcelain platter. He turns round and confronts David's father.

"Meissen porcelain! And you're leaving it here for better times! The finest German porcelain, pawed at by dirty Jewish fingers. Listen, Jew, mark my words: You're not coming back, got it? This is your final journey!"

Without batting an eyelid, he smashes the plate against the wall, shattering it into a thousand pieces.

"That's your future, Jew!" he says, pointing his gloved finger at the pieces. Just then, they hear a scream followed by a shot from the house next door. David grabs hold of his mother, who's shaking. Shocked, his father reaches out for them, as if trying to protect them, he doesn't seem to realize what he's doing.

"*Raus, raus,* out!" shouts the SS officer, waving his hand as if he's swatting at flies. They grab their bundles and cases. David, too, picks up a bundle, and with a shove from the soldiers, they're herded out onto the street.

The first person he can see in the glare of the searchlight, and can hear amidst the clamour of dogs barking and people shouting is Mrs Kaplan, his neighbour. Her clothes are hanging off her like a sack, and she's screaming horribly, while two soldiers are struggling to shut her up. Then she falls down, kicking and screaming on the ground, howling like an animal. He stands still as people swarm past him and then, suddenly, he can hear it: "Eli! They've shot him, my Eli, they've shot him, Eli …"

Petrified, he stares while the soldiers pull her up and slap her until finally, she's quiet. His father pulls him away. They're all ready to go with the sled and their baggage.

"Push!" he shouts and now David's wide awake. He runs to the back of the sled and starts to push, he pushes and pushes, and the sled slides into his father's leg, but he doesn't seem to notice. With the sled's strap over his shoulders, his father runs on ahead, pulling the sled down the road towards the square. David keeps his mother in sight out of the corner of his eye, as she struggles after them with a sack under her arm.

From all ends of the village, Jews dressed in black, wrapped up in scarves and mittens, with several layers of clothing, trudge through the snow and the bitter cold towards the square. Everyone's carrying bags, bundles, suitcases, sacks. Some are pulling sleds, others pushing prams as they force their way through the frozen snow. Some slip and fall, others help them up, all of them manage to reach the square followed by the soldiers in their heavy coats and helmets and the SS men with their snapping dogs. Mrs Kaplan is carried to the square and set down on the frozen snow. Amidst the chaos and the half-light, people trample on her, but when his mother pushes through the crowd to her, she's still breathing. David can hear her calling. He forces his way over to her and together they get Mrs Kaplan on her feet.

Light from the searchlight sweeps over them, then a sharp voice from a loudspeaker suddenly blares out across the square, drowning out the yapping dogs and the crying children: 'Keep calm, nothing will happen to you as long as you do what you're told. The most important thing is to remain quiet and orderly. Anyone trying to escape will be shot on the spot. You are now in the custody of the German army and it is the task of the German army to lead you to a transit camp on the outskirts of Kielce. There you'll be given the necessary provisions and further information.'

The voice drones over the heads of the 267 Jews who've been driven from their homes into the square so early in the morning. Some listen, others just hear the words as one hears the distant voice of a nightmare, but when they hear the promise of work, they begin to feel calmer. There's still hope, still something to cling to. The lights are on in many of the houses and from behind the curtains, shadows of neighbours and acquaintances are recognized. A small group of citizens have come out and stand there freezing and silent at a distance, watching it all. It's an event that will be talked about for a long time. Some Poles shout out over the barking dogs: "Jewish swine, out! Parasites, get lost!"

Mrs Kaplan's legs give way under her and David and his mother have to catch her and pull her up with help from those nearby. "Let me be," she whispers, but how could they let her lay there? She can't stay, no one can, the only Jew who's left after the German invasion of the village is Eli Kaplan, the shoemaker, who could make anything with his hands and sewed boots so the leather sang.

For some days, he's left lying in his own blood on the floor of his house with a bullet in his chest. No one feels like fetching him, no one feels obliged to do the right thing, until one day Tomachevski, the farmer, drives up to the house and carries him out to his wagon. He slings him over his shoulder like a beast and puts him in a sack.

Folk turn away, shaking their heads, from the creaking wagon that slowly carries the last Jew out of the village.

That freezing morning, the people whisper Eli's fate as they move out of the square. They start off slowly, reluctant to leave their homes. Some turn and look back down the road, but are immediately driven forwards by the soldiers' shouts. Others set off automatically over the frozen snow without looking back, but it's as if there is lead in their boots, as if each step is a torment. The young ones help the old people to get through the deep snow, carrying their baggage, while the children start off clutching onto their parents, but soon have to help carry the heavy bundles of clothing, pots and blankets.

As the shabby horde passes the last house in the village and the empty white fields lay ahead in the great starlit darkness, a few of the young people feel a strange sense of adventure. Others are thinking only of escape and secretly begin to plan their flight, as they pull their sleds and haul their suitcases. They know the terrain and all the shortcuts in the surrounding woods and hills, so why shouldn't it be possible − these *goys* don't have eyes in the back of their heads, do they? A peculiar sense of recklessness creeps over them, their hands grow sweaty as they watch the soldiers, who are just shadows and silhouettes in the darkness.

David and his father have laid Mrs Kaplan on the sled, so now David and his mother have to carry most of the baggage. He's dragging a heavy suitcase along when he notices Jakob further ahead in the crowd, with not much to carry.

"Jakob!" he shouts, and Jakob turns round and waits for him as people pass. David lets the suitcase drop, pointing at it, and Jakob nods, he understands. Quickly they put Jakob's bundle on top of the suitcase and then lift it up together. They start to move. It's not too bad. For a while.

After the first kilometre in the biting cold, Isak Schlieferstein begins to limp, his bad leg's troubling him. His suitcase falls from his grasp, but stubbornly he drags his bad leg after him. His wife throws away her bundle and supports him, and they go on together, but more and more slowly, until some time later, they're hopelessly behind. A young man runs back to them, but is abruptly stopped by an SS man, who threatens him with his bayonet.

"Forward!" he shouts, "Forward!"

The young man stands there helplessly, unable to decide which way to go.

"Forward!" screams the SS man, waving the bayonet in front of the young man's face. But the youth is frozen, shocked by this incomprehensible rage, the face contorted in anger and fear, nails him to the spot. He ventures some small, half-strangled sounds of protest, and a second later the bayonet has pierced his breast. He falls over and says no more. It all happens so fast. His family, parents and two sisters stop on the road, the mother screaming, running back to him, the high cry of agony spreads through the masses, so that even more people stop and turn around. A shrill whistle penetrates the darkness. SS officers and soldiers run in from all directions, pushing and beating the confused and distraught group back into line. The young man's mother is also shoved back, and amidst the panic her daughters take hold of her and pull her forward along the road.

Soon calm is restored in the group but Isak Schlieferstein and his wife have disappeared. David's mother keeps on looking back until finally she gives up on seeing them again. Then her stride becomes more resolute, she pulls her coat tight around her body and fixes her gaze on a point on the horizon beyond the farms and fields.

The Schliefersteins have really disappeared, and soon it's as if they never existed. The people walk on and on, but neither the darkness nor their wandering seems to have any end. The road they all knew so well has become unknown and fateful in the course of a winter morning.

Most of them keep their heads up, fighting against the cold and hardship. There's no time to think, there's nothing left to consider. One must simply go along with it and hope.

Slowly the light breaks through the mist, a dim light which slowly outlines the woods ahead. The slender, bare birch trees and the peculiar silence surrounding them in the snowy landscape contrasts with memories of summers past when the green leaves glistened in the sun. Each person has his own experiences in these woods, and maybe that's why they go on quietly, momentarily forgetting their cold hands and feet.

Slowly, tiredness creeps into David's bones, the lack of sleep and the burden of the suitcase are about to overwhelm him. He senses that the suitcase is about to slip from his hands, but Jakob has a good grip on it and tells him to hold on, hold on all the time, and not give up. He thinks he can hear someone laughing, maybe it's Jakob, so he tenses his body and holds the handle of the suitcase as tightly as he can. They walk four or five metres then he can relax again, and he turns his head towards Jakob and nods. He'll make it. If Jakob can do it, he can, too.

But even before they're out of the woods, a young man runs off and disappears like a rabbit between some of the birch trees. The shrill whistle sounds again, the German soldiers block the path with their rifles and motorcycles, and the ones up front stop abruptly. Many people carry on as if nothing's happened, bumping into those in front and pushing them into the angry soldiers, who respond with blows and shoves. Some fall, others push backwards or move out towards the trees, where they're driven back. The shouting and barking of the dogs become louder until the sudden confusion turns to panic, and in the midst of this panic some of the men run off and quickly vanish into the darkened woods.

For a few minutes the Germans are clearly confused and shout at each other, some shoot over the heads of the crowd, others set their dogs after the runaways, and a little later, shots are heard from the woods. An ominous silence follows. In the meantime, people who have fallen over are brought to their feet. They stand and listen, in silence.

Some minutes later, the patrol returns with their excited dogs. They give loud commands and the group starts moving again. Nobody knows whether anyone survived that wild flight through the woods.

A warning is whispered through the crowd that their leader, Antek Blum will hold everyone responsible for their actions. From that moment on, no one thinks of escape.

Now they're out in the open again and they keep on going. Half an hour later, the road rises and heaven and earth blur into one, as the snow falls heavily around them. Everything is grey and white. The elderly and women with bundles or small children in their arms repeatedly slip over or get trapped in the deep snow. The German motorcycles become helplessly stalled so they leave them behind, but onward they must go, always onward. Exhausted, they drag each other out of the snow, bundles and suitcases either slip from their hands or get tossed aside. Now the only thing that matters is yourself and those around you.

David realises that the sled with Mrs Kaplan is stuck, so he and Jakob dump the suitcase and wade back through the snow to his father. They help lift Mrs Kaplan off the sled.

"Leave me be!" she moans again, but they take her under the arms and carry her forward. Jakob slips, she falls down, but they pick her up again. David's father takes her legs and they each take an arm, and in this way they slowly go on.

As they walk along, David searches in the crowd for his mother but he can't see her, and his heart starts pounding madly. He walks on, looking back – there she is, now he can see her, she's still carrying the bundle under her arm. He feels relieved and gets new strength.

It's ten hours before the exhausted flock of Jews reaches the transit camp on the outskirts of Kielce. It's past noon and infants are crying from hunger and cold in their parents' arms. They're led through the barbed wire gate, past a watchtower and into a courtyard in front of two dilapidated buildings that once served as machine rooms but have now been emptied of anything of value. With their few belongings, they're herded together in that desolate courtyard with its view of the white fields beyond the fence. Not far from them, a group of inmates in coats and boots are clearing the yard of snow, while two SS officers, one barking orders with a high, shrill voice, keep an eye on them. Some boys in rags carry the snow away in wheelbarrows, but even before they've cleared a patch, new snow has fallen again.

Four guards from the camp push the group into two lines but some fail to understand what's expected of them and are beaten into place with sticks by the guards. Jakob, David and his father try to get Mrs Kaplan back on her feet, but her legs give way, so David and his father each take an arm, while Jakob supports her from behind. All four stand like that. A guard runs back and forth in front of the group and counts. They repeat this a couple of times. Then the guards stand in a row in front of the group and click their heels together.

David stares at their clean collared necks. They wait and wait. But for how long?

A voice that he recognizes whispers behind him: "Six are lost."

"Don't be so sure," says another.

"I've counted."

"They didn't get Adam!"

"Was it Adam?"

"Yes. He was walking just next to me. He said, 'Now run!' and he ran."

"No, they didn't get him. He's too fast."

Another half an hour passes, the cold cuts into their feet and bones, children scream, people take turns holding them in their arms until one of the guards suddenly breaks in with his stick, beating a father, and stopping this exchange. The father sinks down on his knees and the man next to him quickly bends down and takes the child from his arms.

From the building behind them, indistinct voices can be heard, but the building has no windows and reveals no secrets. The voices seem unreal and far away, as if they belong to another world. The group of inmates clearing snow suddenly leave the square and disappear behind the building. Five minutes later, there's little evidence of their work, and after another five, all traces are gone.

"I can't hold on anymore!" says David to his father, as Mrs Kaplan's legs give way under her again, and they grab her again and heave her up onto her feet.

"You must!" says his father, without looking at him.

Mrs Kaplan begins to moan, but he doesn't understand what she's saying.

"What's she saying?" whispers Jakob behind her.

"She's praying," says his father.

"It won't help," whispers Jakob.

"Be quiet!" says his father, nodding angrily.

But David asks anyway: "How long must we stand here?"

"I don't know," whispers his father. "Keep your eyes open and your mouth shut."

He feels like shouting, feels like letting go of Mrs Kaplan and fleeing from the line – where to he doesn't know. But he keeps on standing. The cold burns into his heels. He turns his head in his mother's direction. She's standing further down the row behind him. Her face is deathly pale, her hair and forehead are hidden under a black scarf. As she sees him, she sends him a faint, tired smile. He quickly turns round and faces forward as he's been ordered to.

Filled with a sudden contempt, he stares at the four guards in their warm coats, who have begun to walk around not far from them. Two of them pace restlessly back and forth in front of the rows of people, glancing at them now and then, occasionally stopping and flapping their arms for warmth. They're bored. The guard who beat them with his stick waves it around as he surveys the yard. David wishes that he'd freeze to death. The two others have just lit cigarettes and are standing there chatting. He can't hear what they're saying, both have stuck their white sticks in their coat belts, one of them's pointing towards him, no, it's not him, it's Mrs Kaplan he's pointing at. He says something to the other guard, who suddenly laughs and shakes his head. A shiver runs down David's spine – in his imagination, they're already on their way towards Mrs Kaplan and … But nothing happens. They keep standing there, talking, but they never take their eyes off them.

Numbed by the cold and the immense effort of constantly supporting Mrs Kaplan's limp arms, he falls into a daze – sees yet doesn't see – that the gate has opened and a new group is being forced into the little square. Driven on by shouts and beatings, they take their places sixty metres from them and are soon forced into silence. Only the crying of the children breaks the grey stillness in the midst of the falling snow.

Another half hour passes, two of the old people in the group collapse, but helping hands pull them up from the snow and support them. The guards are obviously impatient and are discussing something keenly amongst themselves. Apparently there's something or other that hasn't gone according to plan. When two other soldiers bring bread and soup out to the freezing guards, and they're momentarily distracted, small nursing bottles are passed through the ranks from hand to hand to the distressed infants. Where they come from no one knows but they are passed on anyway. But to no avail: the milk has turned to ice and the cold hands can do nothing.

Again the gate is released to allow three open trucks to drive into the camp and disappear behind the building.

In their rows, it's impossible for the people to see what's happening, they can only guess.

A loud crash is heard like a door banging, dogs bark and orders are shouted out from the other end of the building. Polish and Yiddish voices rise above the din, then a piercing cry drowns everything else out. In their rows, people shuffle even closer together, and anyone who still can, including the guards, stares expectantly towards the end of the building.

A woman suddenly appears in the yard with a child in her arms, clutching the child close to her, as she runs wildly through the snowy mist. A guard who's fast on her heels, grabs hold of her shoulder, but she slips out of his grasp and runs further into the open square. Three of the guards immediately block her way and are ready to grab her, but one of them slips over and by some miracle, the woman is able to get past them. Now there are five men pursuing her as she lurches madly towards a fence that she barely notices and goes crashing into it. Somehow, she manages to get back on her feet, still holding her child, even though they are both totally covered in snow. She turns and suddenly faces the five guards who are now blocking her way. Two of them walk towards her, and as if to get revenge for their humiliation, they wrench the child from her arms and push her against the fence. She gets onto her knees and pleads with them to be able to keep her child. But it does no good. One of the guards takes the child, standing with it as if he was holding a stone then strides back across the square. With a lot of shouting, the mother is dragged back to join the people in the yard.

Meanwhile, the three trucks have been quickly and efficiently loaded with inmates from the building and are being driven slowly towards the gate. Silently, the pallid prisoners either sit or lay down in the back and to David, they're just shadows.

"Where are they going?" whispers Jakob, but he barely hears. One of the trucks gets stuck in the snow, its wheels spin then it backs up and goes forward again. The guard with the child walks up to the back of the truck, shouts something and then throws the child in as if it were a ball. Startled, an old man grabs the child and they fall over onto the others in the back. The mother struggles to break free of the guards. When she collapses in the snow, they pick her up and carry her away. The truck drives through the gate and soon disappears into the densely falling snow.

Once again they're left to their guards and the cold and the snow. More time passes, and in the row opposite an elderly man collapses from exhaustion. Before anyone can help him up, two of the guards rush over and pull him out of line. Whether it's for their own amusement or as a warning to others, they begin to roll him around in the snow. More and more snow sticks to his head and his clothes, until eventually he becomes frozen stiff like a long block of ice, which the two guards, still laughing, continue to push around.

At that moment, a young man from Bielino becomes so incensed that he shouts out at the top of his voice: *"Meschugge! Meschugge!* Crazy!"

A guard runs towards the group, but he's uncertain who shouted so he stands for a moment with his stick raised, surveying the rows, then orders a random young man from the front row to step forward and beats him about his head and shoulders.

"Who shouted that?"

The young man staggers under the blows but manages to remain silent, averting his eyes from the guard. Nobody says anything. More guards approach and pace back and forth in front of the group in a threatening manner.

Just then, a Storm Trooper walks into the square, in his long shiny boots and black uniform. He walks casually across the snow while the guards stand in a row waiting, but suddenly loses his footing and falls over awkwardly in the heavy snow. A couple of the guards run over to help him up, but he refuses their assistance and orders them back into position in annoyance. In a flash he stands up, picks up his cap and with a trained movement, puts it back on his head. Angrily, he continues towards them. David can see his outline approaching, like some kind of huge apparition in the softly falling snow.

The Storm Trooper waves a guard forward and points at Mrs Kaplan. "What's she doing here? Remove her, at once!" he says, striding quickly back and forth in front of the rows, speaking alternately in German and broken Polish.

Immediately, two guards grab hold of Mrs Kaplan to pull her out of the row, but Jakob and David's father grip hold of her firmly. David tries to cling onto her arm, a stick flies in front of his eyes, then he feels something hit his head, agony pierces his body – it's white before his eyes. He falls.

He falls and falls and for a long time seems to be running around in an enormous white field. Then it's as if he's flying high above it. He can see himself down there on the white field. Running round and round. Then quiet. Black.

Sounds slowly return to him, whispering voices, a shout and smells – the smell of something burnt. A head that he doesn't recognize bends over him, and his head is lifted up by someone standing behind him.

"Drink!" says the voice and he opens his mouth and drinks. His teeth bite into the metal cup as he drains it. He must have more.

"We don't have any more right now," says the voice. He looks in the direction of the voice and slowly he makes out a shape: it's his father. And behind him is Jakob and his father too. And behind them stands his mother. And they're in a great hall and around them are many others, most of them lying down. It's dark and cold in the hall, his head is aching and when he feels his hair, it's all matted and stiff.

"They hit you," whispers his father. "I could've killed them!"

"It was just as well you didn't try," says Jakob's father, taking Jakob by his shoulders. "He survived, that's what matters right now."

Jakob gives him a thumbs up sign. David slowly sticks his thumb up, too.

"He'll make it," says Jakob's father and leads Jakob further into the hall, where they spread out a blanket and lay down on the floor.

His mother hands him something, which at first he doesn't recognise, but then he sees that it's a wooden bowl and a spoon.

"We saved something for you," she says. "It doesn't taste good; but eat it anyway."

He picks up the spoon and takes a mouthful of the thin soup. It's cold and disgusting; he can't swallow it and spits it out at once.

"Do what your mother says," whispers his father hoarsely, nudging his arm. "Eat!"

In the middle of the hall in the darkness, a voice suddenly complains and other voices make a shushing noise. Again David notices the burnt smell in his nostrils and looks at his father's tired, resolute face. So he takes a couple of mouthfuls of the soup and this time he forces it down.

"Good," whispers his father. "Keep going!"

He eats the rest of the soup, but is still hungry. His mother hands him a piece of bread, which he finishes at once.

"Isn't there any more?" he asks her but his mother shakes her head.

"They took our bread. All we have left is a few blankets and some clothes," she whispers and strokes his forehead.

He looks into her shiny black eyes.

"Tomorrow they'll have more bread," says his father. "Lie down and go to sleep now."

He wants to ask if he really has to sleep there. On the floor. But he's feeling dizzy again so he lies down on the blanket on the floor. His mother covers him with his father's overcoat.

The floor's cold, but he refuses to think about it. He curls up and lies on his side. His mother is also lying down, opposite him, though she's practically hidden under her coat and blanket, only her hair can be seen. Inside the hall, someone coughs, a child is crying, whispering voices murmur in the darkness. Suddenly, he remembers something he has to ask. He prods his mother. "Where's Mrs Kaplan?" he asks.

His mother pulls her coat down from her face and shushes him.

"Why can't I speak?" he whispers.

"You can," she says, "just whisper."

"So where is she?" he asks again softly.

"I don't know, David," she says, "don't worry about it right now."

He can see that she's frightened and lets it go. He tries to close his eyes, but he keeps on thinking about the old lady. He doesn't understand why his mother won't admit that the Germans have taken her. Where have they taken her to? What have they done to her? His imagination conjures up all sorts of possibilities so he opens his eyes and examines the shadows beneath the rafters. Up there it's cold and dark. He starts to shake all over then he feels his mother reach over and rub his arms. Next, she moves closer to him and lays the coats over them both. They fall asleep.

In the middle of the night he wakes up with a start. At first he thinks he's at home but doesn't understand why the room is so big and why there's someone wheezing nearby. Then he realises where he is. He sits up in the darkness and looks around the hall. At first, he can see almost nothing, just faint shapes in long rows. After a while, he can make out all the people. He's frightened by so many pale, silent faces, but he pays them little attention as he can now tell where the noise is coming from. Not far away, lies a small girl gasping for air – he hasn't seen her before and doesn't know who she is. A man in a heavy sweater sits beside her, wiping her forehead with a handkerchief. Her wheezing seems to be growing worse, interrupted only by coughing fits. The man lifts her up from the floor and holds her tenderly in his arms. She's very pale and thin; David wonders what's wrong with her. The man rocks her back and forth in his arms and puts her down again carefully. David would get up and go over to them, but he feels too dizzy so he lies back down and wraps himself in the coat. A terrible fatigue overwhelms him. He sleeps.

When he wakes in the morning, most of the others are already up. He's still feeling tired as he looks around the hall for his mother and father. Everywhere there are blankets, baggage and bundles scattered over the concrete floor, as well as prams and small tables. Here and there, a child lies still sleeping or crying and small groups stand around or sit and eat, whispering to each other. Not far from him, two men are arguing about a blanket. Water's dripping from the ceiling and the wind is howling through a hole in the rafters. Along one wall, four small heaters are burning, giving off a sickening grey smoke that fills the room.

He sees his parents in a long line at the end of the hall. Standing at a table, two women are ladling something out, and everyone's standing ready with bowls and cups. He gets up to go over to them, but suddenly he has to pee. He looks around, but there's no place to go, so he walks unsteadily towards the other end of the building where there's a door. He opens the door, a cold wind slaps him in the face and the door blows wide open. He puts his head down and steps out into the whiteness beyond. He takes a couple of steps along the side of the building when a soldier emerges unexpectedly from the shelter at the end of the building and points his rifle at him.

"Get back, get back!" he shouts.

Frightened, he stands still, crossing his legs.

"But I have to pee," he says in Polish.

The soldier, who doesn't understand him, hesitates a moment and points at him with his rifle.

"I have to pee," he says in German. "Don't you understand?"

The soldier smiles a little, lowers his bayonet, but his face stiffens again. A guard approaches from behind him.

"What's wrong?" he asks.

"The boy needs to pee," says the soldier.

"Oh, he needs to pee!" laughs the guard, before removing his knife and cutting a hole in the fly of David's trousers.

"Piss!" he says. "Piss now!" laughs the guard, unmoving. Then the soldier turns his back and returns to the shelter.

But David's too stressed, he can't produce a drop. He squeezes as hard as he can and stares ahead into space.

"So piss, little Jewish devil!" shouts the guard, pushing him.

David looks incomprehensibly up into the guard's contorted face.

"Oh stop it, Josh, you can see the boy can't go," says the soldier again coming out of his shelter. He puts his hand on the other man's arm and offers him a cigarette.

The guard, a tall thin twenty-year-old with a baby face, stands for a moment feeling agitated, staring at David, then he shakes his head, turns and takes the cigarette.

At the same time, David runs back to the door and into the hall. He desperately shuts the door against the wind and stands there. Ashamed, he looks down at his ripped trousers. His entire body reacts, and he releases a stream down his leg. At that moment he feels completely alone.

In the distance, he sees Jakob on his way over to him, but he doesn't want to talk to him, so he goes towards the wall and sits down on the floor.

Jakob soon finds him but David waves him away with his hand and won't look at him.

"I've got some bread for you," says Jakob and hands over a thin slice of bread. David stares down at the floor and puts his hands over his trousers.

"It's from your mother. Take it now − or I'll eat it!"

Even though he's so hungry his stomach's grumbling, he can't think of anything else.

"You smell," says Jakob, not giving up. "What's wrong with you?"

"I don't smell," he replies, looking fiercely up at Jakob. Jakob bends down closer.

"Your trousers ..."

"There's nothing wrong with my trousers!" he says, trying to cover up his legs with his arms.

"Yeh, they're ..."

"Go away, just go away!"

Jakob stands there for a moment then throws the bread at him, turns and wanders away down the hall.

David can't move; he sits staring at the dry slice of bread on the floor, recalling the guard's angry face, afraid that he'll come after him. His body's so tense, he feels as if he might break into pieces at the slightest thing. He doesn't know what to do or where to go. He looks at the crowd of people in the hall. There are way too many of them. They don't have time to worry about him. And they won't do anything anyway. Not even his father or mother. But why won't they do anything? He doesn't understand.

Suddenly, his mother's standing next to him – he hadn't seen her come.

"Why are you sitting over here?" she asks, but he just looks at her and covers his trousers with his hands.

"Has something happened?" she asks and sits down beside him. He shakes his head and closes his eyes. Gently, she removes his hands from his trousers and sighs a little when she sees the ripped trousers. He turns his face away. Now, she too has seen it.

"Look at me, David," she says and he looks at her. "What have you done? Where have you been?"

"I thought …" he says, "I thought … he'd kill me."

"Who, David, who would kill you?"

"And then … I peed in my pants …"

His mother grabs his arms.

"Now you tell me everything, d'you hear me?"

So he tells her about the soldier and the guard and his knife but he's not sure that she understands so he goes over the whole thing again. Now he can see that she's understood.

"Listen," she whispers, "you have to stay with us, you mustn't go out by yourself, understand?"

Of course he understands.

"Yes," he says and gets up.

They stand awkwardly in front of each other for a moment then she gives him a hug and he feels like he's alive again.

Together they walk back to the tiny space with their blankets. His father hands him a cup full of some sort of black liquid; it's lukewarm and looks like coffee but when he takes a sip, it tastes horrible. He'd like to spit it out, but realises that his father's watching him so he closes his eyes and gulps it all down in two mouthfuls.

"You forgot something," says his mother handing him the thin slice of dried bread, which she must have picked up from the floor by the wall.

"Thanks," he says and eats the bread, too.

He's still hungry and the rumbling in his stomach won't stop, but he decides not to think about it.

He expects his father to question him, but he just sits there in his coat and smokes. His mother gives him a fresh pair of trousers from her bundle and he quickly changes out of the old ones and puts on the new. He sits down close by his father and even though it's cold on the floor, he begins to feel warm again.

The hours pass. He either sits or sleeps or looks around the hall. Smoke and soot from the small heaters has risen to create a grey smog under the rafters, and coughing can be heard from all corners of the room. Somewhere in the dark mass of people, someone asks for water, another sings softly for a small group, a third writes something down, a fourth is searching vainly for extra bread or milk. Some pace nervously back and forth across the floor, most sit passively on their blankets with their bundles and try to keep warm under their heavy coats and jackets.

His mother is sitting down with them and every now and then they massage each other's hands and feet. His father has stopped smoking – the empty cigarette pack lies crumpled up between his legs.

"All we can do is wait," he says suddenly and becomes quiet again.

Several times, a young man with a wild look in his eye, accidentally bumps into them as he edges past, and they've no idea where he's going. Maybe he's lost a brother or a mother, maybe he's mad. Suddenly, he sits down by them and leans his head against David's mother, then just as suddenly he gets up, nods to them and wanders off into the hall.

Most of the people here are strangers. He figures that most of the people from his village are in the other building. Maybe they're better off in there, maybe they can help each other? But when he asks his father, he says, "They're just as badly off as us, maybe worse."

"Why do you think that?" he asks, but his father doesn't answer, just sits and looks out into space.

His mother gets up abruptly and edges past the people sitting nearby. She stops by a man who's sitting hunched over on a dirty sheet. He has a doll in his hands, which he keeps staring at. It's the man from last night, the man with the sick girl. But the girl isn't there any more. Why hadn't he noticed before?

He tells his father about the girl and his father nods, an odd look on his face.

"She's not here any more, David," he says. "She was very ill. She has been for weeks."

"Is she dead?"

His father looks away and fumbles with the empty cigarette pack.

"They came for her this morning," he says, "while you slept."

"Why didn't you say anything?"

His father looks at him blankly. "What should I have said?"

David closes his eyes and tries not to think about the girl. He forces himself to think about the ash trees back home. When that doesn't work, he tries thinking about school, remembering the songs they sang and after that he tries to recall his uncle's stories. He looks at his hands and thinks about what his uncle once told him, that hands were the keys to heaven. "Use your hands well and God will give you everything in return." He closes his eyes and tries to remember his uncle's face but it's impossible. He can't help thinking about the little girl. It's war. She's dead. Maybe they'll die, too. Maybe they'll get sick too, and maybe they'll be taken away one early morning when there's no one to see.

No, he won't think about it. He won't think about anything. He pulls the blanket up over his legs and huddles up against his father.

*

Later that night, when the hall is pitch black and the wind is howling through the rafters and the cold from the concrete floor is cutting into them, he hears his father and Jakob's father whispering together. They think he's asleep.

"There are more than four hundred of us," says Jakob's father. "And rumour has it that more are on their way. There are folk who don't even have a place to sleep."

"Who can sleep in here? Lying right on the floor."

"But you manage to anyway?"

"An hour or two," says his father. "I try to sleep during the day. Sitting up."

"Have you seen the stuff they call milk?"

"Watered down milk once a week."

"The little ones won't make it … This afternoon they took one out. A few days ago, they took three."

His father sighs, he breathes deeply.

"This is worse than I'd imagined."

"Mmm," says Jakob's father and becomes silent. David glimpses the side of his face in the darkness. Some children are crying at the other end of the building. The man on a blanket next to him is saying a prayer, he can smell his bad breath. A scratching sound seems to be coming from the cracks in the wall. Maybe it's a mouse. A man suddenly begins ranting and raving close by.

The only word he can make out is 'cakes'.

"He wants cakes, does he!" says his father.

The two men laugh a bit.

"Any idea where they're taking us?" asks his father after a while.

"Some say the ghetto in Kielce or Rzeszow, others say a labour camp in Skarzyski, where there's a munitions factory by the name of Hugo Schneider, but you can't rely on any of it. Not a word."

"I should've stayed with the group," mutters his father.

"What good would that have been?"

"At least we'd have had rifles."

"You'd be no good as a communist and not much better at knocking people off."

"How would you know?" asks his father in an irritated tone.

"Anyway, it's too late now," says Jakob's father.

They sit there without speaking then Jakob's father gets up and creeps down towards the other end of the hall. David's father wraps himself in his coat and lies down next to him. He tosses and turns.

In the darkness, David tries to imagine his father with a rifle. He remembers the time Tomachevski passed him a rifle to shoot a rabbit in the field, how he got the rabbit in his sights, but couldn't pull the trigger. He used to feel ashamed that his father couldn't be like Tomachevski. Now it's entirely different.

His head hurts and he's feeling sick. He makes himself count to one hundred in Hebrew, but can't get past fifty-two. His stomach's aching and he can still taste the weak turnip soup that he'd eaten earlier. He'd stood in the soup line with his mother, but when they got to the head of the queue, there wasn't any bread left. Among the crowd, people were trading money, jewellery, watches and sleeping places for more bread. Some people had a lot, others had none.

*

At four o'clock the next morning, the door to the building is opened, a searchlight is shone onto the sick and the sleeping, dogs bark and voices shout commands into the dark. The same shouts are heard again and again.

"Get up! Morning roll call! *Schnell, schnell,* hurry!"

Roused by blows from sticks and rifle butts, the people are driven out of the building into the snow. The old, those who can barely walk are dragged along, children who don't understand what's happening are either carried out or hang back among the fearful. Women desperately searching for their children in the confusion are dragged to the side and berated, men who are slow to rise, fight off furious kicks and blows and the sick are carried or helped out.

The shouting and whistles go on and on until the people form themselves into five long rows out in the snow and then the counting begins. A Storm Trooper walks back and forth in front of them in his highly polished boots, counting, while a few guards stand by. The Storm Trooper has trouble walking in the snow and as he stops to write something in his book, he drops his pencil. Immediately, he calls a guard to search for it, takes a few steps back and starts shouting at the people.

"Damned Jews, you don't deserve to live! You deserve nothing!"

With a self-satisfied expression, he looks down at his book and calls a guard over. They stand there for a moment and talk. The Storm Trooper's expression changes. Clearly annoyed, he walks back and forth along the long rows again and counts, in the process knocking a woman to the ground who happens to step out of line. Once more he calls a guard over to discuss the numbers, but something doesn't tally.

Then he turns towards the rows of people and bellows: "Get down! Push-ups! Down!"

Some of them don't understand German and remain standing, while the rest get down in the snow and start pushing themselves up off the ground. The rest quickly follow suit. An older woman falls to her knees moaning and is swiftly pushed down by a running guard, while the children and the sickly desperately try to keep up the pace.

"One ... two ... one ... two ..."

The Storm Trooper waves his arms to the beat and in his agitation staggers a little. One after another people fall exhausted into the snow, only the younger men can keep on pushing themselves up off the snow, until eventually, they too, collapse.

Then the Storm Trooper gives up and walks off unsteadily across the square, disappearing inside a little hut.

"The idiot's drunk," whispers a man next to David, cautiously lifting his head, looking for the guards. His head is big and heavy, as if carved out of rock, everything about him is large, including his hands which he slowly places under his forehead in the snow. His narrow eyes stare at David, his mouth smiles ruefully, "One day we'll get our revenge, one day …"

Then it suddenly occurs to him that it's just a boy he's talking to, and his expression immediately becomes soft and friendly. "Are you alone here?" he whispers.

"No," says David, still exhausted from the endless push-ups.

"Have they beaten you?"

David nods as he lifts his head a little, looking in the direction of the guards.

"If they touch you, you come to me," says the man with a smile, then he turns his head away swiftly.

David lies there for a long time, shaking with cold and looks at the big man's broad neck. He feels as if he's frozen to the ground and lifts himself up from the snow every now and then to get away from the cold for a few moments. But each time he does this, the cold bites into his hands and they burn like open wounds, so he brings them in front of his head and rubs them together.

Some of the children try to get up, but are quickly

pulled back down by their mother or father. They protest and start to cry, but their parents have no other choice.

An hour passes – children howl, older women weep, but the world around them seems unaffected. In the watchtower by the gate, the guards change shift, they chat about the weather or letters from home, as they casually survey the people lying in the snow. There's no reason for concern. Everything's under control and the Jews are frightened as lambs.

The Storm Trooper in the hut takes another sip of brandy and looks at his watch. He gets up and checks his appearance in the shaving mirror on the wall. He sighs morosely at the sight of the bluish bags under his eyes. He's tired of his post, would rather be in Berlin, where he could achieve some distinction and keep an eye on his girlfriend. Why doesn't she answer his letters? Not a word in three months! Is it his fault that he hasn't been promoted ...? He drains his cup and the brandy hits the spot. He gets up, straightens the jacket of his uniform and wonders if he needs his coat but decides that the jacket suits him best. He looks in the mirror and admires his figure. Now back to this blasted work!

He takes a couple of unsteady steps towards the door, straightens up, opens the door and steps out onto the square. The cold wind cuts through him like a knife so he turns on his heel and goes back into the hut and pulls on his coat.

As he walks back to the yard and the hundreds of people left lying there, he has no plan. His mind's a blank, his reactions mechanical. He stands before them and orders them up on their feet. Numbed by the cold, they're slow to rise, and two lie still in the snow. Some men nearby try to help them up.

"Leave them be!" he shouts and stands there silently surveying the rows. The figures simply don't add up; one person is missing and he knows that person must be hiding somewhere. They won't make a fool of him. He stares at the exhausted faces and the frozen shapes and they fill him with disgust.

"Pathetic – you're all totally and utterly pathetic!" he shouts. "Where have you hidden him? Haven't you had enough?"

No one reacts. It's only now that they realize the reason for all this agony. The officer calls two guards over and orders them into the buildings. Then he turns and walks back towards the hut.

David looks up and down the rows as he sticks his frozen hands under his coat. A little way off, he notices a form in the snow. A woman's lying there face down, he's not sure whether she's alive. He doesn't understand why she's just lying there. Instinctively, he turns to look at his neighbour, whose coat only reaches his thighs and whose mittens are full of holes. He's just staring ahead in silence. Maybe he hasn't noticed anything – maybe he doesn't care?

Without moving his great body, he suddenly whispers, "That's how they do it. The more that kick the bucket, the happier they are. And I'll tell you, there are camps that are worse than here."

He looks up at his neighbour's unmoving face and

again sees that strange smile. But he doesn't believe him. Why's he saying that?

"I don't believe you," he whispers.

"Too bad for you," says the man, "you're only a child."

"I'm not a child," he whispers angrily and stares dead ahead.

"How old are you?" asks the man, glancing at him quickly.

"Fourteen," he lies, staring at the guards.

"Why aren't you wearing any gloves? Don't you know you'll die without gloves?"

"Someone stole them last night ..."

"You have to be on your guard all the time, or you won't make it," whispers the man then abruptly shuts up, when one of the guards looks their way.

When the guard looks away, the man tears off his tatty mittens, rolls them up in his fist and quickly hands them to him. But David won't take them – why should someone else freeze for his sake?

"Take them!" hisses the man angrily, poking him.

He takes the mittens and quickly wraps them around his hands and sticks them back under his coat. It helps. After some time he can feel his hands again. He glances over his left shoulder and catches a glimpse of his father. His face is grey and drawn, and he's staring down at the ground. He begins to worry that it's not him but his father who's about to give up. But he can't bear the thought and puts it out of his mind. He can't see his mother and that frightens him.

Occasionally, a car or military vehicle drives past the fence, or people pass on foot, but they all seem like black shadows on the white horizon, and only faint sounds can be heard beneath the silent sky. There's one world outside and one world inside, and the world outside already seems like a distant dream to David. Although he stands there looking at it, he can't see it any more.

Something inside him makes him hold on, and he doggedly repeats to himself: "I will go on, I will!"

In the meantime, the Storm Trooper has paused in the middle of a letter to his girlfriend. He stares at the lines, "I'll soon be with you in Berlin, little Trudi. Promise that you'll write to me right away." Irritated, he screws up the letter; why keep on with this humiliation? Hasn't she already got what she wanted? Next time, he'll arrive unannounced, yes, that's what he'll do. And if there's any sign of someone else, out she goes. Yes, out she goes.

He feels around in his coat pocket for the bottle of brandy, but puts it back when the door opens and a guard enters. The guard salutes him and stands there for a while before the officer responds.

"Any luck?" he asks without looking at the guard.

"The buildings have been searched without result, sir!"

"Search them again, even the toilets!"

"There are no toilets, only buckets, sir!"

The officer turns towards the guard. "Are you questioning the order?" he hisses.

"No, sir," says the guard looking straight ahead.

"*Raus! Raus!* Get out!" he shouts.

"*Jawohl! Heil Hitler!*" says the guard, before turning and quickly leaving the shack.

The officer sits down and stares at the door then holds his head in his hands. Damned woman, can't she see he's suffering? He pulls the brandy out of his pocket and takes a slug. He rips a page from his notepad and tries to write but the pencil remains poised on the paper. His mind's a blank. He doesn't understand. Hasn't he done everything they've asked of him? Hasn't he distinguished himself in this camp? Hasn't he done his duty while the Major has had his fun in Kielce? That Major from Nuremberg, with his endless boasting about women, doesn't think twice about him. But he'd best not underestimate him. After all, he has buddies in the high command.

He gets up with difficulty, leaning on the table and crosses the floor to put on his coat. He walks over to the mirror, straightens up and smiles faintly at his blurred image. For whatever reason, a phrase pops into his head, a phrase that he was always the first to remember at the SS training school in Dusseldorf. He mumbles it to himself: "God be with us."

Morosely, he walks to the door, but as he steps out into the cold, he's 'on duty' again. The rows of people in the square see him coming and timidly straighten up; the guards stand to attention and await his orders. Yet another woman lies prostrate in the snow. The two guards who have searched the buildings for a second time, come running back and report loud and clear: No Jews!

The officer orders another count, and a guard paces briskly back and forth in front of the rows, counting, while the officer steps back, standing astride so all can see him. Everyone waits.

A buzzard glides high over their heads, then suddenly dives and disappears behind some trees on the other side of the fence. David follows it with his eyes and for a few moments forgets where he is.

The cold has clamped an iron grip everywhere. The guard stops in front of the officer, clicks his heels together, salutes.

"422 Jews, sir!"

The officer doesn't register any surprise. He quickly checks his book, the number floats before his eyes: 421.

"Count again!" he orders and the guard again walks along the rows counting out loud.

"The idiot's counted wrong," whispers David's neighbour without looking at him. David wakes from his daze, stares at the officer, but can't think. Before him, the world's turned grey.

The guard again reports back to the officer but the figure's still the same: 422. The officer waves the guard away and stands for a moment on his wobbly legs, surveying the crowd. In his imagination, he's become a great general and the hundreds standing before him have grown to thousands. Once and for all they'll learn just who it is they're dealing with.

"Polish Jews!" he shouts, "you're a disgrace to the German people! Don't expect any mercy. We'll teach you what discipline and hard work really mean. We know you, we know your base instincts, your ..."

The Storm Trooper suddenly stops, searching for the right words. He clears his throat and for a moment looks lost ... an elderly man in the front row takes an exhausted step forward and falls heavily to the ground.

"Take him away!" shouts the officer curtly. Then he turns and just as curtly orders the guards to disperse the flock. Staggering, he disappears across the square and seeks shelter in the hut.

The old man is lifted from the ground and carried away, no one knows where, and a moment later everyone is driven back to the building. The three women who fell, are left lying lifeless in the snow and through a small window their families keep an eye on them, hoping for the least sign of life. Hours pass. Sometime in the afternoon, the three are collected by some of the guards and carried away. By then, they're as stiff as boards.

A few days later, by the time of morning roll call, anxiety and fatigue have taken their toll on the group. Among the new arrivals, a baby is dead and its mother has almost lost her mind. She sits and rocks her dead baby, in a daze, until a relative gently takes the child away from her.

Another woman goes down with typhoid. Quarantine is imposed. All doors are sealed and captivity in the smoky hall is total. The stink from the smoke and the toilet buckets, the unrelenting cold and mounting hunger, all add to the anxiety in the hall. Some prisoners wake in the middle of the night bathed in sweat and wander around restlessly by day. A few determined individuals play chess with coat buttons or keep the conversation going at all costs. A rabbi goes around comforting people and calling them to prayer. Not far from David, he bends over to talk to a man but the man retorts, "Please keep your prayers to yourself!"

The rabbi straightens up with a faint smile, stands for a moment looking at the man, who's deliberately turned his back on him, then he turns in the direction of David's father, edging past some women and putting his hand on his shoulder. David's mother asks him to sit down on their blanket, but the rabbi declines, shaking his head. "I come from Bodzentyn so I'm used to standing up."

David's father stands up too and the two men take stock of each other. The rabbi's eyes shine in his pale face, he gathers his prayer shawl around his black robe which is far too big and tilts his head slightly. "Will you pray with me?" he asks and places his hand on David's shoulder.

"To be honest," says his father, "I don't think it'll do much good here."

The rabbi smiles faintly, his eyes crinkling.

"Am I right in thinking that your heart is set on revenge?"

David's father glances around and whispers, "Yes, you're absolutely right, I've begun to hate these monsters."

"That's only natural but I'd advise you to leave it all to God. It's written in the Torah, 'Revenge and retribution is Mine'."

"That's not good enough," whispers David's father. "I can't forgive them."

"Revenge is fruitless, the sign of God is love … think about your boy," says the rabbi and squeezes David's shoulder.

David looks from one to the other and notices that his father's less sure of himself. He stands shuffling his feet, searching his pockets for a cigarette, although he knows he has none. The rabbi looks into his eyes. As if an idea occurs to his father, a bitter smile crosses his lips, "As you're so sure of yourself, explain if God has so much love, why He lets something like this happen?"

"No one understands the ways of God, not even I," says the rabbi without losing his composure.

"Maybe you believe that all this is a kind of punishment, the more God punishes us, the more He shows us His love?"

"I can see that you're a man of letters," says the rabbi and smiles again sadly, "but you're wrong if you think that bitterness and revenge are the way. No one knows what tomorrow will bring. The only thing we can believe in is our love. Isn't it written, 'For those who love Me and respect My commandments, I'll show them My mercy a thousand fold'?"

David's father sighs, says something else, but the whispered words are lost in the noise from a dispute that's suddenly flared up close by. A woman accuses another of stealing her blanket. The two women are pulling at the small blanket and pushing each other around, until a couple of men separate them. The argument continues, and they stand and watch until Jakob's father raises his voice to comment, "You see how people are; there's no mercy here!"

The rabbi again tilts his head, "An argument makes no difference at all. Think about what I've said."

He nods to David and his mother, turns his back and quickly disappears amongst the crowd in the hall.

Later on, David can see him going around among the sick at the other end of the hall, bending down and talking with each of them and praying. His mother follows his movements too, and when all three are lying in the darkness trying to sleep, she whispers to his father, "You were too hard on the rabbi."

"I just said what I meant," said his father, who is breathing heavily.

"At least he's doing something – you just sit and stare into space."

His father sits up.

"What should I do? There's nothing to do here!" he whispers angrily.

"You could help the sick."

"I've never been good at prayers …"

"There's a lot more you could do."

His father doesn't answer, but remains sitting, staring into the darkness. His mother rolls over and goes to sleep. David wants to talk to his father, but doesn't know how to reach him. It's as if his father no longer sees him, barely talks to him. What has he done wrong?

Earlier on, Jakob had mentioned, "I think your father's sick, he looks sick."

"He's not sick," David retorted.

"He won't even talk to my father."

"That's because he's hardly sleeping. He's really tired," he said, making excuses.

"Why do you always take your father's side?" asked Jakob, giving him a look of annoyance.

"Because he's my father," he said, clamming up.

That was when they were wandering around the hall searching for rats and mice. They had sticks in their hands, just in case, but they didn't find any, although they always heard them at night.

At one point they got some lukewarm coffee, which a man from Suchedniew had warmed up secretly on one of the heaters. Then they played cards with him for a little crust of rye bread. Jakob won, but they shared it with him anyway. The man had a sable coat and looked as if he had money. He seemed to have more to eat than the rest, but like his father, he, too, was withdrawn. The only thing he'd talk about was the card tricks he'd show them when they came by next time. Suddenly, he turned his back on them, opened a small bag and took out a photograph, which he sat looking at for a long time. Jakob asked him who he was looking at but he didn't answer. When they realised that he was crying, they got up and walked away.

"I think I know who's in the picture," said Jakob looking sad.

"Who?" David asked wondering how Jakob knew.

"I think it's one of the ones who died in the yard …"

"One of the women?"

"Mmm … his wife."

"How'd you know?"

Jakob looked at him, irritated. "I don't know, I'm just guessing."

"Did you see him with a woman?"

Jakob shook his head.

"Do you know him?"

Jakob shook his head again.

"Then I don't think you should assume that sort of thing."

Jakob got angry, the corner of his mouth trembled.

"You always think you know what's right and wrong!" he said.

"No," he said, "I just don't think you should make things up about people."

Jakob got even angrier, he'd never seen him so angry before. He clenched his fist, "What does it matter?

We're all gonna die anyway!"

"Who says?"

"A lot of people … You don't get it, do you?"

"I don't believe we're going to die," he said, trying to stay calm, but Jakob was still angry. He didn't want to talk about it any more. He wandered around the hall until he found a spot where no one could see him. He stood there a while and thought about what Jakob had said, but still couldn't believe it. Why should his father and mother die, or his uncle and aunt or his cousins? Why should *he* die? What had they done? Then he remembered Mrs Kaplan, and he felt really scared, hid his face in his hands and felt the tears come. He dried his eyes with his hands and nervously looked around the hall. No, no one had seen him. They musn't see him cry.

That evening he got up tentatively and sat down next to his father.

"What is it? What's up?" David asks his father softly.

His father doesn't react. David tugs at his sleeve, but he pulls his arm away.

"Lie down and go to sleep. Get all the sleep you can!" he whispers.

"Do you want my blanket?" he offers.

For the first time in a long time his father smiles, in an effort, he leans against him and puts his hand on his shoulder.

"No, I don't want your blanket, David," he whispers.

"You need it yourself, don't worry about me."

His father's eyes are black in the darkness, his hands move slowly. David sits close to him for a while until his head drops forward. His father gives him a nudge so he crawls over to his blanket and wraps himself up. He can't think for the cold. He curls up tightly and lays there exhausted and shivering. Finally, he falls asleep.

There is no sign of the Storm Trooper for the next few days so roll call is easier and shorter and they're allowed to wash themselves in the snow. For once, there's more bread and hot soup, with a little meat in the middle of the day. Even the strange liquid that resembles coffee tastes better.

Luckily, during these two days, no one dies, and even though a single case of typhoid is discovered and the doors remain sealed, the mood of the crowd has changed.

Rumours circulate about transportation. The most optimistic among them hope for something better – maybe work – wasn't that what they promised?

It's David's birthday. He doesn't expect to get any gifts, but still feels disappointed when it's the same old routine. In the afternoon, as he's wandering around the hall, Jakob comes over and says that his father wants to speak to him right away. Together, they return to the space where his father and mother and Jakob's parents are located.

"Sit down on the blanket, close your eyes and count to fifty," says his father.

He sits down and counts. When he opens his eyes, three packages wrapped in newspaper are lying in front of him on the blanket. Surprised, he unpacks them: a jew's harp, a pack of cards and two bread rolls. He jumps up and hugs them all one after the other. They stand there silently looking at each other, embarrassed for a moment to be happy in this place.

"Wanna know where I got the cards?" asks Jakob impatiently.

He nods.

"I got them from Mr Osterman!"

"Mr Osterman?"

"Yeh, the one with the card tricks. I went to see him and watched all his tricks and told him it was your birthday."

"But he doesn't even know him," says his mother in amazement.

"He said that David has kind eyes, and that he reminds him of his own son."

They are all silent for a moment, lost in their own thoughts. David eats his dry bread rolls and tries out the harp. It takes time, with a lot of practicing until he can play a whole tune. But then it gets easier. By evening, he's created a small repertoire.

His father sits and listens and nods approvingly every time David plays a song he's learnt at school or something from memory. A little later, he recalls a tune from a Chaplin film that he saw in Kielce, then a passage from a Chopin waltz that he'd heard on the Schliefersteins' record player. Not quite right, but close.

"It was your mother's idea," says his father. "She says you were always good at whistling and remembering melodies. I don't know where she got hold of the harp. Maybe she'd hidden some *zloty*! You never know with women!"

When darkness falls, David feels exhausted and somewhat dizzy. He hides the little mouth harp in one of his pockets. From his happy oasis, where he's been fully absorbed for hours playing the little instrument, the grim reality of the hall returns. Once more he feels the bitter chill and hears the din of all the people crowding in on him. In the dark, he explores the hall. The endless coughing, the grey faces, everyone being caged up — it all seems too much to bear, with no hope of escape. There's a war, but why is there a war, and why is there so much hatred? In his village he never hated anyone, not even people who shouted at him or hit him, but now he hates the Commandant and the Storm Trooper and the guards, and they hate him because he's not like them.

When he lies down to sleep on the floor, he holds on to the harp tightly in one hand. His mother lies down quietly beside him and takes his other hand. They lay like that for a long time, staring up into the darkness.

"Do you think it'll stop?" he whispers to her.

"Yes," she says. "One day it'll stop."

"Do you think we'll go home again?"

"I don't know, David. Maybe we'll find another home."

"Mmm… but where?"

"There's a land called Palestine …"

"I know," he says, trying to imagine it.

He pictures a village similar to his own where all the houses are white and the sun always shines. There are donkeys and palm trees too. And wells full of clean water and orange trees. Oranges are scattered on the ground just for the taking.

But for whatever reason, he can't see himself there. The vision fades away in an instant like a mirage, and soon a dreamless sleep overwhelms him.

He's woken in the middle of the night by a terrific noise. His father pulls him up from the floor and says, "Stay close to me!"

A light pierces the darkness of the hall shining, onto the heads of the confused and frightened people. Orders are shouted, dogs bark ferociously and Yiddish curses fly through the air. Mothers grab their children, fathers collect blankets and baggage. People who are still half-asleep stagger around, stepping on each other's feet. A continuous shrieking whistle from one end of the hall gradually forces most of them towards the great door, where a row of armed guards are positioned alongside the Commandant and the SS officer.

"Children over here, children over here, *schnell, schnell,* hurry!" shouts the Commandant, while a group of SS officers, whom no one's seen before, pull children from the arms of their terrified mothers. Older children are forcefully dragged from the crowd as the Storm Trooper shouts, "Child transportation, deliver your children, child transportation, deliver your children!"

Fathers and other men step protectively in front of the children, but are quickly and brutally shoved aside. David and his parents try to stay at the back of the crowd, but all the time they're pushed forward. Instinctively, David hides behind his father and tries not to see what's going on.

Powerless to prevent it, many of the children are reluctantly let go, some people even push them forward through the crowd. Older boys tear around the hall and hide in the darkest corners, but they're soon found by the zealous SS, who herd them past the guards and into the truck waiting with its motor running in front of the gate.

As the panic mounts, the Commandant raises his pistol and fires two shots up into the roof. The guards brandish their bayonets. When the crowd still presses forward, the Storm Trooper fires his pistol straight at an elderly man, who doubles over, astonishment written on his face, then falls to the ground.

A hush spreads through the crowd. People around the dead man step back while others further away keep on pushing forward. Amidst this sea of humanity many are trapped and trampled. David's mother is pushed forward and as he clings to his father with all his might, David is discovered by an SS officer. The SS man beats his way through to him with the butt of his rifle and reaches out for him through the mob. But his father pushes him away and David is pulled further back into the crowd. Another SS man quickly makes his way towards them. David's father raises his hand but at the same time, the enraged SS man shoots at him and he falls backwards, bleeding, with David still clinging onto him.

People around them back away. It's suddenly quiet around the bleeding man and his boy. David, who was pulled over in the fall, gets up on his knees, gripping his father's hand. He shakes it frantically.

"Papa, Papa!" is all that he can say before his voice fails him.

His father's face is screwed up. He closes his eyes in pain. He tries to say something and a couple of hoarse, incomprehensible sounds come from his lips. Then he falls silent and his head slips to one side. David grips his father's hand while an SS man tries to pull him away. Another SS man arrives and the two officers wrench the kicking boy free from the dead man's grasp. One of them, a tall, sturdy man, picks David up, throws him over his shoulder and carries him off swiftly through the crowd. A shout is heard somewhere in the heaving mob.

David's mother desperately fights her way through the crowd, but she's too late.

On the flat bed of the waiting truck, David keeps on struggling. He pushes his way through the group of children and over to the back board. He gets one leg over the edge when an SS man grabs him from behind and hoists him deeper into the truck. Again he tries to squeeze forward, but at that moment the truck starts moving and he topples over.

"Sit down and be quiet!" shouts a woman in Polish. He gets onto his knees and surveys the motley group of children. Then he realises that besides the SS men there are three women in the truck too. Some of the children sit, others stand, crying or shouting out for their mother or father. Others make strange sounds expressing their sense of total abandonment.

"Shut up!" bawls an SS man, forcing all the children down in the hay. After a while, he lights a lantern and hangs it from the roof. Amidst the chaos, David catches sight of Jakob, and he tries to crawl over to him, but one of the women holds him back.

"Jakob!" he calls and now Jakob turns towards him and gives him a sign.

The truck stops, a soldier throws the canvas to the side and looks in, his face is youthful and without expression.

"How many of them?" he asks.

"Forty-two!" says the SS man.

"Damned job, and in the middle of the night!"

"No problem, I've done it before!" says the SS man.

"Understood. *Heil Hitler!*" says the soldier and disappears.

Again the truck sets off with its noisy engine. The snow-covered road is bumpy and they're tossed from side to side. Some of the infants are crying so two of the women hold them until they quieten and are laid back down in the hay.

David is sitting, squashed up against the back wall of the cab. There's a small bundle beside him but he barely notices it; he's staring blankly into space. When the truck makes a sharp turn, a little girl with long, black hair falls against him but he pushes her away. For a moment they look at each other then she sits down next to him and silently takes his hand. Immediately, she pulls her hand away and stares at it.

"Blood, blood!" she says horrified, and crawls away from him. He wants to hold on to her, but the SS man, who's seated nearby, pushes him back.

"Get back, get back!" he shouts with a voice that echoes through the night.

David looks at his hands and wipes the blood off on his coat. He's in shock; he can't even remember what happened a few minutes ago. It's as if nothing's happened. He's sitting there oblivious to it all. He doesn't understand why there are uniformed women with them in the truck; he doesn't understand what he's doing there. Something inside him protests, there's a furious anger building and he thinks, "I've got to get out and find my mother and father!" And "He's not dead, no, he's not dead."

In the din of the truck, the women again try to pacify the infants. They pick them up and hold them for a while with their stiff hands, and then put them back in the hay. They're just following orders and don't really care, just as long as the SS men don't bother them. One of the SS lights a cigarette, glances at his watch and then studies the children.

They drive for a while and the bundle next to David, which he'd had no interest in before, now starts to move. He looks down and in the darkness he can see a pair of eyes. It's a baby. It starts screaming. He picks it up, holds it tightly in his arms and rocks it back and forth. The crying ceases.

The SS man, who's been keeping an eye on him, suddenly shouts, "See the Jew boy over there, he can make those damned kids shut up!" But the women pretend not to hear him.

The truck rumbles on through the night, sometimes fast and then slow. At one point it stops, some doors are opened and they hear voices outside. The canvas is pulled back and a man with a cap asks, "Hans, got any cigarettes?"

One of the SS reaches into his breast pocket for a pack, taps a couple out, gets up, glancing at the freezing children and hands over the two cigarettes.

"How much longer?" he asks, leaning his long body over the back of the truck.

"Blasted road, at least an hour …" says the voice outside.

"And the car's ready?"

"Yeh, the train's waiting for us."

"The camp?"

"Yeh, same as last time."

"And the others?"

"Either the ghetto in Kielce or selection for the labour camp. Know what the squadron leader said? He said, 'There's no room for them in Kielce, why not take care of them right now!'"

They laugh. A moment later, the truck rolls on.

David tries to collect his thoughts as he hugs the bundle tightly. He looks in Jakob's direction. Jakob points a finger at his temple like a gun and pulls a face.

After half an hour, David has to put the child down. He lays it carefully in the hay. It's sleeping. Others are sleeping, too; many have lain down clinging on to each other. But there are still a few children who are quietly weeping in the darkness.

The women are now sitting passively, close together on the bench along the wall and have pulled a blanket up around them. The SS man is half-asleep behind his great coat. Once again Jakob makes a sign but David looks away, afraid. He closes his eyes.

If they're going to die, let it happen soon. He can't hold out much longer. He tries not to think about his father, but thinks about him anyway. He knows he's dead.

He focuses on his mother, instead, but where is she? Will she be going in the same direction?

The word 'camp' keeps repeating inside his head, but he doesn't know what it means, there's something dark and inevitable about it.

No, he'll think about Palestine. He tries to imagine life in Palestine, but can only hear the rumbling of the truck and the chug of the engine. He opens his eyes and looks over at Jakob, who points quickly towards the back of the truck. He shakes his head. They can't escape, how could they?

In tiny movements, Jakob begins creeping, crab-like, towards the back hatch where, lying on his stomach, he feels around the canvas for the ties. But he can't undo the knots so he takes a penknife out of his pocket. With a glance at the SS man, who seems to be asleep, he quickly gets up on his knees, but is thrown over by a bump in the road. He lies there for a while, catching his breath before he gets up again and cuts the knots with a few quick slashes. Then he crouches back down on all fours.

Feeling both intensely anxious and strangely removed, David follows Jakob's movements in the dark. Jakob gets up on his knees again and cuts another cord, then carefully leans out and looks through the gap down at the snow-covered road racing past beneath him. Grabbing hold of the back hatch with both hands, he swings one leg over and is halfway out of the truck when the SS man springs to his feet and pulls him back in. He throws Jakob to the floor, cursing and beating him, as the lad tries desperately to ward off the blows.

"Don't hit him, don't hit him!" shouts David, trying to get up. But one of the women, who's been woken by the noise, throws her blanket aside and kicks him.

While David's lying there in pain and the SS man keeps on beating Jakob, the truck suddenly begins to lurch from side to side, then it turns sharply to the left and brakes hard. Slowly, it slides back and then they're all shaken by a huge bump. The truck rolls over and everyone's thrown around, up against the roof.

In the ensuing chaos, while the women and children are lying shocked and wounded in a heap, and the SS man is struggling to get to his feet in the damaged vehicle, David sees his opportunity. Miraculously, he's not hurt. In front of him, he can see the gaping canvas flapping and despite the pain in his leg, he starts crawling through the mass of bodies. Foaming at the mouth, the SS man reaches across the truck, trying to get to his feet. But as he puts his weight on his bleeding foot, he shrieks in agony, and falls over backwards.

David hesitates for a moment, before crawling over to the muddy canvas. As he sticks his leg through the gap, he gets stuck. He can feel a hand on his shoulder so he pushes himself forward frantically and slides through the hole onto the frozen snow.

He gets up, stumbles, gets up again then starts running down the road, away from the battered truck.

He runs and runs.

He doesn't know how long he's stood behind the tree. The woods are cold, dark and overwhelming. He keeps peering around until his eyes go blurred. Far away, far out in the darkness behind the hundreds of tree trunks, the road continues. He can't see it, but he knows that it's there.

The woods are still. Now and then a sound breaks through, startling him, making him freeze like a statue behind the trunk of the fir tree. His heart is pounding and his breathing fast. His must calm down, conserve his energy.

He's thirsty too – when did he last have something to drink? He bends down to pick up some snow and sucks on it. But it doesn't help much. He pulls off the big, holey mittens and warms the ball of snow in his hands. He licks it, and gradually it slakes his thirst.

Then he remembers Jakob – where is he, what's happened to him? For a moment, he considers going back to the truck, but how could he help him? He won't be able to run away again, will he?

Even though he's afraid, he starts retracing his steps back to the truck. A large branch suddenly cracks under his foot, he jumps and runs to crouch behind a large tree. He's alone. He says a silent prayer, trembling, but nothing happens. He feels numb. He's still alone.

From far away a noise reaches him and in the darkness he can make out a light between the trees.

A car.

He gets up from the frozen forest floor and runs as far as he can into the woods. Exhausted and frozen, he crawls to the edge of the forest. Beneath the inky sky, the white fields shine in the starlight. The wind has dropped. He looks back but there's only the dark wood.

The snowy fields descend softly, and he can see the outline of two small buildings in the valley. Choking back his fear, he sets out across the fields.

He needs a place to hide; he needs a place to sleep.

As he enters a courtyard from the narrow road, the two farm buildings lie ominously silent before him. He stands with his back pressed against one of the walls for a long time, listening intently to the night.

Swiftly, he edges his way along the wall of the farmhouse and looks in through the windows. In his agitated state, he can see nothing. Only the shadowy outlines of tables and chairs within. When he turns to look at the other larger building, he notices a low latched door. He hurries across the courtyard and tries the latch. The door's open. He walks in.

The stale smell of manure greets him. He's in a small barn. Two cows lie tethered on the hay nearby. One of them calmly turns its huge, heavy head towards him. There's an empty stall next to the cows. He can lie down there.

He creeps past the cows, falls down onto the thin

layer of hay, curls up and closes his eyes. But his throat is parched, his stomach is churning and the nightmare still has its grip on him.

He half sits up and stares at the cows. Their brown, glossy coats shine in the darkness. He used to be allowed to milk Tomachevski's cows, that much he remembers.

He forces one of the cows to get up, and starts pulling on one of its teats. At first, nothing happens then suddenly a stream of milk sprays out. He tries again, this time bending his head down and opening his mouth. The warm milk tastes good as it slips down his aching throat. Then he crawls back to the stall where he curls up and collapses into a deep sleep.

Someone kicks his boot, waking him abruptly. Instantly, he's on his feet but the man is blocking his way with a pitchfork.

"What're you doing here, lad?" he demands, spitting on the barn floor. His shabby clothes hang loose, his broad head gleams in the half-light coming from the small window behind him. His breathing is heavy and his narrowed eyes are suspicious.

David steps back, desperately searching for a plausible explanation. The man jabs at him with the pitchfork, glaring angrily.

"Now! Out with it!" he demands.

David tries to explain: He's completely lost … His father's dead and he doesn't know where his mother is… He's afraid of the Germans – they're the ones who killed his father … He wants to go home, but he can't … He has an uncle in Kielce … but …

The farmer listens, troubled by the boy's words. Finally, he puts the pitchfork aside and scratches his balding scalp. For a moment he's deep in thought. Then he turns back toward the boy, suspiciously.

"Your father's dead, you say?"

David nods.

"And you've no place to go?"

David shakes his head.

"Can you work?"

David nods again.

"You can stay here a few days, if you work. If there's any trouble, you're out. Understand?"

"Yes," says David, looking gratefully at the farmer.

"There's the wheelbarrow and there's a shovel. You can start by mucking out the stable. I'm getting too old for it and my children don't help… Got it?"

"Yes," says David again, breathing rapidly.

The farmer stands there watching as he fetches the wheelbarrow and picks up the shovel. He gets down to work quickly, with the farmer inspecting his every move.

"You're Polish, aren't you?" he asks suddenly, approaching him.

"Of course," says David without looking up.

The farmer stands there for a while, thinking, before asking slyly, "So where *do* you come from?"

David tells him the name of his village, head down, shovelling. The man repeats the name of the village over and over. "That's a long ways away, boy. How'd you get here?" David clings on to the shovel tightly, searching for an answer.

"I ... the Germans took us, drove us into the forest ... they shot my father ... and I ran away... I don't know where ..."

The farmer wrinkles his pale forehead and sighs. David glances towards the door imagining a way to escape.

"Finish up in here, lad, then come and get somethin' to eat," says the farmer, unexpectedly, walking towards the door. As he goes, he turns back once more to call out, "And you'll find the dung heap behind the barn!"

Once David's mucked out around the cows, it takes all his strength to push the heavy barrow round behind the barn and empty its contents onto the dung heap. He walks back to the courtyard slowly and stands there for a long time looking towards the cottage. All those questions.

He's afraid. He pulls his coat round him, feeling a bitter wind blowing over the courtyard. Everything around him is white and deserted. Further away across the fields, the fir trees laden with snow cut a line through the landscape. Up there in the hills, that's where he came from, but it all seems so far away, an alien world he left long ago. He can't go back, but where *should* he go?

A woman's face, wrapped in a scarf, appears at a window in the cottage. A moment later, she opens the kitchen door and David goes over to shake her hand. But she isn't smiling. Her hand is rough and dry. She leads him silently into the kitchen, where the farmer is sitting and eating.

"Take off your coat and wash your hands in the sink!" she says, sitting down at the table, still keeping an eye on him. Her bony figure rocks back and forth on the chair.

"Sit down at the table and eat!" she says when he's washed his hands and stands uncertainly in front of the kitchen sink. She shoves a plate of porridge towards him and points at a chair.

He sits down. The farmer nods and carries on eating from his large bowl. David feels awkward, but is too hungry not to eat straight away. He shovels the porridge down without tasting it. The woman doesn't eat, just sits staring at him.

"That little devil'll eat us out of house and home!" she says as David empties his bowl and hungrily gazes at the pot of porridge on the table.

"Give him some more!" says the man sharply, wiping

his mouth with the back of his hand.

Reluctantly, the thin woman spoons more porridge into his bowl and shoves it towards him and David eats again, more slowly.

"Have you asked him where he comes from?"

The man nods.

"Can he do anything?"

"Don't worry."

"Where'll he sleep?"

"We'll find somewhere."

"I can sleep in the barn!" David blurts out.

They both look at him, astonished. The man nods, gets up from the table slowly and walks into the sitting room. Timidly, David rises from the table, but stands uncertainly, not knowing what to do with himself.

Some days pass, with David sleeping in the barn and working in the kitchen but the woman won't let him be. One afternoon, when they're alone in the cottage and she's got him to sweep the floor in the little kitchen, she comes over to him. She insists on knowing why he never washes himself; he keeps on sweeping as he searches for an answer. She leans against the kitchen table, with her arms crossed, impatiently tapping her foot. There's the hint of a smile curling around her lips, revealing the rotten teeth behind.

"I can't wash in the barn," he says.

Immediately, she pulls a tub out of the pantry, fills it with water and orders him to take off his clothes and wash. He leans over the tub and sticks a finger in the water. "It's too cold," he says without looking at her.

"Wash!" she insists, glaring at him.

He shakes his head despondently.

She grabs hold of his arms, her slight body shaking in agitation. He tries to pull his arms away, but she holds on and suddenly pushes him into the sitting room.

"We'll see if you'll kiss the cross, then, won't we?" she says as they stand in the middle of the chilly room.

He tries to break free but something inside her makes her stronger than him. She pulls him across the room to the wall, where he glimpses a small wooden crucifix. With a self-satisfied howl, she tears the cross from the wall and pushes it into his face.

"Kiss it, kiss it!" she cries, as one possessed.

But he won't kiss the cross, screws up his eyes.

"Little Jew brat, little bastard, you can't fool me," she screams, pressing his head against the cross. "If you don't kiss it, the Germans will come and get you, I swear!"

He starts to purse his lips, wishing he could die. At that moment, the door opens and the woman is startled. The farmer is standing there in the doorway.

"Let him go, you bitch, let him go now!" says the man bitterly, moving towards them.

"You know he's Jewish, a little Jew boy, don't ya!" she whines, gripping hold of him. The farmer says nothing, just nods towards the kitchen, and reluctantly she lets the boy go and retreats like an obedient dog, making faint little whining sounds.

David won't look at the farmer and turns away. The farmer sighs loudly behind him and it's a long time before he says anything.

"You'll have to go," he says. "I won't have all that trouble here. You'll get some food and then be on your way home. It can't be helped."

Out in the courtyard a cat leaps across the snow. From the window, he follows it until it disappears. He clenches his fist. The farmer grabs his shoulders and turns him around. David looks up into his wrinkled face. "Got to look after my own," says the voice before him. "Understand?"

"Why?" he thinks, staring at the old man's face.

The farmer lets go of him and walks into the kitchen, where he stands deep in thought. A bit later, he returns with some potatoes and a couple of eggs. He stuffs the potatoes into the boy's coat pocket and puts two hard-boiled eggs into his hand, then leads him out to the courtyard.

"Go now! Go up to the road and ask the way to Kielce!" says the farmer, standing in the doorway until

David starts to walk. He doesn't look back. Suddenly, he runs. He runs and runs with the eggs in his hands.

Large snowflakes cascade across the fields, whirling in front of his eyes. The grey-white sky seems to have neither beginning nor end. David's tiny figure is barely visible in the mist. As he fights against the wind, his progress is slow and difficult. His heart's racing, and he clutches the two eggs in his mittens, as if they could buy him the world.

Frozen, he searches for the road, but can only make out the bare drifting landscape. He sets out for the few trees visible in the terrain, but they're like a mirage, always further and further away than he has the energy to reach. Finally, he reaches a huge fir and tries to shelter in its gnarled trunk, but the wind attacks him from all directions. He must go on, must carry on.

But which way? To the left, or the right?

He rubs the snow away from his face, ties his scarf tighter around his head, leaving only his eyes and forehead exposed, then makes a decision to go left. Hadn't he come that way? He puts his head down resolutely and tries to remember everything about his mother.

In the midst of the blizzard, with the snow beating down and the whiteness blinding his eyes – isn't that his mother up ahead?

He slips and falls over and gets up again.

Yes, she's over there, waiting for him.

He staggers on for a few yards in the snowy

wasteland, his arms stretched out towards a distant tree.

There, in front of the tree, he lies down, his arm still reaching out…

*

A snow-plough pushes through the desolate landscape, hurling snow aside, making lovely parallel tracks on the road which are swiftly obliterated. In its wake, creeps a dark Daimler-Benz cabriolet.

The snow-plough stops abruptly and a soldier jumps out and trudges through the snow, shouts something indistinctly into the wind and points towards a tree. He's seen something – a large, dark, holed mitten is sticking out of the snow.

With his hands, the soldier digs the child out of the snow, lifts up his stiff body, holds him close, trying to rub the life into him. After several minutes, without any outward sign, David suddenly kicks out and makes a small groaning noise as his legs give way under him. The soldier picks him up in his arms and carries him through the snow to the back of the vehicle, where he shouts to someone through the wind. Another soldier opens up the rear canvas and stares out in amazement. Just then, the driver gets out of the Daimler-Benz to speak to them.

"What's going on here? We don't have time to stop,"

he says irritated, as he pulls on his leather gloves.

"I found this boy under the snow!" says the soldier, showing him to the driver.

"And – so what?" says the driver casting a quick, uninterested glance at the boy.

"I thought we could take him with us."

"Search him!"

As the driver watches impatiently, the soldier searches David's clothes and finds the potatoes, Jew harp and his yellow armband.

"A Jew boy," says the driver. "Leave him be!"

"Then he'll die!" says the soldier, surprisingly sharp, staring ahead.

The driver reflects for a moment before walking back to the car. Soon he returns. "The Commissioner orders him into the car. Can he walk by himself?"

The soldier shakes his head.

"Carry him then!" shouts the driver, clearly annoyed, and hurries back to the car where he opens the door to the front seat.

The soldier quickly follows with David in his arms, laying him gently on the front seat, before the driver slams the door, runs around the car to get in behind the steering wheel, pulling the door shut against the wind and starting the engine.

"Give him your blanket, Müller, and let's get going!" says a voice from the back seat.

Stiffly, the driver covers David with the blanket, puts the car in gear and moves off.

*

The weather closes in around them, the snow whirls against the windshield, the wipers slap monotonously back and forth. Almost silently, the long car glides through the white space. Slowly, the boy comes to his senses. The smell of leather and tobacco reaches him, voices behind him become more distinct, one rapid and stern, the other deep, contemplative. Lying on the seat, he tries to keep very still until a sudden pain in his wrist forces him to stretch out his arms and legs.

"The boy's awake, *Herr Commissioner*," says the driver casting him a brief glance.

"Ask him if he speaks German," says the stern voice behind him.

David sits up in the seat and tries to turn his head, but it hurts too much.

The driver asks him in Polish if he speaks German. Instinctively, he shakes his head and presses himself deeper into the seat.

"He says no, *Herr Commissioner!*" says the driver, glancing in the rearview mirror at the black uniform and the translucent face with high cheekbones.

"Let him recover a bit," says the Commissioner,

"we can try again later!"

A burst of short, hoarse laughter is heard from the back seat before the conversation carries on and the car purrs forward.

Outside, the snow-plough continues to fling the snow aside, some of it landing in dull thuds on the hood of the car. Farms glide past them, the road gradually becomes wider, small clusters of cottages appear only to disappear again. Sometimes they pass a horse and cart with a huddled snow-blasted figure on top, occasionally a military vehicle chugs along in the opposite direction, or a car lies abandoned in the empty white wasteland. He wonders if it's all a dream as he stares out into the grey mist – where is he going, and whose voices are talking behind his back. What do they want from him? Why have they taken him with them?

He has to be careful. Maybe they'll throw him out again if he does anything wrong.

Again, that abrupt, hoarse laughter. He holds his breath and listens.

"So you've personally received instructions from Heydrich … interesting!" says the deep voice. "Why haven't I heard anything about it?"

"It's all very secret, business for the high command and the SS, *Herr Banker*. I have my orders!"

"There must be something you can tell a good friend of the party?" says the banker's deep voice ingratiatingly. The other voice hesitates then briefly laughs.

"You're talking to a soldier!"

"Indeed, but we've done a lot of business together, you and I. I think I deserve a little trust!"

"All right ... But I must have your word of honour that you'll keep it quiet!"

"Of course."

"It concerns our greatest achievement so far," says the stern one. "An operation that requires the utmost discipline and vigilance."

"Get to the point, why don't you?"

"What we're talking about, *Herr Bankier*, is the final solution of the Jewish problem!"

"The final solution?"

"I can't go into detail, but we stand before a heroic task that will ensure our place in history ... future generations will thank us for our commitment to proceed with the severity the matter demands ...

"Excuse me, I don't quite understand ... "

"Oh, you *don't?*" says the Commissioner, cryptically.

"You mean ...? No, I can't believe it," says the deep voice, now clearly agitated. "You mean the time of the Jews has run out, that you've found a way to get rid of them ...?"

"The Jews are enemies of the State and we're determined to exterminate them!"

"But *Herr Commissioner*, it can't be done, no way ...

there are millions of Jews in Europe, it's impossible!"

"Do you doubt our will, or am I to understand that you doubt our efficiency and discipline?" asks the Commissioner sharply.

"Not at all, I wouldn't dream of it, *Herr Commissioner,* it's all so new, I haven't had time to think it through ... "

"Leave that to us! Whatever transpires, there's something in it for you, too. If you know how to handle it right, it will be big business – gold, deposits, bonds ... I'm not at liberty to say any more, it's all too hush-hush ..."

The two men suddenly cease talking and silence pervades. The car glides on as David tries to understand what he's just heard. One word lingers, a word that's too great and terrible for his imagination, his thoughts hazily encircle it: *exterminate* – but it's too unreal; he can't believe it. He can't relate it to anything. And yet he knows that he heard every word, and *this* word too, and because of *this* word, he must get out of the car, he must get away from these people, who sooner or later will do him harm.

From the corner of his eye, he observes the driver, who has his hands on the steering wheel and is keeping a steady eye on the road. His face is fixed and gives nothing away. Once in a while he blinks, it must be the snow blinding him. Behind him, the two men start talking again – maybe they've forgotten him? No, they haven't forgotten him; they're just waiting for him to do something stupid. Why have they picked him up? What do they want from him? Suddenly, he feels hungry and he searches his pockets for the potatoes, but can only find his harp. A sigh penetrates his small body; everything around him is strange and unfathomable, every minute darkness enfolds him. He hides his hands in his pockets and closes his tired eyes.

He senses an ocean of time; the car drives on, he falls asleep and when he wakes up again it's stopped snowing and the snow-plough in front of them is gone. They're passing through a large city with trams and cars. Among the high buildings are the ruins of bombed out facades and walls that stretch up ghost-like towards the sky. Occasionally, there's a huge hole where women and children search through the rubble despondently.

Pedestrians stop to watch the car pass, while German soldiers suddenly click their heels together and stretch an arm out in salute. When the car is blocked by a large crowd of people in one of the streets, the driver impatiently leans on the horn. With shouts and blows, soldiers swiftly force the people aside and the car finally passes through the mass of unhappy men, women and children. An old woman is pressed against the window next to him; her face is forced right up against the glass. For a brief moment she stares at him, terrified, as she beats desperately on the pane. And then she's gone.

They drive out of the city and onto a back road in the snow-white countryside. The wind has died down now, and gradually a blue sky emerges. The two men on the back seat have been quiet for a long time when suddenly the Commissioner leans forward and says, "Müller, let's see what the boy knows!"

"*Jawohl!*" says the driver without taking his eyes off the road.

"Ask him the name of the *Führer*!" he says.

The driver asks him in Polish the name of the *Führer*.

"Adolph Hitler," David answers quietly, staring straight ahead.

"Now ask him," says the Commissioner, "why he thinks we've saved his life!"

The driver asks him, but as he doesn't know what to say and is afraid of saying the wrong thing, he just shakes his head.

"He's not saying anything, sir," says the driver, casting a quick glance his way.

"Tell him, that I order him to answer!"

The driver repeats the demand and instinctively David turns and looks into the Commissioner's pale face with its sneering look.

He quickly turns back and says, "I don't know!"

"He doesn't know, sir," says the driver.

"Tell him, that he owes the *Führer* his life and I expect something in return. Explain to him that we're on our way to Warsaw and I need a young Jewish informer in the city. Let's hear what he has to say ..."

Once again he hears some abrupt, hoarse laughter and before the driver's translated the message, he knows what to do. He begins to cough and holding his head, he slides half way down the seat.

The driver repeats the Commissioner's message, but David keeps on coughing and pretends that he's about to faint.

"What's wrong, Müller?"

David closes his eyes and lets his head fall against the door.

"The boy's ill, *Herr Commissioner*!" says the driver.

David holds his breath as he anxiously awaits the Commissioner's reaction.

"What do you say, *Herr Bankier* …?" says the Commissioner behind him. "Are we dealing with a fake or is the boy really ill?"

The banker, who's unprepared for the question, adjusts his spectacles and hesitates to answer. Finally, he replies, "I assume that the Jew boy is sick from lying in the snow," as he replaces his glasses.

That makes the Commissioner laugh heartily. "That's why you'd never cut it in the police. That little coughing attack was too convenient. And now I ask you, what should we do about it?"

"It's really none of my business, *Herr Commissioner*!"

"Let's just say that it would please me to let you decide the matter! So: should we do away with the Jew boy or give him a chance to think it over?"

The banker nervously wipes his sweaty hand across his brow. "I really don't know why you're dragging me into this." he says weakly.

"Let's just say, *Herr Bankier*, that I enjoy seeing

whether you're man enough to decide the case. Well, what do you say? My pistol is at your disposal."

"Then I suggest you give the boy a chance to recover," says the banker trying to sound decisive.

The Commissioner snorts and once again it's quiet in the car. David keeps lying low in an uncomfortable position on the seat while his mind races over what the Commissioner will do to him if he moves. Only when it grows dark and the men resume their conversation in low tones, does he dare to sit up a little. From the corner of his eye, he examines the door handle, repeating to himself: "When the car stops, I'll jump, when the car stops, I'll jump … "

But the car drives on endlessly. Blackness surrounds them and only the approaching headlights or the distant, blinking lights from farmhouses give him the sense that the car is still in motion.

"Did you really mean to do away with the boy?" the banker's voice suddenly asks, behind him.

But the Commissioner doesn't reply, he just makes a low grunt.

"The Commissioner is asleep, *Herr Bankier*! Don't wake him, he needs all the sleep he can get!" whispers the driver loudly, holding tightly on to the steering wheel.

Some time later, David has the impression of many walls and a town. Here and there, lights are illuminated in the street or in a window. There are many more cars about and German soldiers can be seen crossing the street or standing guard in large, shadowy squares. On a corner, a group of people stand around. One of them shakes his fist at the car, the driver mutters something and accelerates furiously. They turn down a long, wide boulevard and drive quickly for some distance, then the driver slows down all of a sudden before turning to the right. David notices a gate, a light and some guards ... one of them is already walking over to the front of the car ... is it now or never? With his heart pounding, he reaches for the door handle ... the car stops with a jolt, he yanks the handle, leans against the door, almost falls out of the car, quickly gets up and runs off at full pelt. The Commissioner shrieks something inaudible, a door opens, the driver is shouting too, he can hear footsteps behind him ... but then it's as if nothing else exists, except his legs running down the dark boulevard. On and on ... forever ...

Breathless, he stops at a corner and glances back. The boulevard lies empty and deserted behind him. Way off in the distance a figure moves − is it one of them? He runs on regardless, although his legs can barely carry him another step. Having no idea where he is, he runs through a gateway and leans back against the damp wall, stopping momentarily to catch his breath. He stands there in the dark for a long time, all his muscles tensed, listening to the sounds of the street. Suddenly, he vomits, but not much comes out — just a brown spot in front of his boots.

In the murky darkness, he feels his way along the wall, his boots inching their way over the old stones. He comes across a large, wooden door, with glass panels, through which he can see stairs. He tries turning the knob but the door won't budge. He searches further along and soon finds a stairwell, so he quickly steps down to try the door. The ancient hinges creak open to the hallway of a cold, damp basement.

With one hand feeling along the wall, he creeps forward, hearing only the sound of his own breath. The hallway leads nowhere, but next to the far wall is yet another door. He opens it and penetrates a large, dark, shuttered room. As he steps forward, he almost falls over something on the floor. He bends down and fumbles for the object with both hands. He feels a coarse fabric and then skin, a chin and a nose. Terrified, he pulls his hands away and steps back: there's a man's lying on the floor!

Is he dead?

He listens: no, he's breathing, he's asleep.

He turns to go when a thought occurs to him, "If he isn't dead, then he might have something in his pockets, something to eat ..."

Gingerly, he moves towards the body on the floor, bends down and gropes in the pocket of the heavy coat that the man's wearing. He slides his fingers deep inside the pocket, but as he tries to pull his hand out, he can't. Frightened, he wriggles his hand free and is about to get up, when the man grabs him and pulls him down.

"Don't hit me, don't hit me!" he shouts at the man's raised arm. In his terror, everything swims before him, the shape of the man's head, the walls, the darkness.

Suddenly, without warning, the man lets him go. The man gets up, closes the door then strikes a match that he holds up in the dark. David catches sight of the man's face — his cheek is hideously disfigured, his lips are thin and set and although he's staring suspiciously at the boy, David can tell he's afraid too. The man mumbles something, moving closer, searching his pockets — maybe he's looking for a weapon. Whatever it is, he can't find it so he moves away, and with an eye on the boy, bends down and lights a candle on the floor. Quickly, he jots something down on a small notepad, tears the page out and with a sad expression passes it to the boy.

David takes the paper to the light and reads: "I'm a partisan. They did this to me. I can't talk. I'm on the run. Who are you? If you're a spy, I'll kill you!"

David explains who he is and that he, too, is on the run. He tells the man what he's overheard in the car. As he speaks, the man listens with amazement, and when he finally stops, the man goes over to him and embraces him.

For a fleeting moment, he can feel the warmth of another human body. The man, who's only a head taller than the boy, rubs his stomach and points at him. He nods: yes, he's hungry.

Then the man retrieves a canvas bag from the floor and takes out some bread and sausage. David sits down on the man's blanket, and while he's eating, the man produces a bottle of water. Then he sits down and pulls a small flask out from his inside pocket, knocking back the drink swiftly. He hands it over to the boy and not knowing what it is, David takes a mouthful. The liquid burns his throat and makes his cheeks flush. The man smiles at his confusion, but his eyes are still sad and dark, and David can't help but stare at his damaged face. It's a face that both attracts and repels him.

The man writes something else and hands the piece of paper to him: "They poured acid in my mouth and held a lighter to my face. But I told them nothing. They won't get anything out of Vlad."

"Who did it?" he asks in horror, gripping the paper.

The man writes a new note. It reads: "Gestapo. The Devil's hell hounds."

He looks up at the man, who just nods. His eyes keep closing, and he's feeling woozy. The man hands him a new note: "Now we sleep. Tomorrow we go to the ghetto."

Despite the bitter cold, the smell of vodka on the stranger's breath, dogs barking noisily in the streets and the constant rumble of the military vehicles going past, David finally sleeps. He's lying close to the man, floating between sleep and wakefulness, close enough to feel the man's body and hear him sigh. At times, he imagines he can hear the door in the hallway open and the wind tear through the basement – that he and this man are the last people on earth. In his dreams, he keeps seeing the door, still closed, and he doesn't understand how his father has appeared … somewhere in the darkness, watching over him. Then his father's face seems close by; he's smiling gently, more gently than he's ever smiled before … he whispers something to him, but he can't catch what he's saying … he reaches out to him but he can't quite touch him … all he hears is the wind and all he feels is air.

The man wakes him in the darkness. David hurries to get up and while the man packs his blanket and bag into a bundle, he waits for him by the door. His clothes are filthy and stinking but he barely notices; his only concerns are where the man is taking him and whether he'll get something to eat. They walk together down the hallway. As they near the door and the dim light spills through from outside, the man holds him back and hands him a chunk of bread. Then he opens the door cautiously and looks around before giving him the signal to come up.

David blinks in the daylight and the noise from the street unnerves him. The man signals for him to come on while looking up and down the street from the alleyway.

They start off along the pavement, the winter sun gleaming on the snow and the great glass windows. In spite of the array of goods on display in the shops, he stays close on the heels of the man, who's walking briskly. They turn a corner and he recognizes the long boulevard from the night before – now it's teeming with traffic.

A streetcar packed with people goes by, smartly-dressed pedestrians hurry past them, some stand and stare, but most are too busy to notice. They stride along beside a park where children are running around and playing with their sleds and soon they cross a long bridge over a frozen river, with a sign that reads: 'Poniatowsky Bridge'. He remembers hearing about a river that runs through Warsaw, but can't remember its name. He prods the man's shoulder. He turns round nervously and looks at him, uncomprehending, as he points at the river. "What's it called?" he asks, immediately regretting the question.

The man gets out his notebook and scribbles something down. He hands it over with a twisted smile. He reads: "It's called the Wistula. We're on the Aryan side."

They walk on. The sky is blue and everything seems airy and peaceful around them. In the distance, he catches sight of a church steeple and even taller buildings. From the bridge they turn down an immense avenue with trolley cars and traffic. Occasionally, a German military vehicle drives past and then the man puts his head down and walks even faster; David does the same. They turn a corner, the man slows down and they saunter past a café where people are sitting and eating in fine clothes. When he hears music and laughter it makes him wonder how people can be so relaxed – they seem to live in another world, a world that he doesn't belong to. He'd like to stop and watch them, just to share some of the relaxed atmosphere and to take in the aroma of fresh bread and coffee, but his guide has suddenly slowed to a snail's pace for no apparent reason.

Then he notices, a little way on, three SS soldiers approaching them, chatting, not paying much attention. His guide shoves him aside, cuts in front of him, crosses the street and carries straight on. From a few yards away, one of the SS men points at David, the others laugh, but he carries on past them. Without looking back, he continues along the pavement, fearing that at any moment the soldiers might turn around and shout at him. Only when he reaches the next crossroads does he stop and look for his guide but he's disappeared.

He stands there for a long time, searching for him as the traffic flows past before he finally crosses the street and seeks him out in doorways and stairwells. He really needs to find him – now that he's vanished he dreads being alone again. He must find him, even if it's just to say good-bye. Maybe he's found another basement to hide in or another alleyway. He retraces his steps to investigate entrances that might have stairs leading down to basement rooms. He has to tell him that the SS men have already gone and the danger's passed. But most of the basement doors are locked and there's no trace of him in the alleyways. As he's pushing at a door, a man with a broom shouts at him. Startled, he runs back out to the street.

He must go on. But where to? The ghetto, of course. Yes, the ghetto.

He walks down some long street or another without really knowing what he's looking for. He only has the vaguest idea of what the ghetto actually is and that comes from books and folk tales his uncle's told him. As he looks about him, every house and every street corner seems significant. He searches the faces of passers-by, looking for any clue that he belongs among them and is going the right way. But he can't find any clues. No one takes the slightest notice of him and he's afraid to trust any of these smart and self-assured people who seem to know where they're going without a care in the world.

He walks out into a large square, where a long wall immediately catches his eye. A small crowd has gathered in front of a gate in the wall. There's a steady stream of vehicles and pedestrians emerging from the crowd and dispersing in all directions across the square. At the other end of the square, a carousel with screeching children goes round and round. He walks over to it. He can hear music from a loudspeaker. Stalls nearby are selling sausages, bread and cakes, another offers prizes in a tombola. The sky is still clear and blue with rays of sunshine glistening on the snow. All around him there are happy, lively people; he can hear the children laughing, there's a boy waving to him from a horse on the carousel – how he wishes that he could be that boy!

On a platform a group of people are standing, looking over the wall. Some are pointing to something behind the wall, others just stare or exchange jokes. A sign with a yellow Star of David behind some barbed wire catches his eye: 'Jewish Quarter. Infectious. No entry allowed!'

He approaches the shabby crowd in front of the gateway and edges his way forward to the entrance, carefully, without being seen by the guards. A man bumps into him but he carries on, nervously looking around him, nevertheless.

Just inside the gate, he spots the police in their blue uniforms and the German military police too, controlling the flow of people and vehicles. An officer with two armbands carrying a stick and wearing high black boots moves back and forth checking papers. Most of the people show their identity papers without complaint; now and then someone is pulled out of line to be searched and questioned. Two men in dirty overalls are suddenly taken away, protesting, with their hands in the air. A policeman shoves them brutally into a car that speeds away. People turn away and carry on through the gate as if nothing's happened.

David calms down a little as he watches the continual comings and goings, wondering how he's going to get in. He notices that the Jews wearing armbands and arriving by themselves seldom have to show their papers but are often searched and questioned. He rummages in his pocket for his armband, but he can't just walk in, in case they search him and start asking questions. What should he do?

He just hangs around near the gate, going over it all in his mind when the sound of shouting and a barrage of voices from the ghetto startle him. Suddenly, a man grabs his shoulder and whispers to him: "Got you, you little beggar! Come with me or I'll report you!"

Before he knows what's happening, the man's pulled him aside and although he tries to get free, the man has a tight grip on his coat. The man has a craggy face, runny nose and rheumy eyes. His shoes are split and his trousers ragged.

"Empty your pockets!" he says, glancing towards the gate.

David turns out his trouser pockets slowly. Impatiently, the man searches through his coat pockets and finds the armband, bread and harp. Swiftly, he pockets the bread and throws the armband away. As he waves the harp in front of David's face, he shakes his shoulder brutally, demanding: "Give me your money!"

"I don't have any." says David steadily.

"Must be in your boots. I know it's in your boots!"

David shakes his head. The man considers what to do. He's clearly nervous. David notices his hands are shaking a bit.

"Where do you live?"

"Nowhere," says David, looking directly into the man's watery eyes.

"You're lying. A beggar like you lives in the ghetto!"

David shakes his head again. Something, maybe his tone, suddenly convinces the man.

"What're you doing here?"

"I'm trying to get in."

The man examines him as if he's considering whether there's something or other he might steal from him, but the tension's gone. The man lets him go, wiping the snot away from his nose with his hand. Then in a softer voice, he says, "Just wait until the workers return, put your head down and walk in with them. Got it?"

David nods.

The man silently hands him back the little harp before turning and disappearing across the square. He stands there a while looking after him, then bends down and picks up his armband and puts it in his pocket. He passes the time wandering around the stalls, keeping an eye out for the return of the workers. He doesn't really know what to expect but he imagines that some Jews in work clothes will come past and he must quickly take his chance.

The hours pass, a light, fresh snow makes the air grey and covers the square with slush. Lights go on in the windows of the high buildings, obscured by the mist; it all seems strange and distant, like a dark dream from which he hasn't yet awakened. Little by little, the square empties. The carousel stops, the stalls are closed and shuttered. Freezing cold, he grovels around the stalls for something to eat – maybe someone's thrown away a bit of bread. He walks around and around the empty carousel, not knowing what to do with himself. Finally, he sits down on the carousel and clings on to the leg of a wooden horse.

Finally, a line of pale, dirty men cross the square, led by armed German soldiers. Their clothes hang off them and their movements are slow and heavy. Wordlessly, they move towards the gate. David, who's seen them coming, hurries over to the small crowd in front of the gate and waits. Once the soldiers and half the line have passed, he steps cautiously towards the line where two men immediately make room for him, pulling him deep inside the group. Shielded by these tall, thin bodies, he moves forward, unseen. The noise around them grows louder; German voices mix with shouts and the general hubbub. He feels as if he's come to a great square. The men around him disperse; he feels cobblestones under his feet and suddenly finds himself alone among the throng of people on Leszno Street.

Frightened by the barrage of voices and sounds sweeping over him, and the deluge of faces, people, and vehicles, he realises the street is filled with Jews of all shapes and sizes. He is pushed along the street with its high, crumbling walls; people ahead seem to disappear among the strange assortment of caftans, furs and rags. Where are they all going? Then he comes to a point where the crowd seems to stand still, unmoving. He inches his way forward. Children, lying across the pavement or sitting solemnly against the walls, reach out their arms towards him and beg for coins or bread. A few snatches of a song break through: "Because we're young, because we're young…!", the sound of accordion music, dogs barking, horses neighing, all this confronts his senses. Even so, he has only one thought – to find something to eat.

He stops in front of a small shop with bottles, black bread and a couple of cakes in the window – the cakes are old and dry. Inside, a man in an apron and faded trousers hands a loaf over the wooden counter and receives a few coins. His eyes follow the bread from the counter to the customer's shabby bag, his mouth watering. A girl in rags with a cup bumps into David and is soon pushed up against the window by the press of people. She lets out a few soft moans before sinking onto the slush on the pavement, where she helplessly remains. David grabs her thin arms and tries to pull her onto her feet, while she desperately clutches the little cup. Eventually, he gets her up again by leaning her back against the window. He stands there, holding her, listening to her rapid breathing, then tentatively he lets go and steps back. She manages to stay upright but blindly holds her cup out to him again. He's confused; has nothing to give her. He glances up and down the street, notices a man in a shiny brown coat with a walking stick, tugs at his sleeve and points to the cup but the man pulls himself free and walks past apprehensively without even looking. While he tries to persuade other people, without any luck, the girl's legs buckle and her body slowly slides to the pavement, where she drops the cup. Not knowing why, he bends down and picks up the cup, in the bottom of which is a single *zloty*. He hands the cup back to the girl but she just stares into space without moving.

"Where do you live?" he asks, putting his hand on her shoulder.

She whispers something that he can't hear for the noise. He asks again and bends down close to her.

"Mila ..." she whispers, "in the yard ... my mother ... " then coughing overwhelms her.

He gets up and stands for a while, looking at the girl and wondering what to do. For some reason he feels attached to her, he doesn't know why. He turns to a woman passing by and asks the way. Mila is a long street … it's some way … go down Karmelicka, up Pawia, down Zamenhofa and then he'll get to Mila. The woman, dressed in a black coat and hat with a strange red colour on her cheeks and lips, looks curiously from him to the girl and back at him.

"Is she your sister?" she questions him in a harsh tone.

"No," he says, trying to pull the girl up.

"What do you want with her?" she asks severely. But he doesn't answer. With a jerk, he finally gets the girl to her feet.

"Let her be," says the woman. "She's going to die anyway!"

But he doesn't hear this, doesn't want to hear it.

He grabs hold of the girl who is swaying from side to side and in danger of falling into the window. He pulls her away from the shop and holding her tightly round the waist, while she awkwardly clutches the cup, they struggle on through the crowd.

The crowd peters out as they turn down Karmelicka Street and the girl becomes a little steadier on her feet, although she still has to lean on him and they need to rest every few minutes. A German military vehicle cruises past them and he instinctively ducks his head down.

From the backs of carts, people are selling books and pots and pans; an old man walking towards them suddenly opens his coat, displaying several rows of armbands fastened with safety pins hanging from the lining. People with baskets of bread stand freezing on the pavement, chatting or staring emptily into space; he looks longingly at the fresh bread. A bicycle taxi drives up beside them; the boy at the pedals spreads his arms and offers them a place on the vacant wooden seat.

"I'll give you a lift for three *zloty*!" he says, laughing.

David keeps on walking with the girl, pretending not to hear, but the boy stubbornly follows after them.

"There's money in the cup!" he says, climbing off the bicycle rickshaw to stand in front of them.

"It's not mine!" says David, trying to push past with the girl.

"Where are you going?" says the boy, who's a couple of years older than David, tall and lean. A scar shows above his eyebrow, as he squints at them curiously, trying to work it out.

"Mila Street," David says, eventually.

The boy shuffles back and forth in front of them in his worn out shoes.

"You'll never make it," he says. "Jump on, you can pay me later!"

Before David knows it, the boy's taken hold of the girl and hoisted her up onto the seat. David sits down beside her; the boy quickly hops back on his bicycle and pulls away from the curb.

Off they go. He can hear the boy puffing and panting as the bike speeds up. He holds on to the girl, who's slumped by his side, still clutching her cup.

What seems like pandemonium – the swirling crowds of people and traffic assault his tired senses. Grey buildings with balconies and yards filled with rubble glide by. On every corner there are small shops with strange cardboard signs in the windows written in Yiddish. Some of the shops are empty and lie abandoned. Children play in the street with sticks and tin cans. Here, a man in a hat and tattered pants is playing the violin; there, an old woman sings soulfully with one hand reaching up towards the overcast sky. Clustered along the dirty, blackened walls, gaunt, lost souls crouch together in rags. Sometimes David can't help but catch the eye of one of these listless cadavers, drawn in by their despairing look.

From behind the gates and the back yards of the ghetto, the cries of children mingle with sharper sounds like someone beating metal against metal. The hunger that's tearing at his guts has sharpened his senses and given everything a faint air of desperation, like something inevitable finally catching up with him. He can see a rabbi hurrying along, and in the short snatches of old melodies and songs, he feels strangely at home. Then he catches sight of the twisted corpse of a child in an open hearse going by which makes him shudder and draw the girl even closer.

The rickshaw bumps over the cobblestones, turns a corner and stops. The boy leans over to them. "Well, where is it? Do you know the number?"

"No," he says, carefully lifting the girl down to the pavement, where she stands propped up, blankly staring down the street.

"Where do you live?" he asks, holding her tightly.

But she doesn't respond.

The boy gets down from the rickshaw, pulls an apple out of his jacket pocket and holds it up in front of her.

"Do you want an apple?" he asks and laughs a little.

The girl snatches the apple and guards it fiercely, glaring suspiciously at the boy.

"Well, where do you live?" he says unmoved, with a wink to David.

"Number twelve," she whispers and turns away.

The boy looks around quickly, then points towards a gate not far from them.

"It's over there," he says to David, climbing back on the bicycle. Suddenly he looks serious.

"Do you have a place to sleep?"

David shakes his head before gripping the girl's arm tightly.

"Meet me here at the corner at eight o'clock. I'll find a place," he says and pedals off swiftly. And in a moment he's gone.

A sudden jolt of energy revives him as he leads the girl through the melting snow towards the gate. The girl starts trembling all over, drops both the cup and the apple and has to be helped to collect them before entering the small yard, surrounded on all sides by buildings.

Apart from a makeshift shack in the middle, the yard is empty. From windows in the peeling walls all around them, naked light bulbs shine here and there, lighting up the occupants, some of whom peer down on them. There are four entrances with stairs leading upwards, so he leads the girl to each one, asking her:

"Is it here?"

Just as he's about to give up, she seems to come to, pointing towards the shack.

"My mother …"she says, "there …!"

"Are you sure?" he asks nervously, and helps her towards the shack, where a rotten wooden door stands slightly open. The stench of paraffin, mixed with soot and waste, hangs in the air as they go in, and a lamp burns on the table, casting a sharp shadow on the wall. A little light creeps in through a tiny, greasy window. He looks around the small room cluttered with old tools and bits of junk and can hear the soft sound of breathing, but only when his eyes have adjusted to the dimness, can he detect a woman in the corner. She has two sacks tied around her waist and lies curled up on the floor, staring at the ceiling. David goes closer but stops in his tracks, as he notices her fevered look and vacant eyes.

"Water … water …"

Bewildered, he turns, takes the cup from the girl and hurries out of the shack. In the yard, he stands for a moment, looking around as he tries to think what to do next. The girl is sick, the woman is sick – why she's just lying there, he doesn't understand. Why is there no one to help them?

There's no tap in the yard. What's he to do? His shoulders slump slightly then he straightens up, walks over to the nearest entrance and continues up the cold stairway. Half of the railing is gone and the stairs are covered with dust and grime. His footsteps echo on the flagstones, but from somewhere at the top of the stairs he can hear muffled voices. He stops at the first door and knocks.

Some time passes and then steps can be heard behind the door. A girl his own age opens the door a fraction and stares suspiciously at him from the dim hallway. Her jet black hair is tied back with a shiny white ribbon. She grips the door handle, her mouth open.

He reaches the cup out towards her:

"Do you have any water for my cup?"

"I mustn't open the door for anyone," she says. "Only me and my grandmother are at home, the others are at work."

Disappointed, he turns and moves to the next door across the hall. He knocks and waits, but nothing happens.

"There's no one home," says the girl behind him.

He turns towards her and sighs. Her eyes are curious.

"I saw you in the yard …" she says, "in the shack … you shouldn't go in there … they're sick, my father says it might be typhoid. He's spoken to the hospital on Christa

Street ... someone's bound to come and get them."

"Give me some water, anyway!" he says and holds the cup out again.

She cocks her head a bit to one side and smiles.

"What's your name?"

"David," he says and exhausted, he closes his eyes.

She opens the door a little and waves him in. Silently, he follows her down the hallway into a high, white kitchen with a window overlooking the yard. A bare light bulb hangs from the ceiling, two mattresses are spread out on the floor with some piles of clothing and on the table his eyes light on some carrots and potatoes. She fills his cup from the tap. He drains it in one gulp, gazing hungrily at the pot of soup on the gas burner in the corner. She fills the cup again, hands him two carrots and says: "Go now, before anyone comes!"

He'd like to stay here where it's warm, he'd like to talk with her for a while – he's grown so unused to kindness. Perhaps he could tell her about everything he's lost, everything he's seen and heard – perhaps she's come from the country, too, perhaps ... He stands there a moment with his cup, staring beyond her, he can't make himself leave. Suddenly, he remembers his friend Jakob, for a moment he can even hear his laughter, but then he remembers the shadows in the shack and turns with his cup and the carrots and walks back down the hallway, with the girl following after him.

The experience has changed him. Anxiety pierces his

heart; a flash of profound terror grips his mind. He forces himself to go on, searching for some kind of explanation. Maybe it doesn't exist. Maybe he's not old enough to understand, maybe – in spite of everything – the idea of happiness has not really left him. Still, he wishes that the world were whole, especially in this shattered place, especially in this nightmare.

Without looking back, he walks out to the yard, over to the shack. When he enters, the girl's gone and the lamp's out, so once again he feels his way through the darkness and kneels down next to the woman. Her blank look makes him pause for a moment, before he places his hand behind her neck and lifts her small, fragile head, bringing the cup to her parched lips and letting her drink slowly. When he carefully lowers her head, she begins to rant feverishly. He gets up and stands there looking at her but doesn't know what more he can do. He remembers a prayer that he's heard many times in Hebrew school and at the synagogue in Kielce. He folds his hands and whispers to himself:

"*S'hema Yisroael,* Hear Oh Israel, the Lord our God, the Lord is One!"

The woman's ravings stop momentarily. He remembers another prayer, the prayer for blessing. He whispers:

"Ha'gomel le'chaiim tovot, she'gmalani kol tov."

The woman starts to babble again so he takes one of her fevered hands and holds it for some time until she's calm. Then he removes his torn mittens and puts them on her hands before returning to the yard.

He looks for the girl in all the entrances to the stairways, but in the dying light she's disappeared without trace.

He walks out through the gate, and just as he gets to the street he remembers the carrots that he'd stuffed into his pockets. He walks back to the shack and puts them in the window before hurrying out again.

Restless and hungry, he roams the streets.

Long before eight o'clock he's already waiting at the corner of Mila Street. Behind him is a rain drenched poster advertising a performance at Melody Palace: *BOKS*. Torn pieces of older posters advertise new shoes or the excellent services of an undertaker. Beneath a lamp post on the other side of the street, a boy is standing in front of a window. He's selling illustrated magazines, now soggy, hung up on a string. He seems to be engrossed in the magazines and their photos of Hitler and SS soldiers with titles like: '*Illustrierte Presse*', '*Die Wehrmacht*', '*Lustige Blatter*'. No one's buying anything, everyone walks by. The boy stares at David, silently, clenching a small sheet of paper in his hand. But David doesn't feel like talking, just paces back and forth on the corner.

Further down the street an older man with a long, thick beard is seated on a chair close to the curb. In front of him, on the pavement, is a small wooden table and next to him sits a little girl on a stool, which is just high enough for her to look over the table. She's barefoot, something's lying on the table, but he can't see what it is. Someone stops and looks at it and then hurries off in the darkness.

An officer carrying a stick, with a black cap and an armband with a yellow Star of David, crosses the street to quell an argument in a queue. He sends two men packing and once again, there's peace. From afar he hears a clack-clack on the cobbles and as it draws closer, two horses pulling a large, black carriage, turn down the street. The horses are lean and slow, one of them limps and when the driver reins them in, the carriage stops. The driver jumps down and disappears up the stairs and inside a house for a long time.

David stands impatiently, looking towards the stairs, wondering what's inside the house, when the door is abruptly thrown open and a long, narrow coffin is carried out by the driver and an elderly man in a baggy coat. A stocky woman with a black shawl around her head is crying, leaning on a young man with a stony face. The coffin disappears into the depths of the carriage but as the coachman is about to close the doors, the woman tears them open again and reaches out for the coffin with a loud cry.

"There's no time for that, there are too many others!" shouts the driver, annoyed, shoving her out of the way. They hold her back so the driver can climb up on the carriage and get the horses moving. The carriage creaks away heavily, the two men drag the woman back up the stairs and soon it's as quiet as before.

The street empties, the boy packs up his magazines and hurries away. Further down the street, the bearded man with the girl picks up the table and chairs and carries them away. Up the street, a shop door is closed in front of the queue; some people complain, others shrug their shoulders, people disperse. Lights go out, black curtains or sheets are put up to cover the windows and even the streetlights are turned off. Bells ring from a church nearby. People hurry home, directly, disappearing into doorways along the street.

An intense darkness fills the street. In a few windows, small signs still glow; a deathly silence spreads as if nothing's happened, and nothing's ever going to happen. Nevertheless, David keeps on waiting. Distant sounds reach him from the rest of the city, but they're like sounds from an army of ghosts.

The hum of an engine breaks the silence; a car unexpectedly turns the corner with its beams illuminating the street like tiny probing spotlights. It approaches quickly and as he recognizes the shape of a German military vehicle, he presses himself against the wall of the building. At that moment someone tugs at him – it's the boy.

"Come on!" he says and starts running.

David chases after him up the street and through a gateway in a wall. The car stops outside the gateway, shrill German voices echo in the deserted street, boots beat on the cobbles. He follows the older boy across a square, they creep through a hole in a fence and run on over stones and bricks, until suddenly he can no longer see the boy and stands there, lost, listening for him in the darkness.

"Here!" the boy shouts from somewhere to his left.

He runs towards the sound of his voice, finds him and crawls down a shaft into a cellar. When they reach the bottom, they have to crouch down to go any further. Everything reeks of damp and the cold, a rat skitters onto his boot, he kicks it off and hurries on, feeling with his hands along the clammy walls. Somewhere behind him he can hear voices, and like an animal with sharpened senses, he half runs, half hobbles after the boy, scraping the knuckles of his bare hands to reach the end of the passage, where the boy is waiting.

"Sorry I'm late," says the boy, catching his breath as they listen in the darkness of the passage.

They stand there for some time.

"The Germans are gone," says the boy and claps him on the shoulder. "Hungry?" He nods. "Come on!"

They climb a steep fire escape and walk across a stony lot, climb over a fence and turn down an alley, apparently deserted of all life. The boy stops abruptly, knocks three times on a door, and a moment later the door is flung open and a stout, red-faced man stares out.

"Who's there?"

When he sees the older boy, he steps back, letting

them pass without a word. They go down some more steps and continue along a hallway until they come to yet another door. When they go in, a myriad of voices, sounds and smells hit them. The room is full of all sorts of people, mostly sitting at tables eating, while others are playing cards. In the midst of it all, a small, balding man stands on a table singing his heart out:

"I won't come back to you
Only a voice from afar
The dust of the streets is my grave …"

The older lad greets people on all sides and leads David over to a table where they're playing cards. They pay him scant attention. Shortly, the boy returns with a steaming bowl of carrot soup and a piece of bread.

"Eat!" he says, grinning.

He devours the soup and bread so quickly that he barely notices it's burned his mouth and throat. The older lad wanders from one table to another chatting amiably, before he returns.

"You still look hungry," he says, disappearing with the bowl and is soon back with more soup and bread.

"You're a good runner," he says. "We can use you."

He's too hungry to ask anything, just eats the soup and bread.

"I'm Martin," says the boy. "Gimme your hand!"

He holds out his hand and Martin presses his thumb against his.

"That's our sign! You don't have to tell me where you're from, you don't have to tell me anything, the sign's what counts."

David nods and swallows the last crumbs of bread as he stares at the scar on Martin's face.

"A kraut dog bit me," he says, suddenly becoming serious. "I killed it with a rock! Outside the wall on Sosnowa Street ... I was on the way back with a sack of potatoes. They shot at me, but I made it!"

He's about to say something but Martin interrupts. "We've got to fix that hand and then find you a place to sleep. Next time, just keep your hands close to your body, run on and concentrate on keeping your balance. Got it?"

David nods silently, tired.

They quickly get up. Martin says his goodbyes to all around as they leave. A moment later, they're back in the damp alleyway. He looks up. The night sky is icily clear. A mantle of stars shine high above them – their brightness and their remoteness fill David with dread and awe.

They sneak down the emptied streets, past the closed shops and darkened buildings. In many alleyways, people covered in sacks or layers of cloth lie sleeping or moaning. Dogs wander across the streets here and there. At the end of the street in front of the ghetto wall, they notice a Jewish police constable. Martin quickly leads him further along past the walls of tall buildings. In front of one place a boy in rags is shouting up at the windows,

"Bread! Bread! Give me some bread!"

Someone on the third floor opens a window and chucks a package down onto the pavement. The boy greedily throws himself onto it, rips off the paper and begins to gobble up the bread. Suddenly, he's surrounded by three other boys; one of them tears the bread away from him and lobs it to the others. They're gone with the wind – the boy's left empty-handed.

They stop and stand and watch.

"Law of the street," says Martin. "You gotta be fast!"

There are eleven boys sleeping in the same basement room on Pawia Street, not far from the Gestapo's prison. Occasionally, they can hear the screams coming from the cells in the prison when the Gestapo are torturing their prisoners for information. Sometimes they hear the shots when they carry out secret executions at night. But usually, the prisoners are driven out of town into the woods and finished off there.

Martin's given him a blanket and a bed that he's filched from an abandoned flat a few blocks away. Martin's not tired, he's wide awake on the bed next to him and wants to talk, but David is ready to drift off.

"Asleep already?" asks Martin disappointed, getting up on his elbow.

"No," he says, his eyelids drooping.

Two of the boys in the room toss and turn in their sleep, one of them suddenly cries for his mother.

"His mother was picked up on the street one day; he hasn't seen her since …" Martin whispers. "That's how it is here. Be careful at all times. A week ago, lots of us were living in another building but we teamed up with these guys so now we're living here. Next week, we could be living somewhere else … maybe we'll never see each other again."

He nods, but isn't really listening, his eyelids feel like lead.

"Tomorrow, I'll show you how we work. We'll go to the cemetery; from there it's easy to get out onto Smetna Street …"

He's gone, drifted off into a deep, liberating sleep. A bell rings far away, he's on his way out of the village one dusty summer day but something makes him stop, maybe the heat, maybe he needs to rest a while. He hears his father's voice: 'Sabbath is a gift, no matter what one believes, Sabbath is a gift.' A white sheet hung out to dry is blowing softly in the breeze, waving shadows across the grass. He leans back against a gnarled tree trunk and looks up at the bright sky. A hawk circles far above the fields. It keeps on circling, endlessly. Gradually, the light fades. He sees nothing more, thinks of nothing, remembers nothing …

When he awakes the next day, he's alone in the cellar. Confused, he gets up from the bed in the faint light and walks over to the door. As he's about to open it, he hears steps coming up the stairs and stands stock still, his back to the wall. A moment later, someone kicks the door and when he doesn't open it, they kick it again. He hears Martin's voice. "Open up, it's me!"

When he opens the door, Martin steps carefully past him with a bowl of water in his hands. "You stink!" he says. "Get yourself washed!"

For the first time in a long time, he gets out of his clothes and boots, and washes himself with a cloth. The water feels fresh on his skin. Martin, too, takes off his clothes and washes himself. With quick, deft movements, he runs the cloth over his pale, skinny body. In their shared nakedness, they feel like best mates; he gives Martin a playful shove and quick as a flash Martin squeezes the water from the cloth over his hair. They laugh.

When they've dressed again and are sitting on the floor, sharing some bread, he asks Martin where he's from.

"From Lodz," he says, "and you?"

He tells him the name of the village.

"My father was an art dealer," says Martin, "I don't know where my mother is. In thirty-nine we were forced out of our flat and separated in the street in front of our house. My big sister and I were shipped to Warsaw. They ransacked our flat – my father had some paintings by Poussin and Delacroix that he'd bought in Paris. They cut them out of their frames. They took everything – food, jewellery, candlesticks, curtains, tables, and drove away. They burned down the great synagogue and prevented Jews from removing the holy books. The vergers who tried to save the holy vessels and relics were locked inside and died in the fire ... "

Martin stops and looks at him for a moment, as if to make sure he really understands. One of his eyelids twitches but his lips remain tightly pressed together.

"I've been in the ghetto for two years and know what's what. I use my eyes. I've had a lot of money and no money. I've worked for Toebbens. I've made lampshades and marmalade from saccharin and carrot juice, I've begged on the street. I used to go to school in a flat on Niska Street. There we read Mickiewicz, Slowacki and Wyspianski. Do you know Wyspianski's, 'Wedding'?

David nods.

"Let me hear it."

Surprised, David thinks for a moment then remembers the lines:

"Simple ploughboy, you had a horn of gold,
What do you have left now? Just a rope."

"I knew you'd know it," says Martin, "I could tell."

"How?"

"You have my grandfather's eyes; I saw that right away on the street. He was the rabbi in Lodz and read the

Talmud all day long. He had mystical visions and predicted all of this. By the time I was five, he was saying, 'It'll be worse than it was in Egypt.' But none of us believed him."

Martin grows silent again and stares into the distance. He hides his head in his hands for a few moments, gets up quickly and walks over to the door. "Let's get out of this hole," he says and jerks the door open.

They walk over to Pawia Street. It's so bitter, people are walking head down against the cold wind. A beggar lies lifeless under newspapers in the middle of the pavement. Someone's already taken his clothes and shoes, so that his frozen, swollen feet stick out from under the papers that are held down by a stone. David stops to look, but Martin pulls him on. As they pass by an alley across the street from the entrance to the Pawia prison, Martin says "Be careful of that window up there. Sometimes there's a madman on duty and he just shoots at anything down the alley!"

At many places along the street, people are queuing up in front of soup kitchens or employment agencies. A German car full of Storm Troopers in brown uniforms and red armbands drives rapidly past them as they're crossing over the wide Okopowa Street. A little later, the cemetery wall stretches out in front of them. Two horse-drawn hearses with the name 'Pinkiert' painted on their sides move towards the great gated entrance in the crumbling wall. The gates open, Martin starts to run, David follows and they run in with the hearses.

"Don't look down into the graves!" says Martin as they creep past the guard and hurry past the snow-covered graveyard, where a few bare trees stretch their branches towards the heavens. A bit further on, some men and boys in overalls, drag corpses from a cart. Arms and legs are grabbed unceremoniously and the frail, white bodies are thrown, one by one, into a deep pit, whose bottom he can't see. The wind gusts fiercely, blowing clouds of white powder up from the pit and whirling it about, over the freshly dug earth.

He follows Martin's advice and looks away as they pass the pit. At the farthest end of the cemetery, they pass a small snow-covered shack. They go behind some bushes all the way up to the boundary wall. As he keeps watch, Martin kneels down and searches along the wall with his fingers until he finds some loose stones. He quickly removes more stones from the wall until there's a hole that's just big enough for him to squeeze through.

"Come here and look through this hole!" says Martin, rising.

David gets down and crawls over to the hole and sticks his head through the wall. A horse-drawn cart and a tram go by on Smetna Street. He imagines that behind the windows, all the passengers are looking in his direction.

"See that building over there. The red one ..."

"Yeh," David says, looking at the dilapidated,

three-storey red brick building, squeezed between two tenement blocks.

"In the basement of number fourteen, there's a sack of tomatoes. It's hidden inside a wooden crate. You fetch the tomatoes, I'll keep watch and give you a sign when it's all clear. You have to get past the guards on the other side of this wall. Will you do it?"

"OK," he replies, looking along the wall. A couple of people are slowly moving towards the hole but he can't see any guards.

"The Germans go past now and then on their motorbikes so you have to be fast! It's up to you when you make a run for it."

He can feel the tension in his body mounting and swallows hard. Yesterday, he'd stood on the other side of the wall, trying to get in, now ...

A sense of unreality washes over him, before a rush of adrenalin kicks in. There's something he needs to prove.

Just before the people go past, David pulls his head in and turns towards Martin, who's lighting a cigarette. Martin exhales the blue smoke through his nose and looks at him in surprise, then smiles.

"Go now!" he says, pushing him with his foot.

David hesitates a moment, then launches himself through the hole, gets up on the pavement and runs across the street. He sees nothing, just runs as fast as he can. He slips over on a pile of snow near the empty yard in front of the building. The cold sends a wave of pain through his bandaged hand but he barely notices, just hurries on, feeling dizzy, until he reaches the entrance to the rundown red building.

At that moment, two men come out of the door; one of them regards him suspiciously. He turns away, pretending that something on the road has caught his eye. They leave. He waits a moment, then walks smartly into the yard, which is full of rubble and old junk. Some children are throwing snowballs against the wall but they stop when they see him.

"This isn't your yard!" says a little girl, coming towards him but he ignores her and goes down into the cellar of Number 14.

In the cellar, he quickly finds the wooden crate, opens it and pulls the bag out. A hard metal object protrudes from the canvas sack. He feels it with his hand, but doesn't have time to check it more closely. As he walks back to the door, the little girl blocks his way.

"That's not your bag!" she says, peering at him.

"Yes, it is," he says and pushes her aside. She starts shouting so he rushes up the steps and out of the yard.

He reaches Smetna Street in a flash, the girl's shouts echoing behind him. Down the street he can see a guard with a rifle, looking his way. Suddenly, the distance across the street to the cemetery wall seems too far, too hazy and the traffic is too dense ... he feels his limbs go stiff. In the distance, he hears Martin's voice, "Run, David, run!"

But he can't move. In the blur around him, a shadow approaches. It's the guard. He can see his heavy boots and his massive, stony countenance.

"Run! Run!" comes Martin's voice again, more loudly.

In a split second, he's off across the road, shoving the sack through first before squeezing back through the hole. Martin pulls him through the final few inches and immediately replaces the stones in the wall. A moment later, the guard is poking at the stones from outside.

He grabs the sack and they run on into the cemetery.

"Next time! Next time!" shouts the guard angrily. But his words are soon blown away in the wind.

They slow their pace to a steady walk and David can feel Martin's eyes on him. As they approach the gate, he's still shaking.

"Gimme the sack," says Martin, "and calm down."

He hands him the bag and while they walk, Martin pulls something out of his pocket. By the gate, a guard in a grey coat turns slowly towards them. Maybe he knows they're coming, maybe he's heard it all. The guard takes a couple of steps forward, his gloved hands clutching his rifle strap. He's broad and round and breathing heavily in the cold wind. His face is soft and lined like that of an old lady.

"*Halt!*" he says without moving.

Martin gives him what he has in his hand. The guard glances down at the coins and stuffs them in his coat pocket.

"Not enough," he says flatly.

"You'll get more next time!" says Martin, smiling stiffly.

"Who's the boy?" asks the guard. Instantly, his eyes narrow.

"A friend," says Martin. "Won't be any trouble …"

For a second, the guard contemplates something.

"OK … OK …" he says resignedly then turns his attention to something else far behind them. While he's deliberately looking in the opposite direction, Martin tugs at David's sleeve, they open the gate and leave.

On Okopowa Street, old newspapers and scraps of paper whirl in the wind. The overcast sky makes everything, even the piles of rubbish covered in snow, look dark and shapeless. The people swarming along the street pull their clothing tighter and carry on regardless. At one point, inexplicably, the crowd comes to a halt. A sense of panic grows; an urgent desire to break free surfaces. The exhausted, pallid faces stare steadily ahead, revealing nothing. Only the sound of the wind can be heard, a wind that cuts to the bone.

David and Martin walk silently beside each other. When they turn on to Pawia Street, Martin says, "You made it all right, but you think too much." He doesn't reply. Martin stops, hunts for the object in the sack, quickly retrieves it and hides it under his jacket. Martin looks at him with a faint smile. "Want to know what it is?"

He nods.

"A gun!" says Martin and smiles again.

"What are you going to do with it?" he asks.

"Go back to the cellar with the sack. I'll be there in an hour and then I'll tell you everything!"

He's about to protest, but Martin quickly shoves the bag into his arms and runs off down the street. A second later, he's disappeared in the crowd.

Disappointed, David walks along the pavement with his bag, turning into an alleyway to escape the bitter wind. He feels inside the sack for a tomato, and devours it hungrily. Instantly, his face glows, as he savours the taste of the bittersweet juice. Leaning slightly against the wall, in a state of near bliss, he holds on to the heady feeling.

A man in a black leather coat and hat, carrying a cane and a briefcase has stopped in front of the alleyway. It's pure coincidence that he's arrived there in the midst of the teeming crowd, and is staring at the boy. Something about David has made him stop. Maybe it's David's look of innocent enjoyment, maybe the softness of his face. He suddenly remembers his own childhood – summers on the farm: freshly mown grass, dust, and sweat. He shakes off the memory. His gloved hand tightens around his cane.

"No, not now, I don't have time for this!" he mutters, continuing on down the street. He has to carry on no matter what, waking in the night, his body drenched in sweat. Then he has to get up and go on with it all: the numbers, the accounts, the agendas, the requisitions, the minutes of meetings, the petitions, the applications, the inquiries, the telephone calls … endlessly … on and on …

He slams his cane down on the cobbles. Today, he's gone largely unnoticed as he heads grimly towards the town hall on Zamenhof Street. But a woman in rags on the corner of Pawia and Smocza Streets reaches out her hand and shouts his name, "Czerniaków! Czerniaków!"

At odds with his usual routine, he goes into a café, where he nods vaguely at a few customers before taking a seat in the corner. The café is narrow and almost empty. A man in a faded black jacket circulates around the tables, taking orders. At the door, a girl keeps the beggars out. He orders a cup of tea and pulls *'Der Stürmer'* from his case. He scans the first page: 'Julius Streicher warns against the Asian Jews and has found concrete evidence of Jewish vampirism.' Among other things he reads: 'Jews use blood in their wine and for baking; they use either fresh or dehydrated blood from Christian boys for Jewish weddings, for pregnant women and at circumcisions. Especially in Easter week, people should be vigilant in case Jews attack Christian boys to satisfy their animal urges.'

He's feeling nauseous. He folds up the paper and puts it back in his case. He closes his eyes; just ten minutes' peace, that's all he asks. The waiter places a cup of steaming tea on the table and he drinks it, staring absently out of the dirty window. What more can he do? They're attacking him from all sides – oh, how easy it is, to criticize. Hasn't he done everything possible to get the prisoner released from Pawia prison, even asking Commissioner Auerswald to contact the Governor General? Hasn't he worked tirelessly to increase food rations, to get more coal and more water? Hasn't he shown in black and white, how many have starved to death already? Hasn't he led them around the streets, to the workshops, to the hospitals, to see the hardship and despair with their own eyes? To no avail. All those arrogant excuses!

He's clenching his fist under the table; his great body is straining to breathe until he loosens his collar. He must try to stay calm – isn't that what's expected of him? That he walks around the streets smiling, while the earth quakes under their feet?

He sips his tea but it tastes of nothing. The other day, he gave a little speech about the soul and the need for religion. The Council of Rabbis were happy enough. How could he tell them what he was really thinking? Don't they understand that plans are being made – terrible, unbelievable plans? Mass deportation. Mass transportation. That is the terrible secret that he must bear all alone. One day, Auerswald and Höhmann will come and ask for the Council's assistance. No, they won't ask. They'll demand. And what should he do then? Be the Devil's henchman? How will he ever be forgiven?

No, he won't think about it. One day at a time, that's all he can do. He wipes his brow with his handkerchief. It must be the tea, yes, it's the tea that's made him so hot. If only he could stop the thoughts coming for even a second. His mind slips back to the picture of the boy in the alleyway, with his ecstatic face. If only he could be that boy, if only he could be so innocent … free of responsibility … avoid the butchers' clean-shaven faces … yes, they'd tricked him to sit at their table, convinced him that as long as they worked together there was no danger … made him believe that the ghettoes in Warsaw, Radom and Krakow would be safe … but he'd walked right into their trap … and now they were doomed to squirm on the hook … why didn't people realize that they're on the deck of a sinking ship – and that his job was simply to provide the music as the end draws near …

No, he won't think. He can't think. His thoughts slip away like grains of sand … But before he pays and puts on his hat, another long-forgotten memory stabs at him: "Where is Jas, my only child?" he wonders. Tears prick his eyes. He walks to the door, the girl opens it, and with a few coins at the ready, he hands them out swiftly to the beggars outside. The wind blows his coat open; he grabs hold of his hat, slams his cane down on the cobbles and doggedly moves on. He's soon swallowed up by the swarm on the street. With each step, he thinks: work, work, work!

David's been waiting in the basement for a long time before Martin finally shows up. Together, they walk to Leszno Street to sell the tomatoes to a grocer.

As soon as they enter, Martin nods to the stout grocer behind the counter and they pass through a curtain to the back room. A bit later, the grocer, Mr Weizermann appears, breathing heavily. He looks curiously at David and turns to Martin, who's holding the canvas bag in his arms.

"Lemme see them!" he says at once. Martin hands him the canvas bag and with his thick fingers he caresses the tomatoes one after the other, all twenty-four. Apparently satisfied with the produce, he turns towards a cupboard on the wall, opens it with a key and takes out a paper bag. Carefully, he counts the money in the bag, before closing it again.

"How do you keep on getting these tomatoes?" he asks in a tone of astonishment, as he stands ready with the money in the small bag.

"That's for me to know!" says Martin impatiently, stretching his hand out for the money. But Weizermann holds on to the bag.

"Where do they come from?" he asks suspiciously.

"They're grown in a hot-house outside Warsaw, that's why they're small. You should be happy that I can get them; it's winter, Mr Weizermann…"

"Yes … winter," says Weizermann with a mournful smile, handing the money bag to Martin. "You boys don't need to remind me … Do you know what day it is today?"

Martin and David look at each other, mystified.

"Well lads, today is *Hamentaschen* day, the day of lots, Esther's day … so what does that mean –?"

"Purim," says David and smiles a little.

"Tonight, I bet you'll drink so much that you won't know the difference between Haman and Mordechai."

"We don't have anything to drink," says Martin solemnly.

Without another word, Weizermann disappears into the shop and returns breathing heavily with four triangular little cakes and a small black bottle which he gives to David.

"Drink that. You deserve it. I'm not telling you what's in it, mind!"

They both look at the bottle and try to guess the contents.

"It's for me to know …" repeats Weizermann with almost childish stubbornness and glee.

Soon afterwards they leave the shop, and it's only once they're safely back in the cellar with the money, cakes and drink that Martin reveals what he did with the gun.

"You mustn't tell anyone," he says. "Swear it!"

David swears with two fingers on his throat that he won't breathe a word. Even so, Martin studies him warily, with his eyelids twitching nervously. Finally he talks: a man known as Samuel, but who has another nickname too, now has the gun; and it's not the first time Martin has brought guns in.

"What does he use a gun for?" asks David cautiously, imagining the worst.

"I don't know," answers Martin evasively. "It's a secret."

"Is he alone?"

Martin shakes his head.

"How many of them are there?" he persists.

"There are a lot of different groups," says Martin. "Zionists, revisionists and socialists, but not many of them want weapons. They have secret newspapers too, that tell you everything the Germans are lying about. It's really dangerous to get them, but I do it anyway!"

"Aren't you afraid?" he asks.

"They took my mother and father away," says Martin. "I'll do anything to even the score. They won't get me that easily!"

They carry on talking and then Martin opens the bottle with a knife so they can taste the strange apple-flavoured liquid which burns the back of their throats. Martin grows more excited, his eyes gleam in his pale face and he waves his hands about wildly. David feels woozy too and is carried along by Martin's torrent of words as if his thoughts were taking off and floating out on to the streets.

"The future will be different!" he suddenly cries out, imagining his uncle before him.

"What do you mean?" asks Martin, stopping mid-sentence.

"There'll be no more war …"

"Do you really believe that?"

"And we'll be able to walk freely in the city …"

"Not in Warsaw, we won't …" says Martin, shaking his head. "I don't think the Germans are going to just walk away …"

"One day people will be able to laugh and dance again," David says, absorbed in his vision. "And even though you don't believe me, there'll be peace in Warsaw again."

"How do you know?" asks Martin doubtfully, a little in awe.

"I have an uncle in Kielce who taught me that you should never give up on humanity!"

"Humanity stinks," says Martin. "The only thing you can trust is yourself. Where's this uncle now?"

"I don't know," David says in a low voice. "Maybe he's dead …"

"See what I mean!"

But David goes on talking about his uncle anyway until the question occurs to him, "Don't you believe in heaven, then?"

"Heaven isn't for the likes of us," says Martin. "How can you believe in it? Stop dreaming … there's nothing but hell waiting for us."

"If no one believed in heaven, then there'd be no one to believe in hell either," he responds, noticing how dizzy he feels.

"Who says so? Your uncle from Kielce?"

"No ... I say so," he replies, then sinks back onto his bed.

After a while, the other boys return, chatting nineteen to the dozen. Some have smuggled goods from Sosnowa Street, others have slipped through the gate at Grzybowska Street with potatoes, one got hit by a guard, another's been cut, a third sprained his ankle when he jumped off a horse-drawn bus on Leszno Street because there were two Poles chasing him. The bottle goes around and is emptied little by little. One lad starts to sing, others dance on their blankets with improvised hats on their heads. Occasionally, David gets up and fools around with them but his mind is elsewhere. First he feels cold, then hot ... and he can hear a distant voice in his head that he can't quite place, is it his father's or ...? As he slips into a drunken sleep, he fails to notice the sudden deafening silence in the room when the others realize that Yitzhak Breslaw, a boy from Smocza, hasn't returned.

During the next month, David becomes an expert at dealing in black market goods. Slowly but surely, he discovers most of the escape routes and 'safe' houses in the area. From a distance, he can usually predict whether a guard will be prepared to do a deal or whether he needs to find another route. Sometimes he goes out alone, at other times he's with Martin or some of the other lads from the cellar. Sometimes, he wanders around on the 'Aryan' side just to feel free. But all the time, he has his eyes wide open to avoid obvious meeting points and large open spaces. Sometimes he hides in a passageway for what seems like an eternity to avoid suspicious passers-by. He discovers that the ghetto has other distribution points besides the bar in the alley. At certain times, usually in the evening, the place is crawling with Polish and Jewish smugglers, sometimes Germans too, mainly at the cemetery, where there's a rapid exchange of everything from bread to medicine to false Aryan passports. You can't always be sure who you're dealing with and you inevitably have to take risks. But dealing is Martin's business and David learns a little more every time.

They share the money they earn and apart from any that goes on bribes, to people like the porter in the market and the German and Polish guards, or others on the 'Aryan' side, they spend the rest on food and entertainment.

One evening they go to the Femina Theatre to hear the singer Marysia Eisenstadt, the nightingale of the ghetto. Standing at the back of the crowded hall, David can only catch a few glimpses of the nineteen-year-old brunette, who's a slight figure on the stage, but her quivering voice pierces his soul and carries him far away. When they get back to the cellar room, he gets out his little harp and plays some of her songs, to the astonishment of the other boys.

"Why haven't you ever played before?" asks Martin,

clapping him approvingly on the shoulder.

"I only play when I'm happy," he answers, putting the harp back in his pocket. But Martin won't accept that as an excuse and from then on he has to play every evening.

On another occasion, Martin drags David out to the Café Hirschfield on the corner of Sienna and Sosno Streets. David borrows a shirt and a pair of trousers from Martin, and although they're so big he has to roll them up, they're clean and relatively new. A waiter in a coat and tie with shiny shoes leads them casually to a small table in the corner of the big, noisy, smoky room. Martin orders a chicken dish and a glass of wine for each of them. But with a glance at David, the waiter refuses to serve alcohol to minors, until Martin hands him some money. Reluctantly, the waiter disappears into the kitchen.

The café serves the very best food to its cosmopolitan clientele. From the various tables come the smells of roast goose, chicken and duck, or fish in aspic served in fine brass bowls. French wine, liqueurs and cognac are either knocked back or sipped, as the price of gold, platinum, diamonds or even false identity papers are negotiated in hushed voices. The atmosphere is heightened and intense. Older businessmen, who have already made a fortune from dealing in everything from flour to furs, are there with fashionable young ladies, mainly from the tenements in the ghetto, who want to eat dinner with a whiff of luxury. Sixteen-year-old girls are prepared to sell themselves for a meal to the highest bidder, whether he's a black marketeer or a

Gestapo agent. Who can tell the difference, when anything goes? Sometimes one of these girls turns up the next day in a side street with a bullet through her head alongside her lover.

The leaders of the underground front are in the café too. Under the guise of shameless revelling, so popular among the criminal underworld, they can meet together relatively undisturbed while observing the black heart of the ghetto.

On this particular evening, Martin catches sight of Samuel sitting at a table at the other end of the room, but he doesn't go over to greet him. Instead, when a man at the neighbouring table gives him a wink, he goes over to talk with him instead. The tall, blonde heavy set man is dressed in a long casual jacket and smart trousers. There's a menacing smile playing on his lips, and he has a guarded look about him that suggests a cool detachment. He keeps on raising his tall champagne glass to make a loud toast then the two girls and the man at his table make another toast even more noisily and so it goes on.

David feels apprehensive watching the man; he can't understand what Martin wants with him.

"His name's Milek," says Martin when he sits back down again. "They say he's dangerous, but I don't believe it – he's helped me out more than once."

"I don't like him," whispers David, but as he can't say exactly why, and as Martin just gives him his 'I know better than you' grin, he keeps quiet.

"Milek isn't his real name," says Martin, agitated.

"I don't know that much about it but he offered me some jewellery if I do him a favour. And it's not just any piece of jewellery either – it's a solid gold ring!"

"Will you ... are you going to do him a favour?"

"You're in on it, as well. It's just a deal, nothing else – we do him a favour and he pays us for it!"

"So what do we have to do?" David asks sceptically.

"He's loaned some money to a man on the 'Aryan' side ... instead of money, he's going to be paid back in jewellery ... we have to bring the jewellery box back over to him. It's easy!" says Martin, raising his glass of white wine and draining it.

"So why doesn't he do it himself?" asks David.

"Someone like Milek has bigger things to take care of, it's no big deal. Actually, he's doing us a favour!"

"Did he say that?"

Martin nods and having eaten enough, wipes his mouth with the white linen napkin.

"The chicken was good," he says. "Come on. Let's go!"

They leave the Café Hirschfeld where David's had the unpleasant feeling of being watched the entire time. As they walk along busy Pawia Street, where darkness hangs like a blue veil in the windows of the tall buildings, he's trying to decide whether to say 'no' to Martin but remains silent. He doesn't notice the dark shapes shoving past him, barely registers where he's going. He knows that Martin will push him to do it – it's just a matter of time.

And sure enough, as they go down the steps to the cellar, Martin grabs his shoulder and pleads with him, "I've helped you. Now you have to help me. This is important!"

"When is it supposed to happen?" he asks, reluctant.

"Next week!" says Martin, going down a few more steps and opening the door to their cellar room.

David stands for a moment facing the darkness of the cellar. He has little choice.

A few days later he goes back to number 12 Mila Street. It's a sunny day and for the first time in a long time he isn't freezing. In the yard, some men are tearing down the shack. He rushes into the stairway and goes up the stairs. The railing that was broken has been repaired and the stone steps are clean. A smell of soap hangs in the air. He stops at the first door and knocks softly.

Just as before, he has to wait a long time before he hears any footsteps and again the door is opened just a crack. The girl with the jet black hair stares out at him.

"It's me!" he says quietly.

It takes a moment before the girl recognizes him in his new clothes. Silently, she opens the door and lets him into the shadowy hall. The door to the sitting room is open and light from the window reveals several blankets and mattresses scattered about. The door to the next room is closed. They go into the kitchen and then he notices how thin she's become. He immediately hands her the piece of chocolate he has in his pocket.

"Where'd you get it?" she asks without taking it, sitting down listlessly on a chair.

"It's for you!" he says and offers it to her again.

"Mmm ... but where'd you get it?"

Only when he's told her what he's doing does she take the chocolate, break it in half, hiding half in a drawer and eating the rest herself. Slightly revived she returns to her chair but a moment later, she seems tired again.

He tells her that he's heard Marysia Eisenstadt sing but it makes little impression. She looks at him blankly. When he asks about the woman and the girl in the shack, she says nothing, only clenches her jaw and closes her eyes.

"The Germans came and took my father and three other men," she says suddenly. "We don't know where he is. Maybe they've shot him!"

He doesn't know what to say, just puts his hand on her shoulder. Her body trembles, she covers her face with her hands and is silent for a long time. Suddenly, she bursts out crying and curls up in a ball. He pulls her up and stands, holding her. Slowly, the crying ceases and she wipes the tears away with her hands.

"They said my father was a smuggler but an informer at work lied about him because he said what he thought about the boss."

"How do you know?" he asks, letting go of her.

"One of them got away from the Germans in the street and he came here in the evening and told us all about it. The others who work at Schultz, they protested when the Germans came, so they were taken, too ... They came here and pushed us into the kitchen. We heard them shout, "*Los, los!* ..." We opened the door, but they threw us back into the kitchen and threatened to kill us if we said anything ..."

A sound from the next room distracts her and she gets up mechanically, opens the door and goes in to her grandmother. He hears the old lady moaning and through a slit in the door he can see the girl deftly turning her on her side on a wooden bed. The woman mumbles something in Yiddish, "Thanks, thank you my girl," and then, "Shouldn't you be in school?"

He walks over to the window. Out in the yard, the shack no longer exists. The men stack the rotten planks in a pile. Instantly, the memory returns of that fateful day when they were herded together in the village, and he can hear Mrs Kaplan screaming again. He breathes in sharply and struggles anxiously to remember his mother's face. No, no, he won't, he mustn't cry ...

The girl returns to stand by the chair. He turns towards her and stares at her lovely black hair.

"We've almost nothing left to eat," she says. "My mother won't go out begging and she can't find any work. Some new people have moved in here, who beg on Komitetova Street but they have three children. The only one who gives us any food is a man on the second floor. Every evening he comes down with a piece of dry bread and sometimes some potatoes. And my grandmother, she's old and sick, but there's no room in the hospital … Everything seems to be going from bad to worse …"

"Sit down and be still," he says, placing his hand on her shoulder. He notices a glass on the worktop so he walks over to the tap and fills it with water.

"Drink this," he says, handing her the glass. She takes it, but is too upset to drink.

"Drink!"

Reluctantly, she drinks the water and hands him the empty glass.

"Calm down now …" he says softly and now, it seems she's listening. She sinks down in the chair.

"I can help you," he says.

"How?"

"I can get you something to eat!"

"You can't!"

"Yes, I can. I have money. And I can come every day." She shakes her head.

"You mustn't smuggle again, it's too dangerous!"

"I'll manage …" he says but doesn't say any more.

A little later, she sees him to the door. Suddenly, they're both awkward and don't know how to say good-bye. They shake hands then he quickly turns away and hurries down the stairs. When he reaches the street he realizes that he doesn't even know her name.

He has a dream. He's in the black room in the synagogue, where God's name is silent. He whispers God's name anyway, but the word sticks in his throat, and not a sound leaves his mouth.

"Why are you whispering?" asks a voice behind him.

He recognizes Antek Blum's voice and turns, but there's no one there.

"If I don't whisper, what should I do?" his voice echoes in the darkness.

"Shout!" says the voice.

He shouts and a moment later he's awake and staring at the ceiling. The silence around him is overwhelming. Then he can hear Martin's rapid breathing. And then the others in the room. He's not at home here. Where is his home? For a long time he can't sleep.

The next morning he's half asleep as he queues for bread on Pawia Street. The queue stretches out right across the pavement forcing him to balance on the curb. Further down the street, a dark green Mercedes with a closed soft top emerges from Pawia prison with its horn blaring. People jump aside, and a horse and cart pulls up abruptly, blocking the street. The driver desperately whips the bony creature but it won't move on. The car slowly goes round them with two wheels up on the pavement. It carries on, half on the pavement, half off, past the cart and towards the queue.

David's body stiffens, as he has a moment's certainty that this was the car he travelled in to the city. A few moments away from the queue, the car turns back onto the street. But by then the queue has dispersed with people pressing up against each other and against the walls of the houses. He doesn't recognize the driver but catches a glimpse of the man on the back seat, who stares at him through the window with cold blue deep-set eyes as the car passes. His tall, slender body in his grey uniform offsets the bright white collar of his shirt, despite the dim interior of the car. His head is crowned with short blonde hair, combed stiffly back. The eyes sear him like ice.

No, it's not the Police Commissioner, no … and even if it was, the Commissioner probably doesn't remember him. He watches the car until it disappears at the end of the street and sighs in relief.

Reinhard Heydrich, Protector of the Reich, picks up his hat from the leather seat and places it on his head. If he noticed the boy, it was like noticing a spot of lint on his jacket. And yet, the faces in the ghetto made an impression on him, like the expressionless faces of worn-out dolls that children throw in a corner. The more he drives around the ghetto that day, the more he's filled with disgust.

He *is* the future, he …

A spot on his jacket annoys him. It looks like mildew, why didn't he notice it before? He's been on inspection and no one pointed it out … of course not, they're afraid of him, they admire him …

He moistens his index finger and rubs at the spot. Is it gone?

"Klein," he says in his shrill voice, leaning back in his seat. "Have you noticed a mark on my uniform?"

Klein looks in the rearview mirror.

"No, sir. Your uniform is perfect!

The car stops in front of the noisy, restless crowd on Komitetova Street. Slowly, the people part to make way for the honking car – carts, stalls, chairs are all dragged aside while the ragged children, thin men and pale women all shove each other in confusion to try and move aside. The car drives on a bit further, but stops again – a boy's lying lifeless on the cobblestones a little way ahead. Heydrich looks up in annoyance as he's been preoccupied with cleaning the spot.

"Remove him!" he says, casually.

Klein briskly gets out of the car and points at the dying boy in front of the crowd. No one moves. The driver strides over to the boy, bends down, picks him up then throws him onto a cart of potatoes. It tips over with both the boy and the potatoes spilling down onto the cobblestones. Klein quickly gets behind the wheel, closes the door and drives on.

"You really can't see anything?" asks Heydrich. Klein looks in the rearview mirror again.

"I can see a small spot on your jacket, sir!"

"Why didn't you notice it before?"

"My mistake, sir," says Klein turning the car down a side street.

"That sort of mistake can be critical … make a note of it, Klein!"

"*Jawohl*!" says Klein without blinking.

Heydrich now considers where he can change his uniform; he's in a state of strange unrest. He needs to concentrate. For a few minutes he pays attention to his surroundings. Then he orders Klein to drive to the rallying place, and along the way, he studies his map of the ghetto again, noting the most likely route for the forthcoming mass deportation of the population.

He also notes the estimated number of people they can transport daily (around five to six thousand). He's curious to assess with his own eyes, whether the rallying place can perhaps take more than the estimated number. With an effective team and the help of the Jewish police, it might be possible to increase that number daily, depending on the size of the square. The car drives on, stopping occasionally, while Heydrich surveys the world outside – but his thoughts are elsewhere.

They drive through the gate at Stawki Street, cross

Dzika Street and come to the half-empty square with its numerous railroad tracks. He asks Klein to get out and stretch his legs. Klein gets out of the car, while Heydrich remains alone going over his plan, staring at the railway tracks in the square.

A bitter smile crosses his thin lips. He takes out his white gloves and quickly pulls them on. With his hands in his lap, he leans back in the seat and closes his eyes. When he opens them, he catches sight of a dull eye and part of his face in the mirror. For a moment he stares in revulsion at his reflection, then looks away.

He looks over at Klein, pacing back and forth in the square. Simultaneously, Klein turns and looks towards the car, and their eyes meet for an instant. Heydrich gives him a nod and Klein ambles back towards the car. He gets behind the wheel and awaits Heydrich's orders. Heydrich contemplates the square one last time. It seems to him that six thousand Jews are not enough. He makes a note on the map, 'Capacity of the square: 6500 Jews'.

It pleases him to be precise.

On a signal from Heydrich, Klein starts the engine and drives away. Once more, Heydrich's mind turns to the question of how quickly he can change his uniform.

One evening after curfew, David finds himself back in the lively atmosphere of the small bar he'd visited before with Martin. He's come to exchange some black market goods with a man from the 'little' ghetto. He's brought two false passports that he'll exchange for four bags of rice plus a credit note for two bags of potatoes that he can fetch from the cemetery the next day. Like Martin, he's now on familiar terms with the many regulars in the place, and he nods in their direction while the man beside him carefully examines the false passports. He's become one of the motley crew of survivors who struggle on from one day to the next. Although he's grown in confidence, he rarely asks himself what the future might bring. Homelessness is now the norm. He carries out his 'deals' keenly and cautiously, and on the whole people forget that he's still just a child. His seriousness is impressive, yet in his dark eyes you can see the spectre of someone who's come close to the edge. It's as if he's not really there, as if a terrible weight were dragging him toward the abyss ...

A pale, clean-shaven man from Jablonna is playing the violin and two couples are dancing in front of the tables, where others sit and discretely applaud the music.

Suddenly, the stomping of boots and loud shouts from the stairs can be heard. Three men rush out through the kitchen, a woman hides under a table and many others stuff all that they have under their clothing. Some sit paralyzed in their seats, while the couples dance on as if in a dream. Four SS men with their rifles raised run into the room. One of them shoots at the ceiling, and the couples stop dead where they are. Unperturbed, the violinist keeps on playing, while everyone else stares at the door. And just as if he's waited for precisely this moment, a fat Lieutenant with a shiny face makes his entrance with more SS soldiers behind him. The Lieutenant surveys the situation quickly, adjusts one of his white gloves in irritation, takes a few paces forward and with a loose gesture of his hand calls his men forward: "In rows, quick, *schnell*, in rows!"

The violinist stops playing and stands rooted to the spot as the SS men herd folk together and a man who was caught on his way to the kitchen is dragged back on the floor so that all can see. With the butt of a rifle he's hit in the neck and collapses bleeding, pleading feebly for his life. But he's ignored.

They search all the people at great speed. Jewels, money, bags, passports and even David's bags of rice are thrown in a heap on the floor. For no apparent reason, several young men are singled out and pushed towards the exit. From the stairs, dull thuds and loud shouts can be heard. As if it's all a tedious chore, the Lieutenant pulls two women out of the group and orders them to stand still. The rest are driven up against the wall. David stares at a rip in the wallpaper, can feel his legs shaking but slowly he turns his head to glance over his shoulder.

An SS soldier, who looks no older than a teenager, violently kicks the musician, knocking him over. The man crawls confused and silent across the floor. To the laughter and amusement of the SS men he collects his violin and bow with trembling hands, and gets up.

"So you play the violin," says the Lieutenant as he

tightens his belt and strides over towards him. "Play, play your damn monkey music!"

The man, who doesn't understand him, laughs nervously. The Lieutenant takes his pistol out of its holster and puts the gun to his temple.

"Play for the *Führer*," he shouts insanely, "or I'll blow your brains out!"

With trembling hands, the man puts the violin up to his cheek and scrapes the bow across the strings. He starts off by making a grating sound but then he tries again, more carefully. As the delicate melody fills the room, he closes his eyes and his long, pale face suddenly seems transformed. The tone becomes richer and the instrument resonates like a woman's melancholy song.

For a moment, time stands still.

The SS soldiers are clustered in the middle of the room, chatting and offering each other cigarettes or drinking the wine from the tables. The Lieutenant steps toward the two women and loosely gestures to them.

"Undress!" he says, but they pretend not to understand and stare ahead blankly.

"Take off your clothes!" says an older SS man in Polish, as he takes a drag on his cigarette.

Slowly, the two women begin to undress, while the younger SS men stare excitedly and nervously at their bodies. As they stand there in their underwear, they stop and hold on to each other.

"*Los, los!*" says the Lieutenant and waves his hand again.

The men tear the few remaining garments off them. Naked and shocked, they try to cover their bodies with their arms and hands.

"Turn around!" says the Lieutenant lighting a cigarette. His casual air gives nothing away but his thick upper lip trembles slightly. One of the women turns around slowly, but the other stands still. With a look of hatred she stares at the Lieutenant.

"Search them!" he says, motioning two SS men forward.

Through the laughter, two of the soldiers go towards the women while two others hold them tightly. One of the soldiers seems nervous, and hesitates a moment in front of the panic-stricken women who are struggling to escape. But spurred on by the others' taunts and excitement, he quickly removes his gloves, grabs one of the woman's hips, bends down and searches between her legs.

"Anything hidden in there?" says the Lieutenant. The woman screams, but is slapped in the face by the other soldier.

"No, Herr Lieutenant, there's nothing!" says the soldier smirking, and a moment later he searches the other woman too.

"Swine, swine, leave her alone!" shouts a man thickly, turning from the wall and running towards them with a knife in his hand.

The Lieutenant grabs his pistol and fires off a few shots. With the dying roar of an animal, the man falls to the ground, pulling tables and chairs along with him.

The laughter ceases.

"Clumsy Jew boy!" says the Lieutenant, who seems uneasy and appears to have lost his hold on the younger soldiers.

"We have to search. It's our duty. Now, get on with it quickly!"

The soldier who's searched the women gets up and looks uncertainly in the Lieutenant's direction. Just then, the younger, ash-blonde woman with the beautiful curly hair spits in his face.

"She doesn't like you, Jürg. Dance with her, show us what you can do!"

The soldier wipes the spit from his face, but stands uncertainly in front of the woman, who's turned her face away. Something or other, whether it's the woman's obvious contempt for him or the distressing cries from the man on the floor, makes him step aside, shake his head and sit down in a chair.

"Give him something to drink," says the Lieutenant and motions another man forward, who immediately grabs the woman and drags her around the floor. The woman resists initially but a few seconds later her legs give way, yet the SS man holds her up like a dummy and twirls her round and round. They spin around more and more wildly until he suddenly lets go and she falls to the floor.

She cries out, crawls a short distance along the floor and collapses.

The Lieutenant stands there for a moment looking

at her with his trembling upper lip then nods as if in a trance.

"Move out, move out!" he says, turning abruptly and leaving the room.

"Stay where you are!" one of the soldiers shouts to the men lined up along the wall. "Next time, we'll take you with us!"

As if on a given signal, the soldiers storm out of the door. The tramping of boots is heard on the stairs, and just as quickly and unexpectedly as they came, they disappear in their whirlwind of terror.

Like wreckage that has been left behind, the two men and the woman lie lifeless on the floor. The violinist plays on and doesn't dare open his eyes. The naked woman left standing, still hiding her body behind her arms, slowly comes to and takes a few dazed steps towards the men by the wall. A man turns warily, runs up to her and covers her with his jacket. She falls into his arms. Only then does she start to sob.

How he got back to the cellar room, he can't recall. In the middle of the night, he's woken by the uncontrollable urge to vomit. Martin is soon there, beside him, trying to clean the blanket with a rag. They go into the hall, to whisper and in small snatches, he tells Martin what's happened. Martin paces back and forth uneasily with clenched fists. He stops, shaking his head in resignation, searches for something in his breast pocket and hands him a cigarette.

"I don't smoke," says David.

"Smoke it anyway," says Martin as he lights the cigarette. David takes a few puffs and coughs.

"Keep at it," says Martin. "It helps."

He takes a few more puffs and gradually feels calmer.

"Those bastards," says Martin. "Would you recognize them again?"

"The SS officer was fat and ... he shouted like crazy."

"That's Brandt," says Martin turning away.

"How do you know him?"

"I saw him one day at the Café Hirschfeld. He was with ... I'll kill him."

"Who was he with?" asks David.

"Milek ... the smuggler ..." says Martin, reluctantly.

"The one we're working for tomorrow?" asks David, incredulously.

Martin nods silently.

"I won't do it!" says David angrily, hitting the wall with his fist.

"There's nothing wrong with Milek; they only talked together!"

"You're crazy. Brandt's a killer."

"Think what we'll get out of it!"

"I don't care, I —"

"You promised!" says Martin, interrupting him.

"Why does it matter so much to you that we do Milek a favour!"

"I've already told you," says Martin. "He's done me a favour!"

"What's he done?"

"It doesn't matter," says Martin angrily. "Can't you just trust me?"

"I don't trust Milek …"

"He loaned me some money and I promised to do him a favour in return … it's so long ago I'd forgotten!"

"Why didn't you tell me?"

"Because I don't like borrowing money. I'd rather manage by myself."

They stare at each other, both upset and annoyed. Out of the blue Martin sticks out his thumb.

"Your word's your word," he says.

David's trapped … again. Reluctantly he, too, sticks out his thumb. Martin hugs him.

"I knew it. I knew I could count on you!"

Seconds later, Martin walks back into the room. David stands in the hall. The smell of vomit clings to his shirt. Once more he sees the Lieutenant drawing his pistol and shooting the man dead. Nausea overwhelms him so he takes a few more puffs on the cigarette to calm himself.

Memories of another world pass through his mind, a world that used to be, a world filled with fragrance and blue sky. Coughing, he discards the cigarette, goes down on his knees and folds his hands. But his mind is blank.

He gets up and leans against the damp wall in the gloomy darkness of the hallway. He stands there for a long time. Only when his legs are about to give out does he go back in to join the others sleeping in the room.

The next day it's mild like a spring day. From the door that's been left ajar, a ray of sunlight lands on his sleepy face. For some reason, the nightmare of the previous night has vanished. Maybe it's because of the change in the weather and the taste of sunshine, but in his floating, dozing state, he's forgotten it all. A low murmur from the streets reaches his ears, sudden shouts echo in the corridor over the stairs, and the crack of a whip that sounds like a roll of drums, makes him open his eyes.

Only when he sees Martin does he realize what day it is. Everyone else has long gone. Martin's waiting for him and has let him sleep in. Now he'll just have to go with him and whatever will be, will be.

When he's washed and eaten some bread, they go out onto the street.

The spring sun illuminates the teeming crowd. There

seems to be astonishing energy among these people, as they hurry through the streets, in spite of the fact that there's no trace of greenery or flowers, to remind them of Spring. Nevertheless, the faint warmth of the sun reawakens their hopes for a land beyond this one, a land they don't really know. Maybe it's just a childish wish, and this mythical land only exists in their imagination. But today people talk about it as they walk along and David gets caught up in the myth too – Palestine.

As they approach the lane by Bonifraterska Street, they come across a large group of Jewish and Polish police, which makes them grow silent and tense. Near the gate, they stop and wait until two horse-drawn carts rumble by over the cobbles in the direction of the gate. When both drivers are ordered down from the carts and the constables begin searching through the loads, the two boys move along the wall then run quickly in front of the first horse out through the gate. They keep up the pace as they edge their way through the crowd of vendors, swindlers and 'Jew catchers' outside the gate before slowing to a serene pace down Konwiktorska Street and then on to the bustling Freta Street.

As the trams and cars rush past them, making it difficult to see across the street, they find number 17, a mansion in the French style with an imposing iron gate and electric bell system.

Martin presses the bell to Bonachewski. Deep inside the building, a quiet ring is heard. They wait but nothing happens. Uneasy, Martin presses the bell again and they hear the distant ghostly ringing again.

"Are you sure this is the place?" asks David. Martin nods obstinately.

An elderly, grey-haired woman in a crisp white apron opens the door unexpectedly and then with some difficulty, the heavy iron gate too. She surveys them suspiciously.

"Go away," she says. "We don't want any beggars here!"

"We have to talk to Mr Bonachewski," says Martin, undaunted.

"I don't believe you. What would Baron Bonachewski have to do with boys like you?"

"Tell him we're from Milek!" says Martin.

At the name Milek, she changes her tone, a conspiratorial smile graces her lips and she waves them into a grand, dark entrance hall, where their footsteps and voices echo. Massive unlit chandeliers hang on iron chains from the ceiling and a damp, cloistered smell pervades the place as the woman closes the door behind them. She leads them respectfully to a marble staircase in the middle of the entrance hall. They follow her up the dusty and dimly lit stairs, covered with faded carpets. When they reach the landing, the woman promptly unlocks a double door. As they step into a high-ceilinged corridor, the woman rings a small metal bell and an elderly servant in black approaches them slowly from the far end of the hall.

"What are those boys doing here?" he says sourly, not bothering to look at them.

"They've come from Milek," says the woman

nervously. "The Baron's waiting for them!"

"Is that so?" says the servant, turning his flabby neck towards them.

"Since when has Milek started sending filthy Jew boys to us?"

"We're not filthy!" David bursts out.

The servant assesses him with a surprised look on his face before breaking into a sharp laugh.

"So he talks back, does he?" the servant says coldly, dismissing them with a wave of his hand. At that moment, they hear a soft bell from a room at the end of the hall and the servant sighs, shaking his heavy head with its beaky nose in mild annoyance. With the greatest effort, he makes his way slowly back down the long corridor. At the end of the hall, he looks into the room briefly before waving them forward.

"The Baron's expecting you!" he whispers hoarsely, clearly annoyed. They walk down the hall and past him into the room.

The room has a high ceiling, mirrors in marble frames and dark paintings, in which pale, slender, figures with solemn faces adorn the yellowing walls. The furniture, draped in white sheets, is randomly laid out on the parquet floor and sitting at a walnut desk close to the bright, high window is a gaunt, white-haired man whose head is bent over a letter. From the next room, one of Schubert's melodies can be heard from a crackling record player. The room smells of sweet tobacco.

They stand inside the doorway until the Baron absent-mindedly looks up from his papers. He slowly puts his spectacles aside and silently stares at them, as if it takes some time for him to comprehend that two lads in boots and dark, shabby coats are really standing there in his mansion.

"So, you've come from Milek?" he says thoughtfully, suddenly grabbing a small metal bell on his desk and ringing it energetically.

The flabby servant immediately appears at the door.

"Bring us tea and cakes and get a couple more chairs!" he says sharply.

Visibly reluctant, the servant pulls covers off two of the chairs and brings them over to the desk, before he vanishes down the hall.

"Don't mind Boniek, he doesn't like Jews, that's how he's been raised. Personally, I have nothing against them …"

He interrupts himself, gets up from his desk and asks them to sit down on the upholstered chairs. He turns his back to them and stands for a moment staring out of the window. His frail body in the shiny, somewhat faded suit, with a white rose in the lapel, is slightly stooped. Martin gives David a mystified look. The Baron clears his throat.

"You must understand that the world has changed," says the Baron sadly. "Nothing is as it once was, the Polish nation is in danger, it's weak and indecisive."

Then he turns towards them.

"The old rules no longer apply and we have to surrender to the strongest if we're to survive. That's how it is in nature: the survival of the fittest ... you have to form a symbiotic relationship with those forceful enough to be on the way up ..."

"We've come for the jewellery box, Herr Baron," says Martin, impatiently. But the Baron is sunk deep in his own thoughts and doesn't hear. He turns away from them again.

"The Poles are like a shipwrecked people, caught between two giants. We have no discipline ... we are contemptible ... we have to choose sides ... Do you understand?" he says with a sharp, high voice, turning towards them again. "The Germans can assist us in separating the sheep from the goats ... yes, they can help to restore order and dignity. They're like gardeners creating the great gardens of Versailles – determined, precise and ruthless!"

David is beginning to follow what the Baron is actually saying, and wonders how they can escape this place as quickly as possible. But just then the servant returns with a large silver tray, laden with tea and cake. However, Martin's mind is clearly on the cakes, and he polishes them off, one after the other, while pretending to listen to the Baron. As soon as the cakes are finished, he says, "Herr Baron, Milek has asked us to fetch the jewellery box and we have to get back."

Then the Baron, who'd become carried away with his fine speech, stops abruptly and goes into the next room. A moment later, he's back with a jewellery box which he carefully, almost reverently, places on the table in front of them.

"Here they are ..." he says sharply and steps back.

Martin opens the lid and looks down into the cushioned box: pearls, gold rings, watches and jewels gleam inside. He quickly closes the box, and they get up to leave. Martin is about to shake hands, but the Baron coldly dismisses them with a wave of his hand.

"You'll never learn!" he says, turning back to his desk.

They rush down the hall, where there's no sign of the servant, and down the stairs. The woman in the apron is waiting for them in front of the heavy front door and lets them out.

By the time they turn the corner onto Konwiktorska Street, Martin's hidden the box under his oversized jacket. David remarks, "*He's* dangerous!"

"Dangerous, no!" says Martin, keeping his eyes on the road ahead.

"He's working with the Germans!"

"He wouldn't harm a fly. He's just crazy!" says Martin.

"It's the last time I do anything for Milek!" David warns.

But Martin doesn't reply, he just holds the box closer and walks faster.

They approach the gateway and cross Bonifraterska Street, blending in with the huge crowd in front of the gate. They don't have to wait long before an opportunity arises. A German military car stops at the gate and they quickly sneak past it and back inside. But after only a few paces they're stopped by a Polish constable. As agreed, David takes a note out of his pocket and awkwardly passes it to the constable, who hesitates a moment, but then pockets it sharply. They go past him and continue slowly along until they merge with the flow of people on Pokoma Street.

Once they're safely back in their room, they take a good look at the jewels, and as with previous missions, they press their thumbs together. But although they're both relieved, Martin isn't totally happy. "You were too nervous," he says. "It went off fine, why don't you trust me?"

David replies, "I do trust you," but says nothing more.

But Martin continues, "Has it ever gone wrong?"

David shakes his head.

"If you want a new partner, just say so!"

David is surprised by Martin's anger and ashamed of his nerves.

"No," he says quietly. "I don't want a new partner, you've taught me everything …"

"Thanks," says Martin, smiling faintly.

Martin goes out of the room feeling pleased with himself and when he comes back, he has a can of beans and some bread. As they eat, they talk about everything and anything, as if nothing's happened.

Once more they establish a kind of common feeling, that some call friendship. Each boy sees himself in the other as they laugh at each other's ideas. Once in a while, the grim sounds of the ghetto reach them, but today they're desperate to forget, so they switch off to it all as if it's ceased to exist.

In the evening, before the other boys return to the room, they go back out onto Pawia Street to find Milek in Café Hirschfeld. The world and all the noise from the ghetto rushes back at them unexpectedly. All the strange faces, the lost, troubled eyes, are softened by the darkness. They could be faces from a town buried long ago or just the opposite, a new town where people rush around inanely, and where no one has found their place.

They turn down an alley and are walking along casually when two young men suddenly appear from a passageway up ahead and block their path, one of them is holding something under his jacket.

"Where are you two going in such a hurry?" one youth asks as the other makes a grab for David. Martin quickly turns around, but two other youths step out and grab him from behind.

"Hold on to them," says the young man, taking out a pistol, his eyes strangely remote. He walks towards the terrified Martin, who instantly drops the jewellery box on the cobblestones spilling out some of the pearls, diamond brooches and gold rings.

"You know where these jewels come from, don't you?" says the man whose face is half hidden by a cap and large scarf.

"N ... no ..." stutters Martin, struggling to tear himself free. Martin is afraid of the young man's grim half-covered face, the smell of his strong breath, and although he can hear the faint sound of David shouting, in the almost total darkness, it makes little sense.

"Those jewels belonged to Jews and Milek is an agent for the Gestapo ... so what does that make you?" says the voice in front of him.

"I don't know anything about it," Martin croaks, his throat suddenly tightening.

"You're the worst kind, you're a traitor!" says the voice in front of him.

Again David shouts, screeching at the top of his voice, and it's as if this shout triggers an explosion, everything goes berserk. Martin kicks out at the man but instead of buckling over, he points the gun back at Martin. As if time stands still, he senses the approaching bullet. Bang! What should have been a warning becomes an assassination; Martin collapses, bleeding, with a look of astonishment in his wide-open eyes. The youths who are still holding him both fall forward; David wildly kicks backwards too and escapes, fleeing further into the alley. Only the young man who fired the shot remains, frozen to the spot, as if paralyzed.

The shock is instant but the horror long-lasting. The young man slowly turns his head and stares like a sleepwalker into the darkness of the alley. A spot of light that seems to him to be a reflection from David's hand suddenly appears but in reality, everything swims before his eyes and David has long since vanished.

Only now does the young man feel the heat from the barrel of the gun and, in a fit of disgust, throws it away. The two youths pick themselves up and find blood on their hands from the wound in Martin's stomach. They don't know what to do with their hands or themselves. One of them takes a step backwards and with a quick, desperate gesture wipes the blood off on his trousers. He has the presence of mind to cry out, "Let's get out of here, fast!"

The others look at him, startled, as if his words come from another planet. The two younger lads are the first to dart out of the alley on to Pawia Street, then the two older ones separate without a word and each runs in a different direction away from the body.

Martin, or what is left of him, lies there with glazed eyes on the slippery stones. Alone, he came into this world. Alone, he left it.

A quarter of an hour later, a hungry, mangy dog appears by his body. Attracted by the smell of blood, it starts licking at his blood-soaked clothes. A man who's taken a shortcut through the alley stops in front of this macabre sight, unable to believe his eyes. For a few seconds he's stunned, then regaining his senses, he chases the dog away. He stands there for a moment looking down at the pitiful sight, then looking up at the shuttered windows. He clasps his hands together as if to say a prayer, but what can he do? Distraught, he hurries away.

In the meantime, David's making his escape through the streets of the ghetto, running and running without looking back. Beside himself with fear, he seeks refuge under a stairway, where he's immediately chased out by a porter. Once more on the street, he's too panic-stricken to get his bearings. He runs on blindly. He finally finds an empty passageway, where he can slowly, anxiously catch his breath. The minutes pass; they haven't caught him yet. Somewhat calmer, he looks out from his hiding place on to the street, but he recognizes no one among the crowd. He retreats back into the darkness and tries to gather his thoughts. But his small body starts shaking, his teeth chatter and only the brutal need to survive keeps him going.

The horror of the evening's events weighs on him and he realizes it would be unwise to return to Pawia Street. That would surely be the first place they'd look for him.

After half an hour in the passageway, his mind goes blank. Several times he's about to step out onto the street but the feeling of being watched holds him back. *They* have been watching him. But who are *they*? Have *they* been following him all the time? Do *they* know every move he's made?

He'd heard about it before when '*they'd*' taken revenge on someone who'd collaborated with the Germans, but Martin … Martin wasn't a German agent … Martin was just careless … Martin's his friend … Martin's dead …

Like a pillar of black smoke rising before his eyes in the darkness of the passageway, the reality finally hits him.

A strange anger against everyone and everything – including Martin – overwhelms him. How could his friend abandon him? He has no right to! But his rage quickly evaporates and a numbing sense of loss takes over. It blends with the aching loss he feels when he remembers his mother, father and Jakob – yes, the whole bunch of friends and acquaintances from the village, who now live a phantom life in his thoughts. Suddenly, like a voiceless cry in his imagination, he wishes it was he who was dead; but just as suddenly, it occurs to him that maybe Martin isn't dead after all, that he's still lying in the alley and …

Without a second thought, he quits his hiding place and gathers his bearings on the street. Suddenly, his brain is feverishly clear, and he half-walks, half-runs through the crowded streets until he is standing once more on Pawia Street. He turns down the alley which seems even more dimly lit than before. At first, he can see someone lying on the cobbles but no, his imagination is playing tricks on him. The alley's empty, empty and black as the sky.

Two people turn into the alley at the same time. He can't see their faces and hurries away.

A shadow pursues him, although he can't see it clearly. Now and then he turns and finds himself staring into thin air or at people a few steps behind him. At these moments, when he's standing still, he resembles the statue of a child which, for some reason, has been placed in the road and is blocking the traffic. Unaware of the shouts or people pushing past him, he's lost in his own dark and chaotic world. Eventually, a shove nudges him forward and gets him moving again. He wanders aimlessly for an hour in the ghetto. Only when the church bells ring out for curfew and the few lights on the street die out does he come to and remember the girl on Mila Street.

He'd only visited her once with bread and potatoes since he promised her that he'd help. She'd met him at the door and he'd given her what he could but once again forgotten to get her name. She said she'd come back and closed the door on him but although he stood and waited a while, and heard some nervous voices behind the door, she didn't come back. Hurrying along, keeping to the shadows of the buildings on the dark, deserted streets, he's on the lookout for both his pursuers or any police patrols, and he's desperate for some place to belong. This hope, which has no grounding in reality, drives him on. He vaguely imagines being asked in and given a place to sleep, sees himself becoming a part of that damaged family on Mila Street.

But as soon as he reaches the gate on Mila Street and is met by a massive silence in the courtyard he has a feeling that something's wrong. He walks around the courtyard several times but it's not the same. Windows and doors seem to be in different places than he remembers. He holds his head and thinks he's going mad, closes his eyes and looks again; only now the courtyard with its shuttered windows and shadowy doors begins to spin in front of him. His heart's pounding, his mouth fills with spit, a pain pierces his chest. After a few seconds he comes round and gradually recognizes the place in the darkness. He takes a couple of steps towards the door and grabs the handle. But the door is locked. What should he do, he has to get in!

He checks the keyhole and sees the tip of the key sticking through on the other side of the door. Luckily the upper part of the door is made up of small panes. A piece of wood fastened by a thin wire covers one of them. Silent and determined, he removes the wood and sticks his hand through the hole. Standing on tiptoe and stretching his arm down as far as he can, he feels his way down to the lock and retrieves the key with his fingertips.

He lets himself into the dark stairwell with the key and hurries up the stairs, where he hears voices from the rooms behind the doors. With his heart in his mouth, tiptoeing, he knocks on the door but the voices cease immediately and only a whistle through an open window to the courtyard further up, reaches his ears. Even the muffled voices behind the doors further along are silenced. His fear makes him uncertain as to where he is and whether he's even heard anything.

He knocks on the door again and waits anxiously. Suddenly a man's voice from somewhere behind the door is heard. "Who's there?"

He states his name, and when nothing happens, he repeats it.

The door opens and an elderly man in a worn out jacket looks out. His attitude is uncertain; but when he sees that it's just a boy standing there, he runs his hand through his hair in relief and visibly relaxes. David asks after the girl and tries to explain, but the man shakes his head. "She's not here," he says. "They came for them days ago and took her and the family!"

"Yeh, but ... where are they?" he persists.

"I really don't know," says the man, with some irritation. "We've just moved in and want to be left in peace."

All kinds of thoughts rush through his head, he can't speak or leave, just stands there with outstretched arm, like a creature clinging to an invisible thread.

"Couldn't I leave her a message?" he mumbles.

"Don't you understand: she doesn't live here any more!"

"She might come by again," he persists, but realizes this is unlikely.

The man shakes his head, stands a moment, gives him a look of sympathy.

"I'm sorry," he says, takes a couple of steps back and closes the door.

A door that closes, a face that vanishes, a small dream shattered in the midst of this nightmare – he can't take it in. He stands there, nailed to the spot. His carefully constructed world no longer hangs together, the thin thread that had connected him to something meaningful and let him live naturally, has suddenly – like scissors cutting through paper – been torn apart.

And yet he still moves, he goes down the stairs and

out into the courtyard, but instead of going out onto the street, he finds a hole in the fence and crawls into the courtyard next door. He doesn't know what he's doing any more; he stands and stares up at the darkened windows, his mind in turmoil. He considers going up and knocking on the door of a stranger, but can't bring himself to do it. He has the feeling that someone's watching him and turns towards the gate; but darkness is all that he can see. In the midst of his despair, and the cold that has chilled him to the bone, he realizes that it's better to be inside than out. He finds a cellar shaft and creeps down into a cellar, where it seems to be a bit warmer. There – in the impenetrable darkness that enfolds him like a glove – he paces back and forth until he collapses against the cellar wall. On the stony floor, miraculously, he falls asleep. Only the strange noises he makes, like a caged animal, reveal his existence.

He has a dream. He's sitting on an incredibly wide plain, the scent of wheat and clover reaches him, the sun bakes down on his head, the sky is infinitely blue above him. A few soft clouds, resembling the heads of horses or strange shapeless animals, float overhead. He stares at the clouds until they slowly glide away and thinks: if I were a cloud, I could get away from here. He's thirsty. He gets up and starts walking. He walks and walks but sees no one. He follows the clouds. In the distance, he glimpses the figure of a man coming towards him. He's too far away to see his face, but he recognizes that it's his father by his way of walking, and raises his hand to wave. Suddenly, he feels uneasy and goes a little faster … then his father waves back and starts running too. They run and run but get no nearer to each other.

When David wakes up, he finds that he's curled up on the cold basement floor, his body numb. Leaning his hand against the wall to get up, he pulls it away quickly as the cold shoots right through him.

He finally gets to his feet and walks down the hall out to the courtyard, where it's quiet and empty in the early morning mist. The closed windows stare down at him with their smooth, dirty surfaces. Distant sounds from the ghetto reach the yard, and from somewhere a song is suddenly heard. A deep, hoarse vibrato, as if someone, somewhere, is able to celebrate this morning.

Instinctively, he walks out through the entrance and stands indecisively looking up and down the deserted Mila Street, where a couple of lamps burn weakly in the windows of the high buildings. A man turns the corner and walks towards him in a light, shabby coat that flutters like a sail. From a distance, he stretches his hand out towards him and mumbles something indecipherable. He abruptly crosses the street and carries on in his own troubled world.

Feeling faint, David continues along Mila Street, where he finds a woman lying stretched out on a step with a paper sack over her and a bundle at her side. The white face of a child with sunken cheeks stares out, the woman gets up a little when she sees him and asks for money, but he has nothing to give her and carries on.

As he walks through the streets a pale sun breaks through and shouts ring out unexpectedly in the silence. The ghetto is waking up. As if by an invisible signal, a wave of noise erupts, thousands of voices and sounds from yards and houses and squares rise up to the skies. Windows and doors are opened, blankets are hung out, shops open up and the streets fill up with carts, busy people, beggars and children who run about in their ragged clothes.

Today, it's all lost on him, as it seems like a world that he no longer belongs to. He goes towards the cellar room on Pawia Street. The door's locked, and when he knocks, a child opens the door to a room full of people he doesn't know.

"I live here!" he says, staring at his bed, which another has taken over.

"Not any more," says a thin man who closes the door in his face.

The boys have vanished but he doesn't want to think about it, and he doesn't have the energy to look for them. In a daze, he goes back onto Pawia Street, but with no idea of where he's going.

He turns a corner and just stands there, staring at his

face in a dusty window pane; he doesn't know who he's looking at, he doesn't know what to do. He carries on anyway, clutching on to the little harp in his pocket. A man in a suit bumps into him, and the bag he's carrying crashes to the cobbles spilling out a loaf of fresh bread. Mechanically, David picks up the bread and is about to hand it back to the man, when the smell of the bread rouses him, making him hesitate. Annoyed, the man grabs the bread, stuffs it in his bag and hurries on.

Further down the street, he stops in front of a shop window displaying four oranges and three dry cakes, which has the effect of making his mouth water. It's then he realizes that he hasn't had anything to eat for a long time, but the next moment, he doesn't really care and walks on.

On the next street he finds a stairway where he can sit down, and he sits there for a long time, lost in a strange tiredness that never leaves him. Once in a while, he looks up at the people passing by in a blur, and by chance he recognises something familiar: a woman buying something from a stall, he catches a glimpse of her back.

Her dark coat and light scarf and the way she reaches out makes him get up. He hurries through the crowd, but as he reaches the stall, she's gone. Desperately, he searches through the mass of people and cars and again catches a glimpse of the woman further down the street. He edges his way in and out among the crowd and starts running but when he gets to the next corner, he stands there agitated, unable to find her.

He's certain it's his mother.

He runs down the street and looks around frantically, stops and grabs a woman, who turns around and stares at him strangely, he realizes his mistake, mumbles a few words and runs off.

By some miracle, on Dzielna Street he again catches sight of the light scarf and black coat; the woman enters a passage, he slows down and stands watching on the other side of the street as she tries to unlock the door. He's sure that he can see his mother's shoes, the scuffed shoes with thick heels that he'd seen so many times; but her face is only half visible in the darkness of the passage. He's suddenly paralyzed, not knowing whether to feel joy or fear at the possibility of being wrong, his tiny body trembles, his arms stiffen.

The woman can't open the door and stands for a moment shaking her head and pulling at the doorknob, before she leaves the passageway; and then he sees a stranger's face, a face that just looks at him without any sign of interest.

As if in a trance, he crosses the street and follows in her tracks, as if something in him won't let go; but when she vanishes inside a building, he stays back on the street and moves on.

Everything is stranger than before, and as he wanders in this state, the vague thought of ending it all enters his mind. He pushes it away and stops at the corner, standing and watching the noisy life around him. He can hear laughter, men talking and joking with each other on the street. Two girls are playing marbles on the pavement, some boys not far from him exchange cigarette coupons, a lanky salesman calls out for anyone to buy his chewing gum, a frail woman walks back and forth on the pavement offering armbands in different colours. Behind a window people are sitting and enjoying cakes and coffee. He recognizes Café Hirschfeld and then a corpulent face creased in laughter which turns and gazes momentarily onto the street.

It's Milek's face.

David can't take his eyes off him and goes closer to the window, drawn by a mixture of hatred and awe. He stares at his thick neck and sports jacket, and as if from a distant watchtower, notices his manicured hand twirling a cigarette holder.

Milek turns again, still talking, glancing towards the street and his eyes glide over the boy as if he isn't there. Apparently, Milek's seen him but doesn't recognize him. He's turned away and is saying something amusing. His companion, in a German uniform, laughs and gestures with his hand, as if brushing insects away.

David isn't able to comprehend any of this clearly. Not knowing what he's doing, he walks into the café and towards Milek's table, but Milek ignores him and keeps on talking. David steps right up to the table, just stands there and stares.

"The Jew boy wants to talk to you!" says the SS officer casually.

Vexed by the interruption, Milek calls the waiter over and says: "Don't know this tramp, never seen him before!"

"Martin's dead!" whispers David.

"What has it got to do with me?" says Milek and calls the waiter over sharply. "Just get him out of here!"

"It's your fault that Martin's dead, it's ..."

"Out!" says Milek with a sudden burst of rage. He pushes David aside, but again he steps towards the table.

Conversation in the café ceases and the guests turn to watch with unbridled curiosity. The waiter grabs David and is about to throw him out, but the SS officer gestures that he should wait a moment.

"Explain!" he says with a guarded glance.

"There's nothing to explain," says Milek falteringly.

"Do it anyway!"

Unaccustomed to explanation, Milek fumbles for words and leans nervously across the table, but it only takes a few seconds before he's regained his composure and is sitting back in the chair with his usual cynical, charming smile.

"The Jews have shot one of their own, that's all, and it doesn't have anything to do with me."

"Are you sure?" asks the SS officer staring straight into his eyes.

"You know me, don't you, would I ever lie to you?"

The SS officer stares coldly and calculatingly at him then his narrow lips draw back into a smile of approval that freezes to a sneer. He clearly enjoys frightening Milek. But he's already lost interest in the filthy boy, and gives the waiter a sign to remove him before looking back towards the street. The waiter shoves David out of the door and slams it after him.

David finds himself once again back on the noisy street.

*

After sleeping in passageways for two nights in a row and with no food for days, David is wandering among the beggars on Komitetowa Street, when he, too, tries stretching his hand out towards the passers-by. For some reason, many of the beggars in the ghetto gather here. Like a band of lost souls, they sit or stand around in lines on both sides of the street, clutching battered instruments, or their few possessions or simply holding out empty hands. Dulled by the cold, the lack of food and the hopelessness of their existence, they cling to the hope that a passer-by might suddenly stop and give them a coin or a piece of bread.

They're not just on the street, some are sticking their arms out from cellar windows too. Their faint pleas sound like an echo from a shout that never arrives. Many people in the ghetto avoid this street so as not to hear these voices and not to smell the stench from the cellars or get close to the beggars' filthy, louse-infested bodies. Here everyone can see what's waiting for them at the end of the line, and although the ghetto's community service sometimes distributes free bread here, it soon vanishes like coins in the sea. More and more people come every day; most are left to a pathetic death on the cobblestones.

Today, as the rain falls softly and a cool spring breeze pricks his skin, David takes his place by the wall. He stands there for a long time before he finally dares to stretch his arm out. In this exhausted condition, the last reserves of stubbornness and pride make him pull his arm back again; but hunger cuts through his stomach like a knife and the arm, seeming to have a life of its own, pushes itself out again and the fingers on the flat, stiff hand reach out. With his arm outstretched, David looks around, but takes nothing in. He keeps swallowing his spit, until his throat is parched and starts to hurt.

A man lying on the pavement a short distance away, covered in a rag, looks like a dog, while a thin dog sniffing at a heap of rubbish on the other side of the street looks like a child on all fours. The line of beggars on the other side of the street blurs and melts into the walls, the people cease to exist and only the bare walls remain, or they change into a row of children like in the school in his village. He closes his eyes and lowers his arm and leans his head against the wall.

In front of him, a group of ragged children pursue a rabbi, who patiently stops and hands out a few coins, but the children pull and tear at his coat, until he flees in fear down the street with the screaming children after him.

Someone pokes him in the shoulder and when he opens his eyes, he finds himself looking into a lined, mahogany brown face. A man, not much bigger than himself and wrapped from top to toe in rags and torn fragments of old coats, stares at him curiously. Suddenly, he smiles and reveals some brownish tooth stubs. Frightened, David pulls away, but the little man quickly follows and offers him a green bottle.

"Drink!" he says, and despite his mistrust, David takes the bottle and drinks. The fluid burns both his throat and his stomach and wakes him up forcefully.

"Its potato brandy," says the man looking intensely at him with his black eyes before he takes the bottle back. He then hands him a small piece of bread, which David devours in one bite. Overcome by a new and different kind of wooziness, David is about to thank the man when he's disappeared ... maybe he'd never been there at all.

David reaches out his hand again and moves closer to the pavement, struggling to catch the eyes of the passers-by. But most of them either look past him or straight through him, only a few seem to notice him, and even fewer feel into their coats or bags trying to find something before they, too, are gone. Like a dog that only thinks of one thing, his blurry eyes pursue each and every movement of the passing shapes.

When darkness falls, his hands are still empty, and he sinks down onto the pavement and tries to wrap himself in his dirty coat, but the cold from the stones beneath him and the noise of the street keep him awake.

Slowly, the beggars disappear from the street, some seek sanctuary in the courtyards, passageways and cellars – others wander towards the cemetery or roam around until fatigue finally overpowers them at some chance place. A few seek shelter in cafés or beg under the windows on other streets, while those like David remain on the pavement. The most strong-minded wrap themselves carefully inside their possessions. A few who are either too old or too weak simply give up and lay down on the stones. Then Pinkiert's black wagons or boys from the cemetery will find them in the morning and carry them quickly away on their carts.

David can no longer stand the cold so he summons the energy to get up. He walks stiffly a few yards into a passageway in search of a stairwell or a shelter in the courtyard, but as he turns the corner, he trips over a body on the ground. The man shouts and lashes out after him. David gets up again, feeling groggy, and in the darkness he can only make out a shadow and is about to get away when suddenly an arm grabs him and pulls him down a cellar shaft.

"What're you doing here?" says a stout woman, holding him tightly.

"Nothing ..." he says in confusion, he's too tired to resist. The woman stares curiously at him and suddenly opens his lips with her thick, dirty fingers and taps one of his front teeth.

"The teeth are OK," she mutters to herself.

"You can sleep with us," she says. "But tomorrow you have to work! Understand?"

He nods dully. She lets him go then shoves him gently down the stairs. A moment later, he's in a dark cellar that stinks of rats and body odour, but he scarcely notices as his senses give way to exhaustion, and when an arm pulls him down to the floor in that overcrowded room, he collapses and quickly falls asleep among the warm bodies on the floor.

That night he dreams that the shadow in the passage-way was chasing him through the deserted streets of the ghetto and when he wakes, crying out, and half gets up in the pitch darkness of the room, a large, powerful hand pulls him down again and holds him tightly on the floor. He frees himself from the hand and falls back asleep. Later he's woken by a nudge, the dim morning light shines through a small window that gives onto the yard, and the stout woman is bent over a man lying next to him who smells of alcohol. She hits the man a couple of times but he turns over on his side, makes a few grunts then ignores her.

Around them he notices boys and girls of his own age, most of them still half asleep, like a huge bundle of dirty rags, and when the woman orders them up, they get up slowly and apathetically and one after the other go out into the corridor, where they line up. No one says anything; all this happens as if it were some kind of ritual.

The woman now pushes David into the hallway, goes back into the room and soon reappears with a canvas bag. She takes small crusts of bread from the bag and hands them to the children, one by one. Everyone, even David, quickly eats the dry bread and looks longingly at the bag.

"What're you lot staring at?" snaps the woman. "Get

going and fetch some more, or you know what'll happen to you!"

Silently, one after the other, the children go up the stairs and out into the courtyard, where they take turns drinking water from a rusty tap. The water tastes strange, but he's too thirsty to worry about it. Together, they go out through the entrance and spread out silently on the street, where many other beggars have already taken their place.

David takes his place once more by the wall close to the passage and holds out his hand. He stands there like that for most of the day as passers-by ignore him in a long, endless stream. Towards evening, he sinks down on the pavement and hides his empty hands in his coat pockets. Next to him, a frail, old man monotonously cries out prayers in Yiddish at the passing crowd, occasionally grabbing hold of somebody's sleeve or coat. By the evening, he's worn himself out; he turns towards the wall and vomits in a thin stream over the pavement and over David too. David is about to get up, but the man leans over him, shaking, and apologetically tries to dry his coat and trousers with his ragged sleeve.

"Oh Lord, pity me!" he says, looking at the lad with feverish eyes. Then he straightens up, stands tall for a moment with a kind of dignity in his shabby coat, before turning on his heels and staggering off down the street.

When the bells chime for curfew across the ghetto, David's aroused from his cold stupor on the pavement, and although something in him objects, he turns into the passageway to make for the cellar but this time the stout woman blocks his way to the corridor.

"What do you want here?" she says and pushes him back with her heavy body. Then he notices the big stick behind her in the hallway.

"To sleep," he says. "I want to sleep …"

"Gimme your bread and your money first!"

"I don't have any," he says hopelessly.

"You're useless … a waste of time," she says.

"To-morrow …" he says, but stops, aware of his failure. A strange sense of contempt and sorrow envelop him, and as the woman is about to close the door, he turns around and goes up the stairs automatically. She calls after him, but he doesn't hear.

Like a homeless dog he roams around the courtyard looking for a place to sleep, but the doors he tries are locked, and nowhere in the yard is there any shelter. As he turns back onto the windswept street, a military vehicle rushes past, laughing voices hang momentarily in the air, and some boys can be heard shouting further down the street. He follows the sound, but both the car and the boys disappear and he's alone again on the deserted street. It all seems endless.

He hasn't the strength to carry on when he notices that he's standing and staring at something in a window – it's long and black – it's a loaf of bread. He presses his body and hands against the glass, he wants to get in, his entire body has only one goal. He pounds the glass with his fist, but it doesn't break, he takes off his boot and hits the window, but that doesn't help either. Out of breath, he puts his boot back on and walks along a passageway further down the street, urgently searching the yard for a hard object, and just as he's about to give up, he notices a pile of rubbish and on top of the rubbish is a stone.

He grabs the stone and hurries back to the window. Apart from a few drowsy beggars, the street is still empty, but he barely notices, it's as if he's possessed. He taps the stone against the window – it cracks, but doesn't break. He now takes a few steps back, considers the distance and throws the stone with all his might against the glass. A crash is heard, the stone flies through the window, splintering the glass into thousands of pieces. He sticks his arm through the hole and fishes the bread out, and with energy he didn't know he had, charges off down the street with the bread under his arm until he can go no further.

The bread is dry and practically inedible, but he moistens it with his spit and gnaws at it like a mouse, and in the course of a couple of hours he's eaten himself half way full. Exhausted, he sleeps behind the ruins of a house some blocks away from Komitetowa Street. While he sleeps, the hard bread churns in his stomach, and he suddenly wakes feeling as if he wants to vomit, but nothing comes up and he falls asleep again with his hands on the remains of the loaf.

When he wakes a few hours later, his hands are ice cold and the bread is gone. He searches for it among the stones, but as a Jewish policeman is quickly approaching he hurries away and returns to Komitetowa Street, where everything seems to be the same as before. He passes the small shop with the shattered window. It's completely empty now, but he's too tired to feel any remorse and no longer cares enough to worry about being discovered.

The little energy that the dry bread provided, allows him to think, so he chooses a corner of the street where he can stand alone. He rubs his fingers together, pulls the harp out of his pocket and starts to play. After a little while, he can play entire pieces and then it gets easier. He recalls Marysia Eisenstadt's songs and plays them as best he can. All of his senses, his entire body, focuses on the instrument, it's as if he takes off and flies … the passers-by vanish from his sight, he barely notices the sounds of footsteps and voices … when a woman with a bag in her hand stops to listen to him, he stalls and feels embarrassed.

"Keep playing!" she says, laughing.

He pulls himself together and starts playing. She throws a coin at his feet and disappears off down the street. Quickly, he bends down and picks it up, putting it in his pocket. He looks around anxiously, but everything's as it was before and no one's going to take the coin away from him!

He stands on the corner most of the day with his little harp. Now and then, a few boys stop and listen; they shout rude or encouraging remarks at him. A rabbi stops too, puts his hand on David's shoulder and gives him a matzo cracker. His grey eyes sparkle in his bony, bearded face as he reminds David that this evening is Passover Seder, and he should remember to wash his hands.

"You're a true child of God," he mutters, placing his

trembling hand on David's head. A moment later, he's gone.

In the evening, as he rummages through his pockets, he finds he has five *zloty* and enough small silver coins to buy a small piece of dry bread. He tears the bread into three pieces and hides them in his pockets; then eats his matzo cracker and wanders around the streets to find a new place to sleep; but no matter where he looks, everywhere is taken and people chase him away. From the houses, songs can be heard, and after curfew, candles burn in the darkened windows and prayers float up from the cellars. He hears a blessing from somewhere and the smell of celery used for *karpas* reaches his nostrils. He remembers the apple *charoseth* they used to eat in the village years ago at Antek Blum's house; it looked like clay and tasted sweet. His mouth waters so he eats one of the three pieces of bread to numb his hunger and forget.

That night it's blustery, a stiff wind rips at the roofs and tears through the streets and courtyards. In a rubbish heap, he finds some coal sacking and crouches down in a corner of one of the yards. That night, he only half sleeps, the cold creeps into his bones and keeps his eyes pinned to the black sky ... shots ring out in the distance ... engines rev in the next street ... shadows move about ... a frightened cry startles him ... the rattling window above his head is a constant irritation ...

His dizziness returns and a dry, hacking cough rises in his throat but he won't let it come and keeps his mouth shut until he has to give in to it with a small outburst.

*

The next day his fingers are too weak to play his harp, so he holds out his hand again on the corner but no one takes any notice of him and he soon blends in with the wall.

By the evening, he's eaten his second piece of bread and joins two lads begging under the windows and balconies. They're bigger and stronger than he is and he follows them in silence, a couple of paces behind. They don't talk to him but don't chase him away either. When someone opens a window and throws a small bag of potatoes down to them, they take what they need first and one of them hands the bag back to him. He quickly bites into the hard, leftover potato and puts the bag in his pocket.

"What you doing with that bag?" asks one of the boys who's a couple of years older than him, holding out his hand. He gives him the bag and looks away.

"Got anything else in your pockets?" asks the other boy.

"No," he lies and instinctively shows them his hands.

They both look at him suspiciously, but leave him alone

They roam the deserted streets for hours. Sometimes they hide from the Jewish police or a motorcycle patrol which races through the streets. When they happen upon another gang of ragged urchins, they stop and glare at each other, weighing up each others' intentions. One false move could be fatal. David daren't move and can hardly breathe. In the midst of this tension, as if by an unseen signal, they suddenly start walking away without looking back, as if nothing's happened, nothing at all.

At night, these ruffians stick to their own circles, where there's no room for mercy. In the darkness the ghetto bleeds, and behind the curtain of sleep, the orphans, the frail, the elderly crawl along the cobblestones searching for bread or coins which occasionally fall down to them from above. Only a few get so far as to actually feel the bread or coins in their hands.

Earlier that evening, he'd learned to shout "Have pity!" in Yiddish, beneath the windows of the tall buildings, as silent and distant as the heavens above the ghetto.

That night, for reasons unknown even to himself, he's determined to survive. That night, when everything seems hopeless and not a single person has responded to their pleas, the two boys take him to their hiding place in the dilapidated barracks on Leszno Street and share their cold blankets with him in a room that reeks of oil and shit. Once again he's freezing but at least he has the feeling of belonging.

For several days he sticks with the two lads. They take turns begging on Leszno Street and in the evening they share all that they have. He starts playing his harp again and the two lads dance a bit on the pavement. They get other boys to join in, dancing in a line and clapping their hands, and when the tired labourers return home in a long grey stream from the mills, occasionally some of these workers stop and take part in the dance.

One evening as the workers go past, a thin, red-haired man in ragged overalls comes over to him and hands him a *zloty*.

"Keep playing!" he says and laughs. Then all of a sudden he grabs David's arm and pushes him up against the wall, whispering with a deathly pale face: "They've deported thirty thousand in Lublin, do you know what that means? They've shot dozens in the suburbs. And in Zdunska Wola they grabbed ten Jews and made some other Jews hang them right there in the market place! Keep playing, it might be our last day!"

Before David can say anything, the man lets him go and vanishes in the crowd. He stops playing, but the two boys keep on dancing, oblivious. For a long time, he just stands and watches them.

The days are still cold. Spring, which showed its face for a day, has gone again. Among the elegant boots and sable coats, the dismal, pale faces and stooped figures of people literally freezing to death can't be avoided by those hurrying along the streets. Here and there, they step over the limp body of a child lying on the pavement with a vacant stare. The child may simply fall to its knees and remain lying there, like an ember slowly turning to ash. People see this but take no notice and walk on.

Later that evening, as they try to sleep under the blankets, the oldest lad, from Lublin, says, "There was a man from Lublin who told me his father and mother and sister were sent to Belzec … he said it was a work camp, but wasn't sure …"

None of them say anything for a while. They lie there staring up into the darkness. A cold draught slices through them from a hole in the roof so they huddle closer together. For the first time in a long while, David thinks about his mother and father but his memories are hazy. It's as if his mother only exists in his imagination, where her face and movements are vague. Once in a while, he hears her voice inside his head, just a few words said only in the way she could say them, insignificant things like 'wash', 'cake' or 'clothes'. But remembering this seems to drain him. If he doesn't think about her, she doesn't exist. And that's the best way.

"My father sent me to Warsaw," continues the lad. "He said I had to take care of myself and now I don't know where he is or if …"

"There's probably nothing to worry about," says the other boy. Then they both grow silent as weariness takes over. But the lad from Lublin can't relax, he tosses and turns and cries out. David wakes up and puts an arm around him.

"Why does no one hear us?" asks the lad suddenly. "Why doesn't anyone help us? Are we all going to die?"

"I don't think we're going to die," says David.

"Maybe it's better that way …" whispers the lad.

"It won't help anybody if you die," says David.

Finally, the lad falls asleep.

*

In front of the courthouse on Leszno Street, mothers sit with their children bundled up in their arms. Often, a mother tries to rub warmth into the stiff limbs of a dead child, or a mother checks to see if there's still life in the bundle in her lap but quickly withdraws her fingers because the cold from the child's head cuts through her fingertips. And sometimes a child clings to its mother and tries to wake her because it thinks she's asleep.

It's on a day like this in May that German constables force a group of Jews to dance around a basket full of bodies in the cemetery. But this is just a rehearsal for what's to come.

Now that the sun's finally broken through, it shines weakly onto people's faces and reflects in the puddles along the street. David and the other lads are still performing on Leszno Street when he catches a glimpse of a girl with shiny, jet black hair moving among the crowds. He stops playing and runs after her along the pavement. He grabs her by the arm; she turns around and looks at him in astonishment.

"It's me, David!" he says, disappointed that she doesn't recognize him right away.

"You look different," she says. "Are you sick? What are you doing now? Where've you been?"

Amidst the joy of seeing her again, he feels dizzy and begins to cough but he fights it back and holds her hand.

"I'm not sick," he says. "I just have a cough."

"Are you begging?" she asks but he doesn't answer her, and starts asking her questions instead.

"I live with my mother on Krochmalna Street," she tells him, her face suddenly becoming hard. "Grandmother is dead and we don't know where Father is. We were in Pawia prison, but they let us out again ... Why didn't you come and visit us?"

"I did," he says. "But it was too late and I couldn't find you."

Her big, dark eyes are the same as before, but something in her face has changed and he searches for her smile.

"Why do you look at me like that?" she asks.

"I don't know," he says, feeling overwhelmed by a tenderness that silences him. He hugs her and hides his face in her shoulder. He notices how thin she's become. There's so much he wants to tell her but his mind shuts down, he can't let her go and his small body trembles.

Carefully, they separate.

"You must come and visit us," she says, looking at him with a strange, impatient glance.

"I want to ... I will ..." he says.

He stands watching her as she vanishes down the street and is lost in the crowd, then she suddenly reappears and waves to him, and he feels as if the sun's moved a little closer.

That day, he plays better than all the other days put together.

*

The nights in the ghetto have grown milder and the days pass more slowly in the glimmering sun. The streets are recharged with new energy, excited shouts and cries fly out over the general bedlam, and more people are now spending the day out on the street listening to music or looking for any kind of opportunity. At times, the street is so packed that you have to push and shove your way through, you get showered with offers of every kind and risk having your bag or your pockets emptied.

Some thieves are specialists in ripping off any kind of watch in a matter of seconds; others take hats, caps and berets, which can vanish – like a magic trick in a circus – in the midst of the human flood on the street. There are others who have developed a talent for pulling coats off people; even shoes, to the anger and irritation of their owners, can disappear on their own across outstretched hands in the crowd.

Smuggling has now taken on unheard of proportions becoming an even deadlier business. Flour, tomatoes, milk, butter, meat are all brought in by a new breed of smuggler: Christian women of all ages who come in the dark and haul away sacks full of pots and pans, dishes and washbasins, that they push over to the 'Aryan' side through holes in the ghetto walls. The Jews started off selling their clothing, furniture, bedding and pillows. Now they're even selling the kitchen sink.

For those who believe that Spring is a time of renewal and mercy, they're in for new surprises. Early one Saturday morning, on the 16th of May, the bodies of five murdered Jews are discovered. They'd been dragged off in the night by the Jewish police. No one knows their names or asks any questions.

Not a day passes without a raid on the street, where Germans armed with guns round up more Jews for forced labour; not a night passes without a house search, looting, deception, humiliation and murder. The underground newspapers report mass murders and the annihilation of whole Jewish communities in places such as Wilno, Lowno, Slonim, Lvov – who can understand this? People would rather believe that these are exaggerated rumours, turn a deaf ear, and for some reason, prefer to believe that the war will soon be over, that it's not a question of years but of months, and until then, the Warsaw ghetto is the safest place to be.

During these days in the middle of May, David sometimes turns his face up to the sun and lets it tan his winter white skin. It's as if his body is only now waking up from an enforced hibernation. He drinks in the rays of the sun as if it were water, but his chest complains, sending sharp pains to his back when he breathes. The hacking cough clings stubbornly to his lungs and exhausts him. He learns to pace himself and take breaks, hiding the harp in his pocket while the two other lads beg.

One evening as he's playing on the pavement on Leszno Street, he recognizes a lined, mahogany brown face among those who've stopped for a moment to listen to his tunes. It's the dwarf, the little man still wrapped in rags and pieces of clothing, clapping his big hands together madly and whistling appreciatively. In doing so, he drops a walking-stick and David stops playing and picks it up.

"Thanks," he says in Russian, putting his arm around him as he leans on his stick. "You'll make it, you'll make it," he continues in broken Polish and leads him off down the street.

"Where are we going?" David asks, allowing himself to be taken along. But instead of answering, the little man says, "God has sought you out, believe me, Timojan, I know what I'm talking about, he's given you wings!"

They walk some way before the little man stops to catch his breath and he has to support him the last bit of the way to a backyard on Novolipke Street. With renewed energy, the man crawls up the stairs to a gallery in a wooden house and pulls David up behind him with his free, strong arm into a small, stuffy room. With difficulty, he lights a carbide lamp hanging on the wall. His bed is made up of a few sacks on the floor and a brown bottle sits on a wooden crate which immediately passes to the lad. Then he sits down on the sacks, digs deep into his pockets and pulls out a bag of small black cakes that he places one by one on the table.

"Eat and drink!" he says, rapping the little table, and

looking at David expectantly. David reluctantly drinks from the bottle and instantly recalls the strong taste of potato brandy. The man nods approvingly when he takes a second swig. Indistinct in the pale, flickering light from the lamp, his eyes glow like two black points that resemble coal. He turns his face to the door, as if in expectation, then shakes his head, closes his heavy, sinewy hands around the bottle and downs the liquid in one gulp. When he bangs the bottle back down on the crate, he's laughing and crying at the same time. The wrinkles in his dark face crease into a spider's web of fine white lines.

"They almost destroyed my legs," he says, "but nothing can stop Timojan. I'm going back to the forest where I belong, so you can have my room and all that I own."

The little man rummages in his clothing, and from a hiding place under his rags, he suddenly pulls out a small knife, and with a proud nod hands it over to David. The knife's shaft is gilded; it lies light and easy in David's hand.

"Sell it, do what you will with it, it was my father's knife, the gypsy king Vorulef's knife, but it burns in my clothes. I'm afraid that one day it'll have power over me. Knives are like snakes. They kick and spit at me, but they won't make Timojan forget himself … I won't kill … They're going to annihilate us, they're like animals, no, they're worse than animals and although you don't know it, I'm warning you: soon they'll deport us; soon it'll all be over! Timojan can't read or write, but he knows the prayer: 'Let thy soul be still against those who ridicule thee, and let it bear all, as if it were dust.'"

Surprised by this, David nods and looks at the knife in his hand. Affected by the alcohol, he's afraid of it too. The cool, shining metal makes his hand cold, he's about to put it down, but changes his mind. Isn't it a gift, and didn't his father teach him that gifts are blessings? He feels a sense of loss for his father then. He looks at the gypsy, who's scrutinising his every move, but he's no longer listening. A sense of alienation overpowers him. His hand stifles a cough. He asks himself what this person really wants of him and what he's doing there, and even though the man does everything to reach him, he doesn't know how to respond. Anxiety from living on the streets and the threat of sudden disaster are in his blood now, and he hasn't the energy to either think or talk about it. He puts the knife in his pocket and gets up to leave. But the dwarfish man grabs him and pulls him down again.

"You're not alone here!" he says as if he's read his thoughts, and with a strong tug he pulls David close and hugs him. "Save yourself, save yourself from the dogs of Hell, promise?"

"Yes," says David and pulls away.

A moment later, he's standing outside, but then he changes his mind and goes back into the room, where the gypsy has collapsed. He takes out his harp and starts to play. The man stretches out his heavy body on the coal sacks and starts to whistle. His black eyes shine and he rubs them with his dirty, rough hands.

It's only then, when he laughs a toothless grin that David, too, is able to laugh and feel calm.

*

Some days later, the rain pours from the sky and the three boys stand like wet dogs on Leszno Street and try to attract the attention of passers-by. Even in this weather David plays, although the music is practically drowned out by the drumming of the rain on the cobbles.

Every day he notices there are more languages being spoken all around him. Erect, well-dressed German Jews pass him in the rain with their *Jude'* sign on their breast, some holding large black umbrellas. They regard him curiously; their children point at him or stop and look, as if they're tourists. A man he thinks he knows, passes by and tosses a coin at his feet. His head is half-hidden under a wide-brimmed hat that's soaking in the rain, and his smart trousers fit tightly over his black boots. His short raincoat flaps heavily around him as he carries on down the pavement and vanishes in the crowd.

A little later, as he's playing, he guesses who the man is. His hands seize up and he quickly tucks the harp into his pocket and runs after him, coughing. On Solna Street he glimpses the man's boots and raincoat in the dense crowd. A moment later, he's gone again, and then his rain-soaked hat comes into view among the hundreds of scarves and hats and caps. David pushes his way through the hordes of people and watches until the man disappears into a shop.

In a flash David's standing in front of the misted shop

window, watching the man's deft movements: he takes off his hat, pushes his way to the counter and the water from his hat splashes the small woman next to him. She scolds him but he just laughs and sends her away to get him something, his shrill voice piercing the closed door: "Hurry up! I don't have time to wait!"

Instinctively, the man turns his eyes towards the street; his face is heavier than David remembers, his eyes are swollen like two dark holes. David wants to run, but he starts to cough again and stands there, not knowing what he's looking at. His fingers touch the knife in his pocket, but he lets it be.

Milek steps out of the shop with a small bag in his hand and continues down the street, looking dead ahead. David follows at a distance but every time someone comes between them or Milek is about to get away from him in the damp cluster of bodies, he goes faster, coughing and out of breath, like someone bent on a fatal mission.

Unexpectedly, he stumbles, falls over and loses sight of Milek. A moment later, he's back on his feet, continuing down the street and just as he's about to give up, he sees Milek cross the street and stop in front of a window near the crossroads with Elektoralna Street. With a tight knot in his stomach and a sense of unreality, he approaches Milek, gripping hold of the knife in his pocket. An older man walks between them and stops to ask the way; David creeps around him nervously and takes the last few steps towards Milek, who's still absorbed by something in the window.

In a daze, he pulls the knife half out of his pocket. The body before him seems massive and threatening and strangely still. Something in him, a sense of loss and despair, makes him falter in his coat pocket. He coughs and lets go of the knife. Milek turns and, as if sensing the danger, tensely grabs him. "Haven't I seen you before?" he asks. "Aren't you the Jew boy who's been following me?"

"I don't know you!" lies David, trying to break away.

Milek simply stares at him and tightens his grip on his arm. Then it hits him and his wet face brightens up. He smiles arrogantly. "You're the one who caused me all that trouble at Café Hirschfeld, aren't you? You little Jewish shit, I ought to shoot you on the spot!"

"I don't know who you are!" David repeats automatically and turns away.

"You worthless piece of shit, you're nothing, and I'll show you what it means to get in my way!"

"You killed Martin, it was your fault he died ..." says David, facing him.

"Martin who?" says Milek with a cold stare, lifting the boy half off the pavement.

"You know who Martin is," David replies, no longer feeling anything.

With a sudden burst of anger, Milek lifts David off the ground and throws him through the air like a doll. Several passers-by stop in consternation or give Milek a wide berth on the pavement. From a holster under his raincoat, he pulls out a gun and walks towards David, who's lying doubled up in the street, blocking the traffic. Apart from one woman who approaches him, everyone else steers clear; many just stare, but most go on their way. Milek brushes the woman aside with his arm and walks with his gun lowered towards David.

David's on his own, now, more than ever.

But all of a sudden, out of the blue, a young man on a bicycle rickshaw streaks out of Elektoralna Street up onto the pavement and knocks the unsuspecting Milek over. He gives Milek a well-aimed kick in the head too, as he tries in vain to reach his gun.

"Run, run!" he shouts while simultaneously stamping on the pedals, turning the rickshaw around, and before the astonished Milek can even get up, he's already a long way away down Elektoralna Street.

David's off in a split second too. The crowd closes quickly behind him.

*

Later, he coughs up a lot of phlegm and his temperature soars then drops, so that one afternoon he can play non-stop for hours, but another afternoon he just stands there stiffly in the sun with no more energy than to stretch out his hand while his two partners sing and dance.

He goes back to hide in the gypsy's room, where he wraps himself in the coal sacks and sits and stares into the thin air as he tries to recover. In the evening, the lad from Lublin comes to visit him with a couple of carrots and some bread but he's not hungry and just wants something to drink.

"You're sick," says the lad but David won't hear of it and pulls his harp out of his pocket and plays for a bit.

"I can still play," he says. "Tomorrow, I'll be at Leszno Street to help you."

The lad shakes his head and leaves. But the next day, David is going nowhere. As he sits in the room, a world grows in his head. In his imagination, it's already summer and he's walking the streets with the sun beating down on the back of his head. He can smell herbs and spices, people around him are laughing and joking and from somewhere, there's music, music that lifts him up and makes everything clear. Faces come into focus now, voices become more distinct and bodies that were broken seem healed, as if a peaceful hand had touched them all and given them a new life.

But these peaceful dreams disintegrate and give way to a terrible void, a void worse than anything before. Instinctively, he decides to concentrate on simple things: sunlight on the dusty window, patterns in the wooden beams on the ceiling, voices from the courtyard that ring out like music, the banging sound of water in the pipes, the ragged laces in his boots, the sound of his heart beating … In his dream, he keeps going back to the same shop on Mila Street to buy a pot of honey, but no one will serve him, and no one can hear him even though he shouts.

He suddenly remembers a line or two from an old prayer: "Lord, hear me, before I was here, I was nothing; and now that I am here, I'm no more than if I had never been."

He'd never understood that prayer. He wants to be more than nothing. But then, when that terrible pain shoots through his back, he's not so certain. If he became nothing, would his suffering be over?

*

An elderly woman with a child she calls Leila and a younger man who's almost blind moves into the room with him. They've brought their own blankets with them and settle in but don't speak to him for hours. Then the woman tells him off because his coughing wakes the child but the man whispers to her to be quiet and apologizes.

"Please bear with her, bear with her!" he keeps saying, sitting up in the darkness and rocking from side to side. Later that night, David's woken by the child crying.

"God has abandoned us, God has abandoned us!" gabbles the young man throwing up his arms in the air.

"I don't care about your God," shouts the woman. "Get us some food, you lazy fool!"

David hands them some of his uneaten bread, which they quickly devour. But a moment later, the woman harps on, "You're useless, you blind idiot, what am I going to do with your child? If only my daughter were here!"

The man groans, gets up and reaches out for the child. "Give her to me and let us die in peace!"

So it went on, back and forth like a perpetual nightmare.

In the morning, Leila stands there looking at him shyly; she's three to four years old, but too small and undernourished. Her face is a pasty pale colour and the skin on her cheeks is spotted. The woman, who usually carries her around like a baby, has suddenly vanished with the blind man.

"Papa?" she says and looks around.

"He'll be back soon," he says, unsure of what to do with her. He hands her a piece of carrot, but she runs and hides at the other end of the room and won't look at him.

Exhausted, he gets up from the sacks and crawls over to her. She looks at him with great, frightened eyes.

"Don't you want to sleep?" he asks, wrapping the woman's cold blanket around her, but she throws it aside and pulls at the door.

"You have to wait here, they'll be back soon!" he says and lays a hand on her shoulder.

She runs to the other end of the room and sits down, staring at the wall. As he approaches, she crouches down and wraps both her arms tightly around her small body. He returns to the sacks and leaves her alone. After a while, she slowly and silently turns towards him.

He's wracked by a coughing fit and she looks at him

curiously with her tired, green eyes.

"Why are you coughing?" she asks him suddenly in Yiddish, and he's amazed that she can speak.

"It's nothing" he says. "Nothing …"

He starts to cough again and she's quiet and looks away. Her breathing is quick and tense and he has the feeling that, at any minute, she expects him to attack her. She gets up again and slowly walks towards the door. Then she abruptly sits down on the floor and moves her hands back and forth across the dusty wood. Is she cleaning house? She keeps at it for a long time, back and forth, back and forth with her hands.

He thinks about going down to join the boys on Leszno Street but now he must stay and watch her. When will they be back? Will they ever be back? Maybe they've just left her here?

He pulls out his harp and plays a tune but she continues her dusting movements. David gasps for breath and plays on. She gets up and walks over to him and stares at the little harp. She suddenly reaches out and he gives her the harp. She examines it and puts it to her mouth and pulls on the strings. Then she gives it back to him and he carries on playing. Next thing, she's right beside him and struggling to wrap the sacks around them both.

He stops playing; she leans against him and soon drifts off to sleep. He sits there motionless, so as not to disturb her. When he does try to get up, she holds on to him tightly, with both arms. He tries not to cough, but it's impossible. Occasionally, she wakes with a start, once she smiles but he doesn't know whether it's on his account or because she's still dreaming.

He closes his eyes and all of a sudden seems to be flying. He's back in his bedroom in the village; he gets up from his bed and walks over to the window. The two ash trees stand sharply outlined against the sky, the sun shines through the maze of branches. Two long, restless clouds loom over the grass and pass over him at the window; surprised, he looks at his dark hands. A robin's singing somewhere in the distance.

When he wakes up, he's lying on the sacks but the girl is gone. Outside, it's dark. He gets up, confused. The blankets are gone too. Why didn't they wake him?

Again, he's alone.

The next day, on his way along Leszno Street, a military car drives up alongside him; an arm reaches out and drags him into the car. He lands on the back seat with four other beggar boys from the street. The German policeman, who pulled him in, turns around on the front seat and pushes down one of the boys who's trying to escape. "It's like catching pigs," he says, grinning. "What're they going to use them for?"

"Don't know," says the driver, a young SS man with square, close-cropped hair visible under his cap and a massive neck. "The order was as many filthy Jew boys as possible! Half dead, said the Lieutenant!"

The policeman fixes his watery blue eyes on David.

"The last one smells like a pig, too," he says and turns around.

The car brakes hard, the policeman gets out, pulls the seat forward and drags the five terrified boys out onto the pavement in front of Szulc's restaurant on the corner of Leszno and Nowolipki Streets. He herds them quickly into the restaurant, where two men in air force uniforms take over and push them together with four other beggars in a corner.

"Keep still!" says one of them in poor Polish, before turning his back on them.

"They're going to shoot us," whispers a ragged, barefoot boy next to David, clutching on to him.

The restaurant is half-full of Germans in air force uniforms; some of them are under orders from an officer to clear the floor of tables and chairs. A tall black camera has been set up in the room. A cameraman is looking through the lens and discussing something with a blonde officer, who from time to time abruptly turns away and gives orders to all sides. Men hold lamps up in the air and fasten them to high metal rods until the entire restaurant is bathed in a harsh, over-bright light.

At the other end of the room, there are ten tables with well-dressed Jews sitting and eating. Two black-coated waiters pass nimbly between the tables and pour red wine and liqueurs into small, shiny crystal glasses.

Plates and platters loaded with roast beef, fish, bread, steaming potatoes, fruit and cakes are brought out.

"More delicacies!" shouts the blonde officer abruptly and although there doesn't seem to be anywhere to put them, a third waiter appears from the kitchen with trays of chocolate cakes, which he has difficulty finding space for on the tables.

"Give him a hat!" shouts the blonde officer again, pointing to an elderly bearded man at one of the tables. An assistant immediately goes to the tables with a large hat which he places on the head of the bearded man, who stares into the glaring light, in embarrassment. The officer hesitates a moment and then gestures his approval of the hat.

At this interruption, many people at the table stop eating and set their cutlery aside. Confused, they glance out of the window at the street, where a curious and hungry flock has gathered. Others lower their heads and continue eating, ashamed to be caught up in this fiasco. A slim woman in an elegant red jacket, who's recently been brought in from the street and put at a table, demonstratively shakes her head and is about to get up, but is quickly shoved back down by the zealous assistant. Irritated, she brushes his hands away from her shoulders and crosses her arms.

The blonde officer steps forward towards the tables, his attitude is formal but his tone of voice, ingratiating. In perfect Polish, he says, "Ladies and gentlemen, this is all for you. Enjoy this fantastic meal and eat well!"

Only the woman refuses to eat and is soon replaced by another.

Next, they place the filthy, famished boys in a row in front of the tables and order them to stick their hands out. Many of them drool at the sight of the food and beg pitifully for bread and fruit. David suddenly feels the urge to vomit, everything's spinning, his legs give way, but someone holds him up and slaps him across the back. His small body sways back and forth.

"Perfect, perfect," shouts the blonde officer with a smile of satisfaction across his childish face. "Start the camera now and let the wretch collapse in a moment, then we have something to show the world! The rich Jews stuffing their faces while the poor are falling like flies!"

The uniformed men around him laugh and the filming starts. The camera's lens slowly sweeps across the diners and stops at the beggars, who desperately stretch out their hands, unaware of their exploitation.

As if on cue, David falls over and is left lying on the floor.

"Close up, close up!" shouts the blonde officer, ecstatically, and three men quickly pull the camera back and the cameraman eagerly focuses on David's body as it thrashes on the floor.

David notices nothing except the unbearable pain in his chest; he tries to get up, but collapses. At that moment, the shadows around him grow. In the distance, he can hear laughter, a manic, throaty laughter that sounds like the roll of drums, but there are no drums, only the sound of shoes and boots and voices all around him mixing together inside his head.

"We got more than we dreamed of!" says a voice in German near his ear.

"Carry the boy out!" says another.

"Throw him on the street. Pinkiert will fetch him," says a third.

He feels someone lifting him off the floor and carrying him somewhere. Voices and sounds from the street rush at him, lights flash in the corner of his eye. They throw him on to the street.

The shadows merge; their long tentacles cloud his vision. Everything turns to black.

*

He wakes up in a fever and doesn't know where he is. He tries to get up, but his eyes squint at some kind of endless white room, and the noise of whining children assaults his ears. He immediately falls back onto the wooden bed beneath him, his hands fumble beneath the paper sheet, but it's not his legs he's touching ... what is it?

He slowly turns his head. It's unclear what he can see. There's something laying beside him, a skull, a corpse, no, a boy? A foul stink fills his nostrils, he wants to scream but can't, so he turns his head away and dozes off.

He's lying in one of forty beds on the second floor of a dilapidated building on the corner of Leszno Street and Zelazna Street; once a school that's now an infirmary.

In the centre of the building is a large hallway with wide stairs. Nurses and doctors run up and down, as if someone was chasing them. Skeletal children stand waiting on the steps, in their oversized clothes, and sometimes tug at the medical staff's coats or capes to get their attention.

"Aren't you coming to see me?", "Where's my mother?", "Don't you have an apple or a piece of bread?", "I'm not sick any more, am I?", "I'm not going to die, am I?"

Their voices are amazingly lively. Now and then, a nurse stops on the stairs, bends down and speaks with a child.

"We hope your mother will come tomorrow," she says, or, "No, you're not going to die."

But she can't say anymore, she doesn't know anymore, doesn't want to know. In this house, Death can come at any time and you can't survive if you look too closely.

The room David finds himself in, is large with high windows out to the 'Aryan' side, but the many rows of beds don't fill the room. There's room and the need for many more, but there's no money; even the daily emergency rations of weak vegetable soup, bread and watery milk sometimes don't come for long periods.

When the medical staff meet in the morning they

start by mopping the floor to clean away the mess that's collected under the beds from the night before. These starving children all suffer from diarrhoea and at night they blindly search for a toilet or a pot, but often don't make it over to the shallow tin pots in the corners. And even if they do, these pots are quickly filled up and often spill or get knocked over, so that a disgusting stench prevails which can keep even the most experienced member of staff from entering the room.

Two or three children lay together in one bed, many of them so starved they're reduced to skeletons. Others swell up, resembling shapeless heaps. You can only tell they're alive from their eyes; instead of a mouth there's a black hole; their skin is shrunken, parchment-like.

David wakes again from his feverish sleep. Three white forms move around in the room, they go from bed to bed and talk together, but he doesn't understand what they're saying. One of them has a notebook and sometimes jots something down. They carefully check on some of the children, stretching out their thin arms and legs, it's as if they whisper in a secret language. The pain in his chest is gone, and he would like to get up but his body feels light ... maybe he's dreaming, he feels as if he could just get up and go out on the street. But when he lifts his arms, they're like lead weights.

Suddenly, the white forms stand before his bed. He'd like to say something, but he's too tired.

"This is the new one," one of them says. "Where's he from?"

"A man found him on Leszno Street," says another and

as she hands some papers across him, he notices a beauty spot on her cheek. "He was more dead than alive, I de-loused him, gave him some morphine, a small dose ..."

"Is he conscious?" asks the third, who waves his fingers in front of David's eyes. David tries to move his head but fails.

"Diagnosis?" asks the first, an older woman, whose hair is pulled back in a bun at her neck.

"Volynic fever, hunger ..." says the woman with the beauty spot.

"No Pirquet test? No tuberculosis?" asks the third.

"We'll have to wait a couple of days," says the older woman who writes something on the paper.

"Will he survive?" asks the woman with the beauty spot who lays her hand on his chest. He twitches his eyelids and lifts one hand slightly, but none of them notice.

"You always ask the same question," says the older woman in irritation. "Even though you know we can't tell anything without a Pirquet test."

"Miss Natanblut is just a student, she worries ..." says the third, a man with a long, pale face and yellow teeth.

"You needn't defend her. It's probably tuberculosis, and a matter of four to six weeks. That much you know, don't you?"

"Yes," says the young woman, removing her hand.

"Keep him clean and warm, give him something to eat and pray to God. That's the treatment. Understand?"

"Yes," says the young woman again with an impatient nod.

"Perhaps Miss Natanblut is too young to manage this?" asks the older woman.

"She manages fine," says the man with a sigh, examining the boy next to David. He forces the closed eyes open.

"He's dead," he says quietly.

"When?"

"Probably this morning …"

"He's to be removed immediately," says the older woman. "Make sure it's done, Miss Natanblut!"

They move on, he hears nothing more … a black spot on the ceiling keeps flying around, is it a blackbird or a bat?

Then he can see no more, he's drifted off.

Like a tightrope walker balancing on the edge of death, David slowly and miraculously recovers. Over the course of the next three weeks, while he's in the ward, he senses that the woman with the beauty spot is always close by. At first, he glimpses her rarely, or in a hazy silhouette when she gives him water or hot soup and holds his head up. He's not always certain that it's her, but he learns to recognize her hands when they rest on his forehead or tuck his covers tight around him for the night. He begins to know her smell and soon he doesn't have to open his eyes to know she's there, it's as if he can sleep and see her at the same time.

Sometimes she whispers to him, "One day … little friend, one day … little friend …" (and is she imagining it or is there a look about this boy's eyes that reminds her of her father?). On another occasion, as she's standing by his bed, the older woman calls her aside. She hears their voices: "You're spending far too much time with that boy, Miss Natanblut," she says. "There are others here that are worse off than him."

"I'm not neglecting anyone," she responds.

"Let me be the judge of that," says the older woman.

He's afraid that he won't see her again, he has the feeling that she's staying away, but some time later she's there again with a glass of water.

"Take it easy!" she says as he gulps it down.

A doctor with a large head, whom he sees for the first time, is suddenly standing at his bedside. He throws the sheet aside, takes his stethoscope and listens to the chest of the boy lying next to him.

"Tuberculosis," he says "I know the sound. He needs sunshine."

"The station's closed," she says. "You know that, don't you?"

"I was in Pabianice the day before yesterday," he says, wearily.

"You need to sleep."

"I can't sleep, I have to work," he says, stroking his beard.

She looks at him, anxiously, as if there's something she understands but doesn't want to know about.

"First, I hid and then I managed to get out in my car," he says. "I put a Red Cross flag on the bonnet, and for whatever reason, they accepted it ... they came from all sides, rounded up the young children and the elderly and then killed them ... I watched it all from my attic window right above the square ... The worst one was the chief, a Lieutenant Colonel ..."

The doctor pauses and looks vacantly out over the beds.

"You don't have to tell me any more," she says and lays a hand gently on his shoulder.

"You don't understand. They stood in rows and he ordered them to sing Jewish songs. They sang them out of tune mostly, some of the children sang beautifully ... Then he started to teach them a German song, 'Moses'. He sang it over and over again until they finally all sang it together. When he was satisfied with this, they were shot, shot down like rabbits.

The doctor covers his eyes as if the entire tragedy is right there in front of him and he can't bear to see it again. The shock is too much. Like a man hit by a bullet, the doctor staggers backwards and falls into the arms of Adina Natanblut. She holds him up, as best she can, while calling for help. Soon they take him downstairs to the doctors' room where he's laid on a bed. For a long time, he lays there ranting and raving, until a merciful soul gives him an injection to sedate him.

In his drowsy condition, David has overheard every word of the doctor's story, but not knowing what to make of it, he dozes off again into an uneasy sleep.

There are other days when, despite his fever, he wakes up feeling refreshed. On such a day, he gets up from his bed in his sick clothes, and walks past the rows of starving children and out onto the stairs. His only thought is to go out into the street and feel the air but as he goes down a few steps, he grows dizzy and has to sit down. A moment later, he has company. Two kids his own age, a boy and a girl, come and sit down next to him and start asking: 'What's wrong with him?'; 'How long's he been there?'; 'What's his name?' He answers them slowly, as best he can.

The girl's face is pale and gaunt, but her eyes shine. Her brown hair is cut into a bob as if she'd had a basin on her head. The boy calls her Sarah. He's tall and thin and is constantly holding his stomach, even when speaking. Blue veins protrude around his throat.

"They play with the children!" says the boy and looks at him as if he clearly understands how stupid they are.

"What do they play?" David asks, uncertainly.

"Yeh, well, 'house' and that sort of thing. But not with white bread and Sabbath fish, they don't have any. There are candles and dark bread and then there's a father and a mother and others pretend to be their children. Yesterday, they had real honey cakes and some beetroot."

"Are you sure?" asks Sarah in amazement.

"It's only with the small kids," says the thin boy, shaking his head. "They think that …"

"What?"

"Well, the little ones think that this is a completely normal life … and they're just like normal kids … "

"Maybe they don't know anything else," says Sarah.

The boy shakes his head again and gets up from the stairs. He stands there thinking, seriously, and can't make up his mind whether to stay or go. The girl turns towards David, who's not really listening.

"I'd like to be able to play," she says. "To sing and be normal. I used to sing all the time …"

"Why don't you sing now?" he asks.

She shakes her head.

"Why not?" asks the boy, suddenly curious.

"My throat hurts," she says and gets up.

"How much?"

"A lot," she says and opens her mouth, so he can look down her throat.

"Maybe tomorrow?"

"No, in a week or so, perhaps …"

"I'll play my harp too," says David, slowly.

They look at him in surprise so he tells them about the little mouth harp that's in his coat pocket, but he realizes that he doesn't know where his coat is anymore.

The weather improves over the next week or so. The sun shines in every day through the dusty windows and the street outside seems to grow busier. Almost every day he explores the three floors of the hospital, avoiding places that are restricted, because of the danger of infection. He gets used to the sight of sick children and the never-ending activity in the wards. One day, he helps Miss Natanblut by carrying bread and water to a small room all the way up at the top. There, he recognises the tall, thin boy he'd met on the stairs, now lying in one of the five beds. His face is as white as the sheets, his eyes strangely large, and as David hands him some bread, the boy doesn't recognize him. He takes the bread limply, but drops it.

David picks up the bread and puts it near to his mouth, but the boy turns away. Miss Natanblut carefully gives the boy something to drink from a mug. His head falls to the side, but his eyes are still open.

"Is he dying?" he whispers in her ear. She nods.

"His name is Celek," she says, standing for a moment in front of his bed, then walks over to the door.

"Come on," she says, looking sadly at him. David

silently shakes his head and she lets him stay. He pulls out his little harp, which he's recently tracked down, and shows it to the boy.

"I found my harp, Celek," he says. "Remember, what we said?"

The boy doesn't move, but a girl in the next bed, with a tiny blue scarf on her head turns towards him.

"Can you play?" she asks softly, her breathing troubled. He nods.

"Will you play for us?"

He nods again but then instantly rushes out of the room. He searches the building for Sarah and finds her asleep in a bed in the room below. He wakes her gently.

"Will you sing for Celek?" he whispers.

"You want me to sing now?" she asks, surprised.

He nods and points up at the room where Celek's lying. She gets up and holds on to him to steady herself.

"He's really sick," he says, but won't say any more.

"OK, but what should I sing?" she asks.

"Do you know any psalms?" he asks.

They both think for a while.

"Open up thy heart now …" she suggests. "Shall I sing that?"

He nods. She's still clinging on to him.

"Can you stand by yourself?" he asks, uncertainly and looks at her grey face with its dark, lively eyes. In answer, she lets go of him, stepping deftly to the side. Together, they go up the stairs to the small room. As they walk in, the four other children are already waiting, excited in their beds. Only Celek remains where he was, staring blankly ahead of him.

Sarah goes over to him and takes him by the hand, and then he moves his eyes and mumbles something that they don't catch.

Sarah begins to sing. Initially, her voice is hoarse and hesitant but soon it regains its tone. Her slight body vibrates with concentration as she gives herself over completely to the Yiddish words:

> "Father, thou art good!
> Let our prayers and atonement
> Reach you. Let the rest of
> Our life be from this day forth
> For thy joy.
> And let us pray now
> For forgiveness."

David picks up on the tune and starts to play too, so that soon the room is full of sound. When Sarah stops singing, he has to go on. In his imagination, he's back on Leszno Street with people swarming around him, and the noise from the street ringing in his ears. As if under a spell, he plays and plays, until he suddenly realizes where he is, and lets the harp drop.

Celek has closed his eyes, his face looks relaxed, the blue veins in his throat can no longer be seen. It looks as if he's asleep. They all look silently and expectantly at him until the little girl with the blue scarf says, "That's how I'd like to sleep."

Then they all know. David puts his ear to Celek's chest but can hear nothing.

"Why are you doing that?" asks Sarah.

"He's dead," he says, uneasily.

"I know," she says. "Like a boy next to us. 'He got a peaceful death' said the doctor."

The girl with the scarf hides her face in the pillow and weeps. Then Sarah cries too, it's as if she's smiling and crying at the same time. The others remain quiet in their beds.

"The soul lives on," David says to comfort them. "One day we'll all be resurrected."

Sarah nods.

And he recites a *Kaddish* that his uncle had taught him long ago in a life that no longer seems to be his own. And the children mumble after him: "Therefore we trust in you, Lord, our God, that soon we may witness Your power and Your glory, to deliver us from all the evils of the world ..."

He pauses and swallows. A fly is crawling over Celek's motionless eyelid. He turns away.

Later that night he has a dream. He can hear his mother's voice whispering in the breeze. He goes out onto the deserted streets, following the sound, as if spellbound, until he reaches a place where three dwarf musicians are playing the flute and violins.

"Where do you come from?" he asks.

But they ignore him and walk on.

The gateway at the end of the street is open, with no guards in sight.

The sounds from an amusement park and lively, happy voices stream towards him. As he walks down the street, he can see Krasinki Place in the distance, where a carousel is turning. His mother is there, sitting on the carousel, on a white horse. She's holding onto the horse and doesn't hear him even though he shouts at her.

As he walks through the gateway, an arm grabs hold of him and he stares into Milek's fat, shiny face.

"You won't get out of here unless you bleach your hair!" he sneers.

He tries to tear free but can't and reluctantly agrees to bleach his hair. With his new white hair, he finally approaches the carousel and waves frantically at his mother. Their eyes meet, but she doesn't recognize him.

The carousel goes round and round without end.

"Where will you go?" asks Miss Natanblut one day at the beginning of July. His bed has been taken over by another patient and he's been allowed to sleep in the doctors' room for the past two weeks.

Since then, he's helped her de-louse the newcomers, with her wearing a plastic overall in the bathroom, and helped pass her the needles full of glucose which give the sick an instant boost. As if by magic, a child's face would light up momentarily, but it only lasted a few hours before they were overcome by fever and lethargy again. He learned to spot the symptoms for typhoid fever, diarrhoea, malnourishment and nettle rash; words like 'meningeal tuberculosis' and 'chest emphysema' were no longer strange to him; he'd handed out barbiturates and witnessed many blood tests.

Around this time, food supplies improved, and everything from sugar beets to black sausage to real honey became available, which helped some of the children recover. But the most essential medicine gradually stopped coming. He noticed that many of the doctors numbed themselves each morning with small drafts of the pure alcohol that stood in clear bottles in the doctors' room and he thought: perhaps this is why they can still smile at the children.

One day, the hospital was visited by an SS officer and two soldiers who, despite the protests of the doctors, searched the building for members of the resistance, known as the *Armia Krajow.* They dragged two seriously ill fourteen-year-olds down the stairs where the doctor from Pabianice and Miss Natanblut stood in the doorway and blocked their way.

The SS officer, a tall, broad-shouldered man with a nice sun-tanned face, drew out his pistol and held it cheerfully in front of Miss Natanblut.

"If I was you, I'd get out of the way now!" he said.

"Are you really so cowardly that you have to remove sick children and threaten defenceless women!" demanded the doctor from Pabianice without flinching. The SS officer resolutely turned the gun on the doctor.

"Oh, a man who speaks up for defenceless women, how interesting!" he said and held the gun to his temple. "Do you think that your profession protects you?"

"I have no illusions," said the doctor, still calm.

"You know then what's waiting for you if you don't move immediately?"

"Yes."

"No matter what you say and no matter what you do, you're in my hands. Do you understand what I'm saying?"

"Yes ... here and now you can do with me whatever you wish but somewhere beyond all this, your power has absolutely no meaning," said the doctor, whose large face showed a trace of a bitter smile.

"Aha, we have a philosopher," said the SS officer. "God is dead, don't you know that?"

The doctor from Pabianice looked the SS officer

straight in the eye. For an instant the two men took the measure of each other.

"The boys stay here!" said the doctor firmly, controlling his fear.

The SS officer's lips quivered, he laughed abruptly, then unexpectedly re-holstered his gun, turned and ordered the two soldiers to release the boys.

"They've got a week and then I'll be back," he said without looking at the doctor. Quickly, he disappeared out the door.

The two soldiers took a couple of steps forward, unsure how to react, then they, too, rushed out of the open door.

For two days, the doctor silently enjoyed his new reputation as a hero who'd put his life on the line to save the boys, but then he was seized by a patrol and accused of collaboration with the resistance. The same evening he was shot in Pawia prison.

David doesn't know what's worse: to do nothing or to make a stand against the impossible. That day, he tells Miss Natanblut: "I'd like to fight too, but I don't know how."

"Keep yourself alive," she says. "You're only a boy."

"Why should I stay alive when the Jews will die anyway?"

"That's exactly why ... because so many will die, you must live!" she says and smiles.

He can see how tired she is and that she, too, is on the verge of giving up. But a moment later, she says, "You can't stay here any more, we need the bed in the doctors' room. I've found a job for you and a place where you can sleep. Can you wash dishes?"

Of course he can, she doesn't even have to ask. She hands him a note with the address of a shelter. Again, he notices the beauty mark which is black like a small flower.

"You're cured," she says. "Go out and help the others."

They hug each other and she holds him so tightly that he feels like crying, but he doesn't. There's a blurry white spot in front of his eyes, that slowly cracks.

"Go along now!" she says, seeing him still standing there.

And so he goes off, rushing down the stairs.

*

For a long time, the view from the hospital windows had been his only contact with the ghetto, and he'd gotten so used to being in the ward that the outside world had paled into insignificance. When he'd stood at the window, he'd longed for the freedom of the streets as if it were a dream. But whenever the thought of leaving the hospital occurred to him, the streets of the ghetto seemed hostile, like a nightmare, and he couldn't imagine going back there.

At first he was overjoyed by Miss Natanblut's offer of work and a place to stay, but as he ran down the stairs and approached the front door, his heart was pounding so hard out of fear at what he might see, that he stalled. Had it not been for the fact that a visitor arrived just then and opened the door, he wouldn't have had the courage to leave.

Now he's standing in the turmoil of Leszno Street and all the faces and the traffic and the bright sunlight hit him like a wave. Tentatively, he takes a couple of steps along the pavement and notices how easy it is to walk. Just walk along and feel what it is to be alive.

As if tipsy, he stumbles along the street, bumping into people but the longer he walks, the easier it gets to adjust his movements. After about an hour, he's practically regained his old skill of weaving in and out of the crowds and is soon moving freely through the swarms of people on the streets.

Without giving it a second thought, he's in front of the Tlomacka synagogue, a decaying building with a columned entrance that he'd passed by many times before, but always felt too insignificant to visit. It was Martin who'd told him all about the beautiful curtain on the tabernacle with its palm-like field of revelation, and about the hand-carved wooden doors that are like doors to the deepest secrets, and about the heavy golden chalices that require two hands to lift. But surely it must all be hidden away by now. Aren't there Jews living there – Jews from Germany?

Just as he's going up the stairs, a rabbi opens the great door to let a group of German Jews go out, so he waits until they're all out and is about to go in, when the rabbi closes the heavy door without noticing him.

He knocks on the door and the rabbi opens it again.

"What do you want here?" he says, squinting. He has a long grey beard and thin white hands. David feels faint and doesn't know what to say. The rabbi sighs impatiently and is about to close the door again, but his long robe gets caught. Deftly, he pulls the garment out of the way but looks curiously at the lad, leaving the door ajar.

"Do you have an errand here?" he asks, helpfully.

The old man coughs and steps from one foot to the other in his worn out shoes, which David can't help staring at.

"They're like my father's ..." he says, eventually, shaking his head and turning to go, but the rabbi calls him back and lets him in.

The high-ceilinged room he enters is dusty and peeling, cluttered with bundles and suitcases sitting on planks along the walls. From one of the rooms beyond comes the sound of a child crying, and other raised voices echo strangely. Light from the narrow windows reflects distorted, white shapes on the bare walls and onto the hunched figure of the rabbi as he signals to David to follow him.

They walk down a long corridor and with some large keys the rabbi unlocks the door to a little room then, with difficulty, he sits down on a chair behind a heavy square wooden table. The rabbi coughs and points silently at a stool in the corner, where David perches. Along the walls are shelves lined with books, on one of the walls hangs a magnificent prayer shawl, and in a corner behind the table he notices a small chest.

In the sharp daylight from the window, the rabbi seems grey and tired. He's still wearing his long robe and hat and although he coughs again, his voice is soft and alive, almost a whisper.

"Your father is dead …" he says and folds his hands. "How can a boy bear it?"

"How do you know?" David asks in surprise.

"Your eyes, my friend, it's easy to read the eyes of children! And my shoes! Your father's shoes were also worn-out?"

"Yes."

The old man sighs and looks up towards the window.

"Everything's worn-out, even charity," he says, as if to himself. He then turns his eyes back towards him.

"By the rivers of Babylon we sat down and cried," he says and looks at David inquisitively. "Do you know the psalm, have they taught you?"

He nods.

"So you know that Moses spoke harsh words to the Lord and that he said: 'Innocent children were killed and their parents had to endure the despair of slavery'. It's written in the Book of Lamentations. Everything in history repeats itself, my friend. The Romans destroyed the Temple, the Germans destroy the synagogues; again we're being tested. Do you understand?"

"Yes," he says, wondering why the rabbi's sharing all this with him.

"Do you know the story of Choni, who dreamed for seventy years, and when he awoke everything was so changed that no one understood him? So have we dreamed, and now there's no one who understands us. Do you know about all our suffering and what we believe? Do you know about the martyr Rabbi Ishmael? As he lay with his neck bared for the executioner, he was asked by the emperor if he still trusted in God, and do you know what he replied? He said: 'Even though he kills me, in Him I trust'. Therefore you must believe. Do you?"

"Sometimes, I think I do ..." he says, uncertain under the rabbi's gaze. "But people die ... so I don't know what to believe ..."

"What have you done? Do you beg?"

"I used to beg and play my harp," he says and is about to say more, but is afraid that the old man wouldn't understand.

"May I see it?" the rabbi asks, curiously.

He takes the harp out of his pocket and hands it over. The rabbi examines it carefully with his nimble fingers.

"During their imprisonment in Babylon, the Levites hung up their great harps in the trees and destroyed their own fingers, refusing to play for King Nebuchadnezzar, but you, you must play in the streets ... Understand?"

"I've been sick ..." he says and wonders if he should tell the rabbi about the hospital, but is silent.

"I'm sorry ..." says the old man and puts his hands on his head, "there's no Hebrew school any more and you're just a boy, but still you have to work out what you'll do.

Have you had your Bar Mitzvah?"

David shakes his head.

"Do you want something to eat? Is that why you've come?"

"I'm not hungry," David lies so as not to embarrass the old man, but the rabbi pretends not to hear and stiffly gets up and pulls out a slice of bread, which he hands to him over the table.

Together, they eat the dark bread that tastes like sawdust, and neither of them speaks. The rabbi's movements become increasingly slow and his breathing heavy, his eyelids close over his bloodshot eyes and in the middle of a mouthful he falls asleep.

David feels embarrassed, because he'd said very little and didn't really know why he was there. He sits for a while, observing the old man, as his nostrils flare open and closed with his breathing. He doesn't want to leave, the old man sleeping near him makes him feel safe, in a way he hasn't felt for a long time — his coat and hat, his gentle mouth and sharp nose, like the beak of a hawk that reminds him of his uncle — and even though the distance between them is great, he senses a connection of some sort. He carefully gets up and gently touches the spines of the leather-bound books. He reads some of the titles: *Rabbi Nissims Chibbur Jafe, Talmud, Ta'anith, Talmud, Aboda Sara.*

Shouldn't he say good-bye?

He quietly opens the door and goes back out to the street.

*

The shelter on Dezielna Street is made up of a long, narrow dormitory with rows of bunks, a makeshift dining hall with benches and worn wooden tables and a small kitchen with a stove and a sink. Every day, Luba Lewin heats up a weak vegetable soup on the stove in two large boiling pots, and serves it, with a lot of noise and commotion, through a small hatch to the long line of homeless people and beggars who file past. From the start, Mrs Lewin shows him how to hand out the tin plates, collect up the food coupons or the twenty pennies for a bowl of soup and a small piece of bread. Many in the queue, which runs through the dining hall and right out onto the street, have neither coupons nor money, but they still get their soup, paid for by the community charity. From day one, he sees the same listless, smirking or pleading faces return to the hatch to ask for more but Mrs Lewin, who has an eagle's eye, quickly sorts them out and never gives free soup to the same man twice.

The dining hall is always crammed full of people, who use it as a sort of waiting room, games room or place to sleep. Especially so at midday, when the dormitory is quickly cleaned and those who are too weak or too ill, are given a thin slice of bread at their bed, while the others are chased out, crowding into the dining hall. It's then that the fighting for a place becomes fierce and hard to stop. Often, they shove and push, or trip and tear at each other's clothes.

But sometimes, to Mrs Lewin's dismay, music and laughter can break out in the midst of this seething tumult, when two of the men climb onto the tables to sing and dance.

After the meal, the tin plates and spoons are left scattered over the tables, and there's not a drop of soup nor a crumb of bread left. David collects the plates and spoons and washes them in one of the huge pots, and then he sweeps the floors and empties the overflowing latrines. That's his job.

But it's not long before he also starts caring for the sick and malnourished in the dormitory. Many of them no longer have the strength to get up and their hair is thick with lice. He gets water from the kitchen and washes their hair with soap which he's bought with his first week's wages. The bedridden are full of gratitude for about a day, until they're re-infested with lice, which crawl all over their clothing and over David too, as he sleeps in a bunk in the dormitory, tossing and turning from the bites in his scalp.

One day, there's no water, another day, no gas for the stove. It often stinks of the excrement on the dormitory floor but he does what he can. Mrs Lewin watches him with concern, fearful of him taking on too much.

"You won't last long, you need to take better care of yourself!" she says, as she stares down into her pots.

Every other day a man or woman dies in their bunk and the tired, black men from Pinkiert's make their routine visit to the shelter. They silently come and go after dark with their long wooden coffins which they quickly nail shut. Often, there are two in each coffin; at other times there's no coffin available, so he helps them carry the body out to the black hearse. At the cemetery, they bury the dead in the early hours of the morning, most without clothes, simply covered in white paper, they're lowered down into a mass grave. Because of ground water, they can't be buried very deep and there's not enough earth to cover them all.

A madman runs into the street behind the coffin shouting: "Did the dead man leave his ration card, did he leave a ration card?"

One morning, Simon Tenenbaum, a forty-year-old man from Bodzyn, who's bedridden, calls him over to his bunk. Knitting his eyebrows together, he whispers: "I'll tell you a joke and you don't have to laugh. Got it?"

He nods.

"A tailor tells his workers off because they made a pair of trousers that wouldn't fit. But they said to the boss: 'For dying in, these are fine.'"

They both laugh a little; Simon asks for a cup of water and when David comes back with the water, Simon insists on telling him another joke. With his lank hair and bad breath, his pale cheeks and feverish eyes, David thinks: "He'll probably die soon, I probably won't see him for much longer" but he nods anyway.

Simon's mind wanders a little before coming back to tell his joke: "Two Jews are on the gallows. 'The situation isn't so bad' says one to the other, 'apparently they've run out of bullets.'"

They laugh together once more and Simon tries to sit up and pat David on the shoulder but he collapses back with a cry of pain and slowly dozes off.

Pinkiert's van came for him that evening.

*

David dreams that Simon's sitting in the ash tree, that he's a crow whose cawing wakes him up before the break of day. Alone, the crow sits among the bare branches, staring at him until suddenly, it falls to the ground like a stone. Then beating its wings rapidly, it rises up and vanishes over Tomachevski's fields.

*

Two weeks pass and every day and every night, he's approached by ragged, destitute souls who ask for advice or food or money. He barely sleeps any more. They take up all his time and all his energy. As Mrs Lewin predicted, he must slow down and think of himself.

But what does that mean: to think of yourself? Does he have any choice?

In the middle of the Sabbath, a few days before *Tisha Be'av*, a Jewish policeman shows up in the tiny kitchen and asks for some soup. The heavy man, sweating in his jacket and boots, pushes his wide-brimmed cap back and wipes his forehead with a white handkerchief. As he eats the soup, complaining to Mrs Lewin about the endless heat, he keeps a beady eye on David.

"Is that the new boy?" he asks with a nasal voice, sticking his hands under the tap to cool them.

"That water's for drinking!" says Mrs Lewin without looking up, as she ladles the soup onto the plates that David hands her.

"I asked you a question!" he hisses, holding his wrist under the cold running water. But his words are drowned out by the hundreds of needy people in the dining hall. Annoyed, he grabs his whistle and blows.

"Quiet, quiet!" he shouts and walks to the door. At the sight of the agitated policeman, a hush descends in the crowded dining hall. They all look at the policeman, cowering and hunched in the queue. He turns back to Mrs Lewin.

"Well?" he says, drying his hands on his white handkerchief.

Without looking at him, Mrs Lewin replies: "David Rubinow has been hired by the congregation. You don't need to know any more. You should be concerning yourself with the rumours about mass deportation."

"Rumours?" he says, pulling his cap down. "They're just rumours."

Mrs Lewin faces him.

"Is there any truth to them?" she asks and looks him

straight in the eye, pursing her lips.

"How should I know? What does that have to do with this?" he says, casting a disapproving glance at David, who's still standing with the plates in his hands.

"They say they have trucks ready at *Umschlagplatzen* …?"

"That's something totally different. People are being sent to work camps … I don't know anything, anyway … the only thing that interests me is whether this lad here has a work permit!"

"They say that *our* police will lead the action, is that true?"

"No," says the officer, angrily. "We've not been told anything, and now I want an answer to *my* question, understand?"

"How can God Almighty allow it, how …?" says Mrs Lewin, covering her face with her apron.

The officer suddenly grabs her arms and shakes her.

"Answer me, answer me *now*!" he shouts.

"No," she shouts, "he hasn't got a work permit, what does it matter now?"

She tears herself loose and looks at him with contempt.

"Give him your money, David, give it to him!"

In a panic, David rummages through his pockets for the money, but he has none left, so he bends down, opens the little money box with his key and hands the officer five *zloty*, but he shakes his head stiffly.

"That's not your money," he says. "You'd better come

with me!"

"Take it!" pleads Mrs Lewin.

The officer hesitates, then reaches out and pockets the money. He adjusts his jacket, gives them both a disdainful look and leaves the kitchen.

"I'll be back!" he shouts from the dining hall, but his voice gets drowned out in the hungry, seething chaos.

He dreams that night that he's a sparrow, hopping about on the flagstones and pecking at breadcrumbs, worrying about the things that might get thrown at him. He darts up and down above the pavement, before swooping and soaring higher and higher, up and up, until the street disappears beneath him … there's a labyrinth below him now and he no longer recognizes the ghetto… he can't see any people, maybe they're not there any more … he glides for a while and then flies up closer to the sun … everything around him is growing very hot.

He wakes in his bunk bathed in sweat, not knowing where he is.

What is a rumour, if not a half truth coupled with fear? Like a swarm of flies, it invades an entire city and grows in strength as it goes from mouth to mouth, confirming people's worst fears and often surpassing the actual events. Sometimes, though, the rumour can announce the truth in a chillingly clear form, before being official. People try to deny it, but often in vain.

On Sunday the 19th of July, a lovely sunny day, some people on Dezielna Street stop and turn their faces towards the sunshine and the blue sky, while others seek refuge in the cool shadows of the side streets. There are also a few who have gathered in random groups to noisily discuss certain rumours. A strange nervous quietness prevails like the silence before a storm. A battered car drives down Dezielna Street and stops close to the shelter. A door opens, a man with a heavy face and sharp nose and strong, calm movements steps out onto the street. Shading his eyes with his hand, beneath his black hat, he looks up and down the street and steps up onto the pavement. With a tense and tired smile, he addresses a group of passers by, the beggars and street children, all of whom have already gathered around him.

They recognize him immediately as the chairman of the Jewish Council, Adam Czerniaków. He searches for words, shifts from Polish to Yiddish (which he's not comfortable speaking), puts a hand on the head of a dirty little boy then quickly removes it, smiles stiffly again, and speaks in a strong clear voice:

"You've nothing to fear, there'll be no deportations. Commissioner Auerswald and the Germans have assured me that there is no truth in these rumours!"

Questions rain down on Czerniaków, as more and more people arrive from back yards and flats. The traffic comes to a standstill, cart drivers and coachmen get down off their vehicles and rush towards him, and David and Mrs Lewin join the growing crowd around him. Czerniaków tries to answer as best he can, but there are too many questions and under the protection of his two assistants, he begins to walk further down the street, where he stops to repeat his assurances to the unbelieving throng. A beggar suddenly shouts: "The Germans are coming! The Germans are coming!"

A hush comes over the crowd pressing in on Czerniaków and his smile vanishes as he's pushed some way down the street. He shouts out forcefully: "Don't be afraid!"

But his words are lost in a flood of shouts and his assistants swiftly pull him out of the crowd and shove him back into the waiting car.

The car starts, but youths start booing him and block its path. One of them climbs onto the bonnet and beats on the windshield, the driver honks the horn and drives a forward a few feet, but has to stop. Czerniaków holds his head up and still tries to smile, but the splitting pain in his head is about to lay him out on the seat. That morning he'd taken some cybalgin and several drops of valerian for the pain, "What good will it do, what good will it do?" he keeps whispering to himself, as he tries to smile at the many-headed monster outside the car. He closes his eyes and doesn't notice the three Jewish officers who have appeared and stoutly removed the youth from the car bonnet. With their piercing whistles and strong-arm tactics, they shove the people aside and finally the car can move out.

The crowd gradually dissolves, still discussing and arguing, some are on Czerniaków's side, pleading for calm, others will have nothing to do with the old man's assurances; some feel betrayed and curse the congregation. "Nothing, they've done nothing for us," shouts an elderly man, waving his stick in the air. "They're nothing but German lackeys." "What would you do?" shouts a young woman, "I wouldn't give tuppence for your common sense!" "We'll kill all the Germans!" shouts a ten-year-old boy, chucking a stone at a wall. "God has betrayed us! God has betrayed us!" wails an old woman, stretching her arms up to the heavens.

A little while later, back in the kitchen, Mrs Lewin says to David, "Czerniaków didn't look well, I was afraid they'd hurt him."

"No," says David "no one would hurt Czerniaków …"

"Why ever not?" she asks, stunned.

"The beggars like him, there are a lot of people who like him, but they don't know what to do."

"Do you know him?" she asks sceptically.

"No," he says "but I've lived on the street and I've heard

what he does for the children."

She stands there looking at him, shaking her head.

"You're a strange lad," she says and starts chopping up some dried up carrots.

The sun continues to shine as dark rumours spread and bring things to boiling point. Wealthy and well-informed Jews desperately try to get false passports. They pay exorbitant bribes to get their family out in time. Others ignore the danger and live as if the worst could never happen. Some wall themselves inside cellars, attics, corridors and backyards. They build makeshift rooms behind cupboards and furnish hiding places under the floorboards or up in the roof space. But for most, the great mass of poor, homeless people, these rumours are little more than extra salt on the wounds of their already agonizing existence. A few even imagine the possibility of something to eat, maybe a job somewhere in the East, where it's said that the Germans are constructing whole Jewish towns.

On Dzielna Street, there's a new rumour that Czerniaków is being held prisoner in his own office and that the German police have arrested several members of the Jewish Council, including Gepner, the leader of the charitable institution. It's also thought that a Jewish policeman by the name of Ajzenstajn has been killed because he refused to assist in the deportation — and not only him but twenty or thirty other Jewish officers too, who refused to obey orders. On Karmelicka Street, people say that the Germans raided houses and threw people into their trucks, killing twenty or thirty in a single night. What should one believe? Judgement

Day is at hand … who will come to the rescue?

No one comes.

On Wednesday, the 22nd of July, the impossible happens. Sometime in the morning, hundreds of Jewish officers, soldiers and Ukrainian mercenaries invade the streets. The sound of their shrieking whistles sends people into a wild frenzy. Shops close, squares are emptied, children are abandoned … Trucks with SS drivers at the wheel fly around corners, shooting at people randomly as they run along or walk. Unrelenting terror is unleashed, as the ruthless hunt for Jewish flesh gathers pace. Confused and panic-stricken beggar children, and the old and weak are herded together, swept into trucks and driven off with shouts and screams. From loudspeakers throughout the ghetto, German voices pour forth assurances or issue dire threats and warnings. Posters are quickly pasted up proclaiming that "All unproductive elements should meet at *Umschlagplatzen*". People flock to employment bureaus, desperately trying to secure a work card, or what's known as a 'survival ticket'.

At Toebben's and Schultz's workshops, the doors are firmly closed to people who arrive with a sewing machine under their arm, hoping for a last chance of a job. Rumours have it that a sewing machine can save your life. Consequently, the streets are full of people running around with old and useless sewing machines madly looking for the sweatshops that are allowed to work for the Germans, but everywhere the doors are barricaded. The lucky ones are already holed up and despite connections and bribes few are able to join them. Offices for the Jewish self-help organization are deluged by all manner of people asking for charity, begging for help – but who can help them?

At 103 Zelazna Street, Major Hoefle establishes his staff of transferral clerks. A special SS group, an annihilation unit, is organised in a short space of time to be the spearhead for the operation. With meticulous foresight, the Germans force the Jewish police to man the front line, where they confront their own people in these final hours.

Their first targets are the prisoners in Pawia and Gesia prisons and the 'unproductive elements' in the shelters. By midday, twenty Jewish police have appeared on Dzielna Street and block it off with mounted police and barricades. While one group of officers remains on the street with raised batons, another group quickly breaks into the shelter and with a lot of loud shouting and much blowing of whistles they order everybody out. There's a huge amount of panic, and the homeless who are queuing up for food, flee in all directions. Some try to force their way outside but are met on the street by the police with batons; others hide under the tables, momentarily, until one after the other is hauled out by the officers, either kicking wildly or pleading for their life. A few flee upstairs to the dormitory, where they hide under bunks, but to no avail. The officers work unstintingly and don't care whether someone is healthy or sick. Everyone's to go, the dying and the starving are both pulled out of bunks, carried, pushed or dragged along the floor and out into the street, where they're loaded onto the truck. All the others are herded together in the middle of the street, where, still pleading and praying for their lives, they are forced to stand and wait.

David and Mrs Lewin are to leave too. At the appearance of the officers, David instantly hid in a kitchen cabinet, but was pulled out by an officer and beaten. Accustomed as he is to resisting, he kicks the officer in the shins. With a roar, the policeman buckles up, giving David time to unlock the cellar door and bolt down the stairs. In the damp cellar shaft under the house, where few ever go, he runs on in the darkness, and after passing a couple of doors, he reaches one that leads to a courtyard further down the street. He'd checked the route in advance, of course, and after the first wave of panic, knows exactly what to do. He hears footsteps behind him and raised voices, but in four paces he's up another cellar shaft, through another door and out across the courtyard.

By the fence, he suddenly discovers a policeman who's already raised his stick to beat him. He quickly turns around and races back towards the entrance and out onto the street. Up ahead, in front of the shelter, most of the police are busy controlling the crowd. He runs to the other side of the street that's deserted, and although two officers set off after him, he reaches the barricade without difficulty, ducks under the beam and rounds the corner into the wider Smozca Street, where he hides in the first passageway he finds, to catch his breath.

He counts the minutes as he anxiously clings to the wall

of the dark passageway. What should he do? Where should he go? In the distance, he hears shouting and gunfire but the street in front of the passage is ominously empty and quiet. A speeding military vehicle rumbles past over the cobbles and disappears. A few minutes later, a woman with a child in her arms runs out of a side street, shouting. She runs from door to door, pounding on them with her fist, but no one opens. Finally, a little way down the street, a door opens and an arm pulls her in.

A truck turns the corner and drives past the passageway. From his hiding place, he fleetingly glimpses the truck from Dzielna Street, with the sick and homeless packed like cattle in the back. Next, he can hear Yiddish voices shouting, coming closer, the sounds of footsteps and the low drone of hundreds seemingly in a trance. He holds his breath, pressing himself even closer to the wall. First come the shadows, then the policemen and with them a huge flock of beggars and vagabonds. He glimpses many people from the shelter and then, too, Mrs Lewin. He's stunned. All at once the deportation has become a reality. She turns her face and looks into the darkness of the passageway. For a brief moment their eyes meet, just a bleak glance from a stooped figure, and then she's gone.

He can do nothing, he's not even sure if she's seen him. He hangs back in the passageway until he's certain that the Jewish police are out of sight. What should he do, where should he go?

He tries to think clearly. He can't go back to the hospital or the synagogue, as they're no longer safe. He's got to get out, he has to escape but where can he go? And how?

He's heard that the soldiers have surrounded the ghetto …

Then he remembers the girl on Krochmalna Street but he's never been there and hardly knows her. The more he thinks about it, the more the idea seems absurd. Suddenly, a group of beggars appear on the street, with no police in sight. He hears one of them say "Even Chaim's gone to *Umschlagplatzen*, he says there's bread there!"

"How can I get some bread?" asks another.

"Idiot, you just go there!"

"Isn't it dangerous?"

"It can't be worse than this, can it?"

One of them laughs a loud, hoarse laugh and the voices die out. Again there's no one in sight. Terrified, he waits in the passageway until nightfall, then sneaks out and heads in the direction of Krochmalna Street.

Apart from the sleeping beggars, curled up on the pavements, the streets are deserted and the lights in the windows are fewer than before. Rain suddenly pours from the sky over the ghetto and it's hard for David to find the way. On one street he almost runs smack into a brick wall outside Toebben's workshops and has to retrace his steps. At other places he runs past small groups of lost souls. He pays little attention to the dead bodies which lay strewn on the pavement; they're merely obstacles that he has to step over. He picks up the pace of his running, and feels a strange joy in just moving. All the time he can hear a noise ahead of him, like the noise of a huge animal crying out. As he reaches Ogrodowa Street to search for the entrance to the bridge over Chlodna Street, he lands, unexpectedly, in a sea of shivering, homeless Jews. He pushes his small body through this flock of lost souls, who, for some unknown reason have gathered there. Above them, the tapered windows are wide open; lost bags and possessions have been scattered across the square. Children howl, men fight, women pray, everything's in chaos and all the time there are hands tugging at him, pushing him backwards but gradually he reaches the edge of the crowd and slips over the bridge. Again he starts running. On and on.

On Krochmalna Street he finds the right stairway but the door is locked. He bangs on the door fiercely but can't bear to wait outside. In the dim light of the hall, he finds an empty tin can which he throws up at the window on the first floor of the decaying building. A face appears behind a dark curtain, and soon he hears footsteps on the stairs. The door is opened slightly and a little man with a long beard and suspicious eyes appears in the doorway.

"What do you want here?" he asks.

"I know a girl here," he says. "She lives here with her mother."

"What's her name?"

"I don't know … but they lived on Mila Street, and she has white ribbons in her hair …"

"I don't know anyone with white ribbons, and it's too dangerous to let strangers in," says the little man, keeping his eye on the street.

David carefully takes the knife out of his pocket and passes it to the man, handle first.

"Take this," he says, "and let me in!"

The man glances at it without taking it.

"What do I need that for?" he says, "I already have a knife … do you think you can bribe me?"

"Can't you just let me in for a moment?" he pleads. "And if the girl doesn't live here, I'll leave."

The man scrutinizes him closely. Something – maybe David's persistence – changes his mind. He suddenly opens the door and says: "She lives on the second floor but be out by morning, OK?"

He nods and rushes up the dark stairs and knocks on the door on the second floor. Again, a man opens the door. This one is tall and thin with glasses and a dusty jacket. He glances at David nervously, as he tries to explain but when the man hears his name, he pulls him inside the stuffy hall quickly and calls for the girl. For the first time, David hears her name, Eva, and they awkwardly embrace. She doesn't seem at all surprised to see him and kisses him on the cheek. Her black hair shines under the bare light bulb in the hall, and he notices that it's longer than when he saw her last. He stands there looking at her, amazed that she's there in front of him.

"It's my birthday," she says. "I've been thinking about you!"

He doesn't know what to say. She takes his arm and leads him through two rooms stuffed with mattresses and blankets. A slight, grey woman greets him and speaks to him as if she's known him for some time – it's Eva's mother.

In a corner of the cramped kitchen, Eva lights a Hannukkah candle and they sit on the floor and talk. They discuss everything that's happened, but David avoids talking about the dead bodies he's seen on the streets. He keeps looking into the girl's dark, burning eyes which seem different somehow. He takes her hand and holds it tightly, and she's quiet, smiling dreamily. He just wishes the moment could last. He'd like to give her a gift, but what can he give her? He takes out his harp, dusts it off and plays a tune. But then he notices how tired he is ... his fingers can barely play, he feels himself nodding off and he mumbles something about the danger they're in. Eva says she knows about it, but today is her birthday so she doesn't want to talk about it until tomorrow. Tomorrow, they'll hide ... they've already rebuilt a cupboard which they'll push in front of the door to a bedroom. The back wall of the cupboard has been made into a special door that can be opened by an invisible latch ... they can hide inside ... there in the room behind the cupboard ...

But he doesn't hear any more. Still holding the girl's hand, he falls asleep from exhaustion, so they carry him into one of the rooms and lay him on a mattress.

He dreams that he and Eva have hidden in a suitcase, where they whisper to each other, but he can't hear what she's saying. "Speak up," he says, but he can only hear the sound of wind whistling through the cracks.

Then they wake up, open the lid of the suitcase, rub their eyes. Before them there's a mountain of wooden legs, glasses and human hair. "Where is everyone?" Eva asks, feeling lost and confused. "This isn't earth," he says, "it's still a dream." He takes her hand. They lie down again in the suitcase and close the lid. They fall back to sleep again in the darkness.

They have no time to hide. Early the next morning, a Jewish policeman kicks in the door to the flat and three officers barge in, shouting, with raised batons. They force the frightened sleepers onto their feet, tell them to dress quickly, collect their belongings (fifteen kilos maximum), and go down to the street. From the hallway and out in the street, they can hear footsteps, whistles and angry voices. In a matter of moments the tenants are scuttling around in panic. One young woman gets up from her mattress with a child in her arms and pleads for her life, but an older officer swings his baton wildly in the air shouting: "Orders, orders!" A man attacks one of the officers and tries to hold him down but is clubbed in the neck by the others. An elderly woman refuses to leave her mattress and clings onto it defiantly until two officers heave her off and throw her into the hall. Eva and her mother who, like everyone else, have slept in their clothes, quickly pack their suitcases and go out to the stairs. David follows them carrying a bundle that he's collected together in the midst of all the confusion.

But it's chaos on the stairs with people shouting, running up and down, as some try to go back for something they've forgotten. From the windows, both tenants and police are throwing out clothes, chairs and other objects. A man tries to shimmy down on a sheet, but loses his grip and falls with a thud onto the stones, where he lies. In some flats the officers run amok and smash everything and from there, the screams of their victims fill the street.

German soldiers suddenly materialize, jumping out of their vehicles and running up to the flats. Swiftly, they haul away furniture or carry off valuables, loading it all into their trucks then driving off.

Through continual beatings and repeated shouting the Jewish police herd the masses into groups. A few fortunate people pull out gold watches or bracelets and manage to bribe the police to turn a blind eye, as they scramble away like mice through passageways or rainy side streets.

Some members of families take the opportunity to run away and hide, when in the midst of the commotion, they're left unguarded. But the Jewish police have their own special tactics. They catch the children, and with the children the parents return and with the parents, the grandparents return.

In the group around David, two men have got hold of a Jewish officer and dragged him into a porch. They push the terrified man up against the wall and cover his mouth.

"I know you, Leib," says one of them, threatening "we went to school together, remember?"

"They're going to kill us," says the other angrily, "your own people ... how can you ...?"

The officer's words are muffled behind the man's hand, so they let him speak.

"You don't understand anything," he whimpers "... four heads every day, that's the order or we're shot!"

"I feel sorry for you, Leib," says the first man, wearing a stained overall. He spits in the man's face. "Swine!"

They let him go, and he collapses humiliated and crying. They stand there a moment and look at him, then a whistle shrieks close by and they run off across the courtyard.

David tries to keep close by Eva and her mother. He takes the mother's suitcase, but is often pushed or shoved aside in the uneasy moving throng. Someone suddenly steals his bundle and vanishes off down the street, where he's caught by an officer who rips the bundle from his arms and kicks him back in line.

The whole street is teeming with nervous, confused people, who are unprepared for what lies ahead. There's little opposition although in the last half hour their entire world has fallen apart. After the initial shock, most of them have accepted their fate, any trace of resistance or hysteria has been stamped out by the police and now a strange sort of hush has come over them. It's the kind of quietness you might see in a defeated elephant that's been chained to a post for weeks. Consequently, a few hundred Jewish police manage to drive thousands of people together then divide them into marching groups without much difficulty. With their shrill whistles and orders in either Hebrew or Yiddish they set the first column in motion down Krochmalna Street and soon it reaches the bridge over Chlodna Street making it sway and creak under the enormous weight.

The rain becomes torrential, a heavy, grey rain that sticks to the faces and the streets. Through the windows, tenants on the half-empty Leszno Street watch the endless stream of marchers, in apprehension of their own destiny. In many places, they open the windows and throw bread or vegetables down, shouting hoarse farewells. Beggars and other homeless waifs and strays retreat in terror from the marchers but a few tired or ignorant souls join the column, either through a misguided belief in the rumours of a brighter existence or perhaps out of despair. Others join them in the hope of finding their children or family members. Those who'd previously escaped, and found that later they regretted it, come back to the column. You can see them running up and down beside the sea of people in a frantic search for familiar faces.

As the last flank of the column turns into Karmelicka Street and the trolley bus on Leszno Street starts moving, a previously unnoticed German military vehicle turns the corner from Orla Street and blocks the path of the horse-drawn trolley bus. The driver gets up quickly and pulls hard on the reins to bring the vehicle to a lurching halt. Before the passengers can react, four SS men jump out of the car, point their weapons at the trolley bus and order everyone out.

One after the other, the nine passengers step down with their arms raised. They're shoved into the middle of the street where two of the SS men quickly search them. Then one of the SS men points his gun at a well-dressed elderly man with trembling lips, shouting, "No work papers, Jewish traitor!"

The man falls to his knees begging for his life, but the SS man laughs and fires two shots directly at his temple. Bleeding, the man falls. Another, younger man impulsively steps towards the dead man and kneels down, raising his arms up and lamenting, *"Schma Yisroael, Schma Yisroael!"* before another shot ends his life. A couple of SS men push the other passengers up against a wall and take everything of value from them while a pair of them discuss their forthcoming lunch. Then this pair finish off the passengers one by one with a quick shot to the back of the head. As if rehearsed, the four SS men get back into the car and are gone in a trice.

Only the driver, who's witnessed it all from his seat, is still alive. He sits there in shock until some of the residents nearby dare to come outside and pull him down.

At this time, Czerniaków's sitting at the desk in his office on Zamenhof Street. He's locked himself in, oblivious to the picture of the prophet behind him on the wall. Through the closed window, he can still hear the distant drone of the thousands on the move through the ghetto. He's calm, but it's the kind of calm you only know if you've decided to end it all.

As late as the previous evening he'd believed that he and the Council could accomplish something. But it was all in vain, everything was finished. Today Worthoff and his colleagues from the transferral staff demanded that he prepare a child transport list – a figure of ten thousand was mentioned.

"Only children?" he asked, hiding his terror.

Worthoff nodded, handed him a document and asked him to sign it. Just a formality, his signature. He stared at the document, but the letters blurred and he didn't have the strength to lift his pen. Worthoff cleared his throat impatiently and adjusted his collar. His uniform remained impeccable and the distinct scent of shoe polish wafted from his highly polished black boots. In his eyes there was a flash of contempt for Czerniaków's indecisiveness.

"We have, according to your wish, exempted the vocational school from the list," he added laconically. "Also the husbands of working women have been exempted … I'm prepared to speak with Major Hoefle about the orphans, so you've gotten what you wanted …"

"H – How many days a week will the operation last?" Czerniaków asked, to buy the time he needed to collect himself.

"Seven days a week," said Worthoff, indifferently.

Czerniaków asked them to come back, and it took some time before Worthoff understood what he meant, he'd been so certain that he'd sign the document, that he hadn't foreseen the possibility. Now, the thought of returning to his superior without this signature made him feel anxious. For the first time, he gave up on any pretence of politeness. He got up and slammed his gloves angrily on the desk.

"We're not asking you, we're giving you an order," he said "we're cleaning up and nothing can stop us!"

He abruptly reached across the desk and seized the document and with a curt "Heil Hitler!" left the office with his silent colleagues trailing.

So they'd trapped him, caged him in a room where he no longer knows who he is any more. Is he a butcher? Is he the one to seal his people's doom?

He glances down at his large hands, picks up his pen and continues writing in his diary. Carefully, he dries it leaving a few blotches on the paper.

He clenches his jaw. They'd already taken his wife hostage. And Major Hoefle had been so kind as to inform him that she'd be shot if the transferral didn't go ahead as planned. The first of many ...

Still, he hadn't gone to pieces. He'd kept his composure. That was yesterday, after all. Or was it? Time no longer seems to exist.

He leafs through his diary and the thought occurs to

him that he would like to kill that man. That damned, slick murderer. But hadn't he negotiated with them to save his own neck? Like a good Jew … like a calm Jew … a Jew with no tears.

Hadn't it always been for the sake of the children? Wasn't it for their sake that they'd established the gardens on Nalewski Street and Nowolipki Street and celebrated their opening with music, fine speeches and songs? And he'd stood there, beside the newly planted flowers, and spoken of the future, of the children, of hope …

He had to believe them … he had to go on smiling even after everything had long since become impossible. He had to hold back the tears every single night and in return all he got was a throbbing headache.

He'd allowed them all to deceive him – of course, they'd denied knowing anything about the deportation. How Höhmann had laughed when he'd asked anxiously about those rumours … oh yes, that laughter burned in his mind now so much that his head nearly exploded … and he replays the discussion in his mind, with Höhmann waving the idea away like an annoying fly: "*Quatsch, Unsinn!*"

They'd fooled him – yes and no. He'd known that the end would come. It was a game they all played, and he played it for the sake of small improvements. And he'd provided the music.

He looks at his large, white hands. What haven't they already signed? Are they really his hands? He closes his eyes. What he wouldn't give to live till the end of the war and just a half an hour more.

But his bitter chalice is filled to the brim. He has to show them that it's not possible to deal with murderers, that it's all over. They'll call him a coward, they'll call it escape …

But sorrow, pity … They're not just words …

He takes out a sheet of paper and writes to his wife:

"They demand that I should sacrifice my people's children with my own hands. I have no other choice than to die."

An hour later, he crunches his teeth together and cracks open a cyanide capsule inside his mouth.

His heavy feet thrash about on the floor at the moment when the world turns white … as the prophet on the wall steps forward translucently, he's thinking of his son … His mouth opens, he grasps the arm of the chair, everything lets go, his feet hit the floor.

*

Shortly before they reach Stawki Street, a group of ragged children run into the huge column of marchers. The children have only a faint idea of what's happening in the ghetto as they swarm among the marchers, begging for bread. Confusion grows in the column and both the Polish and the Jewish police as well as German soldiers start running along side the marchers, beating and threatening people back into line.

A small boy grabs David's hand and clings on as people around them frantically push and shove back and forth in the now motionless crowd. A shot is heard from the other side of the gateway and cries for help echo. The boy is terrified and holds onto David with both arms, making him drop his suitcase. Suddenly, the column starts moving again and they're pushed forward through the gateway.

"The suitcase, the suitcase …" he frets despairingly, as they're forced to keep up with the column's shuffling gait.

Between two tight lines of Jewish police on Dzika Street, the column is led over to the rallying place at *Umschlagplatzen*. A wave of sound hits them – raised voices, the neighing of horses, barking dogs, shrieking whistles but amid all the noise there's a strange quiet as if thousands were holding their breath. Behind the barricades and mounted police, there are armed German soldiers and Ukrainian guards with machine guns watching as thousands stream into what was once a market place.

Purses, suitcases, prams and carts loaded with the sick and dying lie scattered across the square, as new groups of weary marchers appear from all sides. Trucks full of captives drive up to the square and unload their cargo, ambulances drive back and forth from the hospital on Dzika Street where hundreds are waiting for transport. In the middle of the square, there's a group of white-coated doctors and people flock to them in the hope of getting something to eat or a bed in a hospital. Those who aren't sick pretend to be, while those who are sick pretend to be dying. The Jewish doctors make the most rudimentary examinations before writing out sick notes which the SS officers disregard as it pleases them.

Lost children search among the crowd for their parents and parents search for their stray children. Jews with money search for Jewish police who they can bribe, but many Jewish policemen are busy searching for their grandparents, as it's only now that they realize that their older relatives have been assigned for deportation.

A long train made up of dirty, brown cattle cars cuts through the mass of people. The cars stand there, their insides emptied and their doors agape. Like abandoned dungeons they await their residents.

When the column from Krochmalna Street flows into the square, the mass of people grows dangerously large and the barricades are swiftly removed. The 'volunteers' are sent back to the ghetto, and others slip away, thereby saving their lives for a couple of days or weeks.

David's still searching for Eva and her mother in the tightly packed crowd, when far ahead he catches sight of the white ribbons in Eva's hair. He tries pushing forward, but there are too many people and he can't get the boy through. He bends down to the boy, who has close-cropped hair, and is clinging on to his legs.

"What's your name?" he asks.

But the boy just stares at him and doesn't reply. David gets up and holds on to the child tightly.

Time passes, they stand and wait, the rain drenches them. David tries to work out what's going to happen, but he can't think clearly. They're going to be taken away, maybe they'll die, but he doesn't want to die, he wants to run away, to escape. He focuses his mind on that word – escape – and feels in his pocket. Yes, he still has his knife.

All around him rumours are flying about the place they're going to, but he doesn't bother to listen. The boy nudges his leg.

"Adam!" he says softly.

"Your name's Adam?" David asks, looking down.

The boy nods and is quiet again.

Up ahead a whistle is blown and an order is shouted out in German. Slowly, the people begin to move forward. One woman bumps into him, declaring, hopefully, "Finally, we're leaving!"

Another begins to cry, becoming hysterical, shouting farewell over and over until a man grabs her and covers her mouth.

As if in a trance, the thousands inch towards the train. There's an open area in front of the train, where the Jewish police armed with batons and the SS armed with guns, are directing people to line up for 'selection'. Three groups of SS officers are positioned there, some counting, others selecting. One of them, a youth not much more than a teenager, is shouting the loudest and pointing right and left with his whip. Puffed up by his authority, he snorts like a blood-crazed bull. His lightning quick decisions separate fathers from their children and women from their husbands.

Many of the young people and those who are able to

work are sent to the other side of the tracks where waiting trucks will take them to nearby work camps. The old men and women, the children and the sick are assigned to the cattle cars, with few exceptions. Most people show their papers, but here stamps and signatures count for nothing. Once in a while, an SS officer would pull one of the sick out of the line to demonstrate 'charity'. Many people realize only too late what the selection process means and when they try to find members of their family, behind the back of the SS youth with the whip, a blow or a kick swiftly forces them back into the cars.

When David and Adam get up to the youth, he steps towards them with his left hand raised. Adam suddenly breaks free and runs off towards the cattle cars. Like a frightened rabbit, he ducks down and crawls under one of the cars. Two Jewish police run after him, one grabs his foot but he wiggles and kicks until his shoe comes off, then crawls further under the wagon, gets up and disappears among the masses on the other side.

David is startled by a blow.

"That was planned! You planned it!" shouts the little SS man.

Shaken, David holds his cheek, unable to speak.

"Answer, answer me!" shouts the SS youth, grabbing his collar.

A Lieutenant Colonel steps forward.

"This has to be fast, Brünner, let him pass!" he says coolly and with his index finger signals the next person to step forward in the line.

In sudden doubt over his authority, Brünner raises his hand as if to strike David, then changes his mind and turns his back.

David is momentarily left alone, but feels too dizzy from the blow to take in what's happening. As he walks slowly towards the cattle car, a Jewish policeman gives him a shove that makes him fall over. He gets up, takes a few more steps and instinctively reaches out at the opening to the cattle car, where an arm swiftly pulls him up inside.

The first thing he notices in the dim, damp box, where strange faces turn towards him, is the smell of hay. He crawls past dozens of legs to reach the side wall, then sits down with his back against it.

"Papa, where are we going?" asks a six-year-old girl nearby with a small suitcase in her hand.

"I don't know," says a young man with a wet coat, holding her tight.

"Treblinka!" pipes up an unexpected voice from the shadows.

"Is there a playground there?" asks the girl.

The young man looks towards the opening where two women are crawling in. The noise of the people in the square seems far away. A shot is heard in the distance.

"I don't know," he says and smoothes her wet hair. "It's all right …"

An older man throws a suitcase in on the hay and with difficulty clambers up into the car. He looks around, confused, adjusts his glasses, gets up, grabs his suitcase and stands close to the opening.

"Move!" says a young man in a ragged jacket as he struggles to heave a feeble old woman up into the car. She hangs there a moment in his arms and his legs start to buckle.

"So help me!" he shouts.

The older man sighs, lets his suitcase fall, reaches out and lifts her up.

"Mein Gott," she whispers as she tries in vain to get up from the hay. "I can't stay in here!"

The cattle car is already half-full, and every time someone else comes in, the rest move closer together. Some people sit, others stand; the foul-smelling and terminally ill lie down, often babbling incomprehensibly to themselves. One woman kneels down and wipes their faces with a handkerchief. The rest try to keep their distance but as more and more people enter the car, they're forced to get closer and closer to the sick until they can't avoid stepping on them.

At one end of the car, pushed right into a corner, there's a rabbi who keeps kissing his prayer shawl as he rocks back and forth, mumbling prayers to himself. His beard has been shaved on one side of his face so that he looks like two different men. David tries to catch the man's eye.

Outside the car, the din mounts as people with suitcases

and bags run back and forth in panic. Children call out fearfully. Names in many languages whirl through the air, a man sticks his head in and shouts "Esther, Esther!"

But no one reacts and he vanishes again.

More and more people clamber up into the car, and soon it's so full that David is pressed against the wall. He gets up and works his way towards the long back wall. At the top, a little way down from the ceiling he notices a small air vent covered with chicken wire. He can escape through that, for certain. He forces his way through the bodies until he's right under the vent then slowly turns so he has his back to the wall. From here, through the narrow gaps between people, he'll try to find a man who can help him climb up. But the crushing continues, even more people get in and he's shoved right up against the back wall.

"Stop pushing,!" he shouts and gets an elbow in the stomach. He slides down the wall and lands on the floor. A woman steps on him and shouts "God, my God, a child …"

Outside a whistle is heard, the door slams shut, everything is suddenly plunged into darkness … keys rattle and with a few sharp jolts the train departs.

As the air inside the car becomes increasingly clammy, David's eyes adjust to the darkness, he looks up at the vent, rises to his feet and reaches out his arm …